ROBERT L. SWITZER

The Lady PROFESSOR

Bink Books
Bedazzled Ink Publishing Company • Fairfield, California

978-1-945805-12-7 paperback

Cover Design
by

DESIGNS

Bink Books
a division of
Bedazzled Ink Publishing, LLC
Fairfield, California
http://www.bedazzledink.com

Dedicated to the Memory of my Mother,
Elva Allison Switzer
(1907 – 1977)

ACKNOWLEDGMENTS

I am most grateful to C. A. Casey, my editor at Bedazzled Ink Publishing, above all for believing in Emma's story and taking a chance on an unknown, first-time novelist, but also for her thorough and thoughtful editing of the manuscript, polishing the writing and curbing my excesses.

It is a pleasure to acknowledge the years of constructive criticism and encouragement I have received from the members of Champaign-Urbana's distinguished Red Herring Fiction Writer's Workshop, especially from its longtime leader, Elaine Fowler Palencia, who is the author of splendid prose and poetry and a gentle, but firm exponent of the craft of creative writing.

I also gratefully acknowledge others who read the manuscript of *The Lady Professor* and offered both criticism and encouragement: Peter Beak, Chip Burkhardt, Bob and Judy Jones, and Clark McPhail. Two real-life lady professors, Susan Martinis, Professor of Biochemistry, and Brenda Wilson, Professor of Microbiology at the University of Illinois, Urbana-Champaign, shared their comments and insights on the manuscript. These reader friends contributed many improvements to the manuscript; the flaws that remain are my responsibility alone.

Special thanks go to my life's companion, my wife of many years, Bonnie George Switzer. The example of her self re-invention as a fine artist in midlife spurred me to strive to become a creative writer in the years after my retirement as a biochemistry researcher and educator. *The Lady Professor* is a novel about a life in science, but it is also, in part, a story of love and family. Most of what I know of love and family I learned with Bonnie; some of what I learned permeates this novel.

CHAPTER 1
1985

HER GRANDMOTHER'S SUMMONS had come to Maria printed in an unfamiliar hand, not her usual neat graceful script, which had been always written in black ink with an old-fashioned fountain pen, the kind with a sharp metal nib and a little rubber bladder inside. She had dictated this note to her nurse; that fact alone was painful evidence of her advancing disease, of the urgency of her request:

> *Dearest Maria,*
> *I hate to intrude on your medical training, which I know is most intense just now, but I beg you to come and see me while I am still able to talk to you. There are some things I must tell you, not least among them how much I treasure you. Please do not delay.*
> *Love, Grandma*

Maria managed to negotiate two days off and hurried to her grandmother's home. She still had a front door key left from her younger days, so she let herself in and stood now in the big front room enveloped in a nostalgic fog of memories provoked by the odors and sight of the room.

The rooms looked very much as they had during the years when she came here as a girl; they were furnished with dark Victorian furniture, heavy drapes pulled back, thick Persian carpets, and with light filtering in through the surrounding trees. A soft odor of furniture oil and old books permeated the air. Ranks of bookshelves lined the walls, every shelf packed with neat rows of books and unbound scientific journals. The many papers on her large desk lay in neat piles; a dust cover shrouded her old Underwood typewriter. Stacks of books, journals and unopened mail lay on the dusty dining room table. She must be no longer able to keep up with it; she would hate the disorder and neglect.

Maria had only gradually come to realize what a remarkable woman her paternal grandmother was. Throughout her childhood years she had simply been her "Grandma", though there had always been a special bond between them. She had loved visiting her in this old house at the edge of the campus with its upstairs rooms—her personal museum—

full of taxidermically mounted animals and birds, carefully labeled specimen boxes with glass tops, bottles of pickled creatures—fish, amphibians, snakes—even ugly parasitic tapeworms, which she told Maria had been removed from the intestines of animals. She had been fascinated and frightened by a little yellowish near-term human fetus floating in formaldehyde; it was a little boy, his small, perfectly formed genitalia proved that; a purple umbilical cord dangled from his belly; his eyes were closed and his face was scrunched up in a worried expression. "He was stillborn," Grandma explained matter-of-factly in response to her nervous questions, "That happens sometimes, but not often. Sometime I will show you the entire collection of preserved human fetuses at the Natural History Museum, so you can see all the steps by which a fertilized egg, called an ovum, develops from the earliest stages into a baby like this one. Come, I set up the microscope in the next room. I thought we would look at the slides of insect mouth parts today. We can see how they are adapted to the insect's life habits." Small and neat, gray hair clipped short, quick precise movements, intelligent dark blue eyes behind wire-rimmed glasses. Her gentle hand on Maria's shoulder as she peered into the microscope as strong a declaration of love as any words.

She was always keen to share her love of biology, eager to engage a willing student, even if—no, especially because—she was her granddaughter. During the many hours they had spent together, she had amused her, she had taught her, she had challenged her, and now she realized that she had molded her in her own image into the physician-scholar she was training to become. In high school and college, she became aware that her Grandma was also known as Dr. Emma Hansen, Professor of Biology at Harrington College, and that her life had followed an extraordinarily challenging path. The youngest daughter of a hardscrabble farm family, she had somehow managed to scratch out a college education and to become one of the first women to earn a Ph.D. in biology from Cornell University in the 1920s, a time when women were strongly discouraged or even banned from graduate study. She was the first female appointed to the science faculty at Harrington, a small liberal arts college, and in time became a respected biology teacher and established the only active scientific research program in the college until the appointment of younger faculty in the 1950s. At the time of her retirement in 1970 she had been universally regarded as the most eminent scientist in the college.

A WHITE-CLAD nurse stepped soundlessly into the room, startled her from her reverie.

"Oh, Dr. Bellafiori, you're here. She will be so glad to see you. She has been somewhat agitated all day, knowing that you were coming."

"How is she?"

"Not well, I'm afraid. Weaker and losing weight. She can still get to the bathroom with a walker, but I worry about her falling when I'm not here. She absolutely refuses to go to a nursing home. She needs to have around-the-clock care."

"Oh, my. She has always been so capable, so independent and dignified. She's been a widow for decades, very self-sufficient. I can imagine how hard all this is for her to accept."

"Yes, it is."

"Is she in pain?"

"Yes and it is getting worse. Metastatic to her bones, as I think you know. I've been giving her Percocet p.r.n.—as needed. And she is using quite a lot. Is there more you'd like me to do?"

"Oh, no. You should follow her doctor's orders. I'm just starting my residency. It would be inappropriate for me to supervise her care. Just think of me as her granddaughter."

"Yes, well, please go in. I know she's eager to see you."

"MARIA, OH, DEAR girl, come here." A weakened, wavering voice, not as Maria remembered it.

"Grandma!"

Grandma was propped up in bed with pillows, emaciated and pale, but smiling. Maria embraced her carefully, as though the bones that she could feel so easily through her flannel nightgown might break—as indeed they could—and kissed her dry cheek. She tried to hide her shock at the deterioration in her health since she had last seen her.

"I'm sorry it's taken me so long to come to see you. The internship was just grueling. I couldn't get away."

"Oh, I know. I've never understood why medical schools abuse interns the way they do. It's just hazing, like in the military academies. Graduate schools are more humane, especially nowadays. And effective, I daresay. Is it better now that you are in your residency?" Her eyes drew her in with well-remembered intensity.

"No, it's just as bad. And with more responsibility. It took some pleading to get away."

"I'm sorry. I wouldn't have asked you to come if it weren't important."

"I know, Grandma."

"You must miss the research lab. Have you decided on a specialty?"

"I'm pretty inclined toward oncology. I think there are going to be some exciting opportunities for research. New discoveries about oncogenes, genes that normally regulate cell growth but go haywire in cancer. They might be targets for new therapies."

"That's wonderful, Maria. You really must choose an area where you can do research. Use that fine mind of yours." Still encouraging, prodding, setting the bar as high as she could possibly reach.

"But, Grandma, that's enough about me. I came to see you. See how you're doing. You sent for me."

She waved a skeletal hand dismissively. "Oh, that's clear enough, isn't it, dear girl. I suppose I am paying for all my exposure to x-rays back in the 30s and 40s. The cancer is quite advanced now. I intend to die soon."

"Oh, Grandma. Don't talk that way." She bit her lip. How could she be so matter of fact about it?

"Now, hush. You know I've always tried to do things rationally. It's time. My disease is progressing rapidly, and I will soon become incapacitated. Intolerably so. I'm eighty-five years old. I can no longer do useful work. I need to do this while I can still think clearly. And I need you to help me." She broke off abruptly, closed her eyes, and gripped her blanket with her fists. Muscles tightened in her face.

"Grandma, you're in pain, aren't you?"

She did not speak, but nodded slightly.

"Aren't you taking your medication?"

"Some."

"What do you mean, 'some'?"

"Maria, dear Maria, listen to me," she said softly. "You are my favorite grandchild. They say you shouldn't have favorites, but I'm sorry, I do. And it's you."

Maria fought tears. "I know. I guess I've known that for a long time. I think my brothers knew it too, but . . . but, maybe it doesn't matter now."

"Yes, it does. Because I want you to help me. "

Maria raised her hands to ward it off. "Grandma, I can't—"

"Oh," she interrupted. "I won't ask you to violate your medical ethics. Just tell me how much I need. The pain pills. I've been saving them, not taking them except when it gets really bad. I've hidden them away where she can't find them. And I won't tell you where they are either."

"Grandma, please . . ."

"Now, Maria, listen to me." Such strength, such determination. It had brought her this far, and it would take her the rest of the journey. "Listen now, my dear. You know how I hate messes. Hate being dependent. I'm going to do this anyway, so just help me to do it right. I've talked to my lawyer. Got my affairs in order."

"Shouldn't we call Dad and Mom?"

"No! Bring them all the way back from Africa? Spoil their holiday? No, wait until after. Your father is just like his father, dear Joe, so emotional, so passionate. No. I need calm now. No scenes. Peace." Weak as her voice was, it was whip-taut with determination.

The knot in Maria's throat blocked a reply.

"I just need two things from you," Grandma said quietly.

"Two things?"

"Yes, now first, tell me how many of these pills will I need?"

"Grandma . . ."

"Maria!" The familiar tone when she disobeyed.

"OK." Maria sighed and picked up an empty vial from the dresser. Her grandmother weighed less than a hundred pounds now, perhaps only eighty-five to ninety. "These are 7.5 milligrams of oxycodone plus 325 of acetaminophen. I'd guess thirty at one time. Unless you've been taking them regularly and become habituated. Then it will take more. Forty, even fifty." She broke off, choked back a sob and covered her face with her hands.

Her grandmother stirred in the bed, groaned and with obvious effort leaned over to tug gently on Maria's hands. She pulled them to her lips and kissed them.

"I'm sorry to put you through this. Please try to think of it as an act of love. You're the only one I can trust."

Maria couldn't reply, but fished in her purse for a handkerchief and dabbed tears from her face.

"There's one more thing. Something else I need for you to do."

"What's that?" She feared to ask, but knew there was little that she could refuse.

"Look in the top left drawer of my dresser over there. There's a key in the back behind my jewelry case. So-called jewelry." She chuckled. "It's all cheap costume stuff that I rarely wore. Find it? It's a key to the metal file cabinet by my desk out in the living room. Unlock it and look for a thick, sealed manila envelope in the file called 'Am. J. Genet.' *American Journal of Genetics*. Top drawer. Bring it in here, please."

Maria went to the living room and fumbled with the key to the file cabinet. She was crying again, so she paused and took a few deep breaths to get herself under control. Grandma would want that. She found the file exactly as described. She returned to the bedroom. Her grandmother was lying back on the bed with her eyes closed, lips parted, exhausted by the effort of their conversation.

"Remove the letter on top. The handwritten one from me. There's a longer typewritten one under it," she whispered. "Read it. Take your time. Read it carefully."

As Maria read, she became more agitated. Her pulse throbbed at her throat. "This is incredible. Grandma, I can't believe this."

"Shh. Finish reading it. Then read my letter on top."

She completed reading; her hand trembled as it held the document. "You want me to send these letters to the editor of the *American Journal of Genetics* to be published? My God."

Her grandmother did not sit up, did not open her eyes. "Yes," she said softly. "After I'm gone."

"It'll cause a huge scandal. What if he refuses to publish it? He probably will."

"Tell him you'll send it to the *New York Times*. And if he still refuses, do it."

"Oh, Grandma, why now? After all these years?"

"This is not about settling scores, Maria. All the principals are dead now. Or soon will be. This is to set the historical record straight."

"What if they don't believe you?"

"Oh, the truth will get out. I trust the historians."

"You think they have more integrity than scientists?"

"No. I just know academics. Careers are made by overturning the conventional wisdom, the established order of things."

CHAPTER 2
1912

THE SKIES DARKENED to a glowering blue-gray in mid-afternoon, and heavy wind-borne snow began falling soon after; slanting sheets of white obscured the pupils' view of the surrounding fields. Miss Connor was forced to light the kerosene lamps because the daylight from the tall schoolhouse windows became too dim. A cold draft chilled the older pupils, whose desks were ranked along the west wall nearest the windows and distant from the coal-burning stove in the center of the room, but Emma Hansen was warmly dressed and so absorbed in solving algebra problems that she didn't notice the approaching snowstorm until an especially strong wind gust rattled the windows.

It would be a cold walk home through snow-clotted roads; there would be no shortcut through corn stubble. She would much rather stay here in her favorite place, the Hamilton Grove School, warmly encouraged by Miss Connor, than trudge to the big old farmhouse where evening chores and an ill-tempered mother awaited her.

Emma dwelt in two worlds, both situated in the undulating fields and woods of a northwestern Illinois farming community and peopled by second- and third-generation northern European immigrant families like the Hansens, but separated by a mile and a half: the world of the little one-room country school where she now sat, and the world of the farm where she lived with her parents and her siblings: three older and one younger. She much preferred the school. Although she was not yet thirteen, she was in the eighth grade because she had skipped third grade. If some of the sixth and seventh graders called her teacher's pet, she didn't mind, because it was true, but well deserved. Besides, the younger pupils adored "Miss Emma" because Miss Connor had deputized her to teach them reading and arithmetic; they flocked around her, competed to hold her hand. And—*mirabili dictu*—they learned as quickly under her guidance as they had from Miss Connor. Emma was the only eighth grader, so Miss Connor had designed a special program for her: algebra, Latin, English literature and grammar, geography and world history. It was not the standard eighth grade program prescribed by the county superintendent of schools, but his visits to the many rural schools in the county were so infrequent that he would never know.

Next spring, however, Emma would be forced to emerge, an uncertain butterfly, from this cocoon of success and approval; she would graduate from grade school and leave Miss Connor and Hamilton Grove School forever. She hoped to go on to the nearest "high" school in Stanton Mills, twelve miles away, but Emma knew little of high schools. Her two brothers and her sister had completed their education at eighth grade; she knew that it would be a struggle to persuade her parents to allow her to continue her education. It was an enticing, if slightly frightening prospect; she was prepared to fight for it.

EMMA STAMPED THE snow off of her rubber boots and removed them on the back porch before entering the house. Tracking wet boots into the kitchen would earn a scolding. Inside the kitchen she hung her coat and knit cap on a nail. Adjacent nails where her father's, Bjorn's, and Henrik's coats normally hung were bare; they must still be out working. She stood by the great iron kitchen range and rubbed her cold hands together close to its hot surface; this was the warmest place in the house and welcome after the long walk home in blowing and drifting snow.

"Emma, don't dawdle," her mother called out from the front room where Emma guessed she was nursing baby Aaron. "Fetch the potatoes from the cellar and get them peeled and on to boil. Bring up a jar of string beans too. Papa and the boys came in early from cutting wood because of the snow. They're milkin' now and they're going to be hungry."

This was good news. If her father and brothers had been still working in the woods, Emma would have been sent to the cold barn to milk their five cows by hand. She and her mother had done it together until this summer when the baby was born after a very long labor. Aaron had been born "arse first"; Emma still cringed at the memory of her mother's cries and moans. Now her mother was burdened with the care of an infant and ill-defined—to Emma anyway—"female troubles," so many of her farm and household chores fell to Emma. She retrieved a dozen musty potatoes from the root cellar and sat at the kitchen table to peel them with her Latin text propped in front of her; she could memorize vocabulary words while she peeled the potatoes, saving the peels to feed to the chickens.

"You'd get that done faster if you'd get your nose out of that book," her mother scolded as she entered the kitchen. "Honest to God, child. Kirsten would have had them boiling by now."

"Yes, Mama." Emma closed the offending book and worked in silence while her mother shoveled more coal into the kitchen range and filled a frying pan with pink sausages.

Kirsten does everything right, everything better than me, she reflected. But she's not here, is she? Kirsten, seventeen years old, had been hired out as a live-in servant girl with the Reinhardt family, who were Catholics and had a large number—a "litter" her mother derisively called it—of young children. "God knows, we need her back since the baby was born, but we need the money too."

It was far from the first time Emma had heard that remark. Kirsten only returned to the family home on alternate weekends, and with the snow filling the rural roads as it was tonight, it was unlikely that her brothers would take a team and sled to bring her home this weekend. That was all right with Emma. She would have the bedroom they shared to herself. Cold as it was, she could wrap herself in quilts and read as late in the night as she wished. Miss Connor had given her *Tess of the d'Urbervilles*. Emma read with fascination at the guilt and shame visited on poor Tess through no fault of her own—Tess, a milkmaid like herself.

"Now set the table, Emma. Honestly, child, do I have to tell everything? Get your head out of the clouds."

STAMPING OF BOOTS announced the arrival of Emma's father and brothers on the back porch, and a gust of cold air blew into the kitchen with them. As they hung their coats and caps on nails behind the kitchen range and laid their gloves to dry on the floor next to it, a familiar odor filled the room, an amalgam of the rich organic smell of cow manure and horse urine, of spicy hay and sour milk—the smell of the cow barn. To it was added the nip of male sweat; the family had its last weekly baths five days ago.

"Snowin' like hell out there," Bjorn offered. "They ain't goin' to be no school tomorrow, I don't think. The teacher can't get there if it keeps up like this." Like his father and younger brother Henrik, Bjorn was tall and fair, already muscular from years of fieldwork and cutting and splitting wood. He patted Emma's head. "You'll be sorry about that, huh, Miss Bookworm?" She did not reply. Bjorn, six years older than she, seemed almost like another parent; she was more fond of gentle

Henrik, who was only two years older and never teased her about her bookish ways and still played with her in their rare free time.

"Wash up now," her mother said. "Supper's ready."

After a perfunctory recitation of the usual prayer, the family ate hungrily. There was little conversation beyond requests to pass dishes until the meal was finished, when Emma's father scraped back his chair and began speaking almost as though he were thinking aloud. "That snow is gonna slow us down if it gets too deep. We need to get them big oaks snaked out of the woods and cut for the framing of the barn addition. And the boys have got a couple wagon loads of fence posts cut that we need to sell."

Emma's mother's mouth tightened. The barn addition was a source of contention between her parents. Her father had come home a few months ago and announced, "I've been talking to that Swiss cheesemaker, Tschudi. He says he'll buy all the milk we can bring him, a dollar a hundredweight. I figure if we put an addition on the barn, we can milk more cows, store the milk in cans in the cow tank overnight so it won't go sour and haul it to his factory every day. Be good steady income."

"How many cows?" her mother had asked warily.

"Oh, ten, twelve; maybe work up to more later."

"Who's gonna milk all them cows? Not Emma and me, like we do now. Not that many. And with the baby and all."

"Oh, me and the boys will pitch in."

"What about the hogs? We're feedin' them the skim milk now."

"There's a lot of whey from cheesemakin'. Tschudi needs to get rid of it anyways. So we can haul it back for the hogs. It's good for 'em. Along with corn like we do now."

"And how're we going to pay for the cows? That's a lot of money."

"We'll have to borrow enough from the bank to buy half a dozen or so. Pay it back from the milk money. Then, if we keep all the heifer calves, we can grow our own herd in two, three years."

Her father's expression made it clear that the decision was made and no further discussion was welcome.

"Well, just don't come to me when it's hayin' time, or threshin', or plantin' time and you can't keep up with milkin' all them cows," her mother muttered.

Emma knew that a good portion of the extra chore would fall to her, and she dreaded it. Already her hands ached after milking five cows. A dozen more? It was too much. Secretly she had begun plotting her eventual escape from the drudgery of the farm: she would become a schoolteacher like Miss Connor. Already she was teaching the little ones, and Miss Connor called her "my bright young assistant."

WINTER EVENTUALLY GAVE way to springtime, Emma's favorite time on the farm. A canopy of white and pink blossoms covered the orchard's apple, plum, and pear trees. Fresh grass and swaths of yellow dandelions, tender leaves on the trees replaced the melting snow banks and mud of early spring. There were fields to be plowed and planted, but today, in respect of the Sabbath, no fieldwork would be done.

Henrik and Emma were free to pursue a favorite shared pastime. Henrik had helped Emma with her collection of wild bird eggs from the beginning two years ago. Finding the eggs of meadow and ground birds—meadowlarks, bobolinks, red-winged blackbirds, pheasants— had been relatively easy. Henrik often spotted their nests during his work in the fields and alerted Emma.

Raiding the nests of birds that nested around the buildings and in nearby trees—pigeons, sparrows, starlings, grackles, robins, barn swallows—also presented little challenge, as Henrik was willing to climb the trees.

Emma punctured each end of the eggs with a needle and blew the contents out. She had learned to candle the farm's hens' eggs before they were sold, so she could tell whether a wild bird's egg contained an embryo that was too large to be expelled. Those eggs were returned to their nests, although Emma had broken a few and studied the stages in their development from bloody spot to tiny bird with huge closed eyes, naked pink body and a rubbery yellow beak. The empty eggshells were preserved with a drop of camphor and placed in cotton-lined boxes with neat handwritten labels identifying the species. Emma also kept written notes about the location and construction of the nests, undisturbed if possible, but retrieved from trees by Henrik if necessary.

Now it had become more difficult to add new specimens to the collection. Emma and Henrik hunted for birds whose nests were harder to find or raid, such as woodpeckers, owls, and secretive woodland birds. Henrik had spotted a crow's nest at the top of a dead hackberry tree hidden in the farm's woods. He planned to climb it and retrieve the eggs for Emma's collection. If he succeeded, it would be a triumph. Crows were the most intelligent of birds; their nests were difficult to locate and perched precariously in high, inaccessible places.

As they headed for the crow's nest, they crossed a stony outcropping in the hilly pasture that lay between the farm's gently rolling cultivated fields and the twenty-acre woods at the northern edge of the farm. A killdeer fluttered on the ground a few feet from them uttering its shrill "Kill-DEER!" cry and dragging a bent wing behind so that reddish under feathers were displayed.

"Look, she's pretending to be hurt, so we will try to catch her and not find her nest," Emma said. "Most birds just fly away or scream at you. Isn't she clever?"

"You've already got killdeer eggs, haven't you? Do you want to look for her nest?"

"No, let her go."

As they approached the dead hackberry tree, Emma felt a shiver of fear. "Henrik, it's taller than our windmill, and the nest is way up at the top. Be careful."

A large saucer-shaped mass of sticks lay wedged in a crotch formed by three small branches some forty-to-fifty feet above them. Two black crows circled warily.

"It's OK, Emmie, I'll just shinny up there and lower 'em in the sack the way we said," Henrik replied.

The plan was to place two or three purloined eggs in a cloth sack and lower it gently to the ground with a length of binder twine so that his hands would be free for the difficult descent. With that, Henrik was up the tree, searching out branches to brace his feet and pull himself up. He moved quickly but carefully. A few dead branches were too brittle to support his weight and broke off and clattered to the ground.

Emma watched nervously.

As Henrik approached the nest, the crows cried out loudly and flew at him. He ignored them and let out a whoop when he secured a position at the top of the tree from which he could reach into the nest. "Eggs! A whole clutch of 'em!" He wobbled as he wrenched the sack from his back pocket.

"Hang on, Henrik!" Emma cried out. "You almost fell!"

"Don't worry," came his cheerful voice from above. "I've got three of 'em in the sack. Let me get fixed tight here and I'll lower 'em down." The sack slowly descended, swaying and bumping branches gently.

Emma reached up eagerly and pulled the sack into her hands. "Let go the string," she called. "I've got it."

Inside the sack were three pale blue-green eggs covered with dark brown speckles, larger than most of the eggs in Emma's collection, but smaller than the hen's eggs she gathered daily from the henhouse.

"Do they have babies in 'em?" Henrik called down.

Emma held an egg toward the sun and squinted, twirled the egg gently. "No! They're perfect. Just yolks. Now come down. You're scarin' me up there."

Henrik crept down the tree more slowly than he had ascended it. He felt for supporting branches with his feet.

Emma watched his fumbling moves nervously, called out when she could warn that he was missing a branch or tell him where one was near his foot. She relaxed and returned to studying the eggs when he was about ten feet above the ground. She heard a sharp snap and little cry. She jerked her head around and witnessed Henrik landing on his side at the base of the tree.

"Henrik!" she screamed.

He lay still for a long time, then rolled over onto his back and groaned.

Emma knelt by him, her hands fluttering, not knowing if or where she should touch him, finally caressing his face. "Are you all right? Please, be all right."

"I guess so," he mumbled. "Knocked the wind out of me." He sat up, then fell back with a cry. "Oh, my leg hurts like hell."

"Do you think it's broke?"

"I dunno. Have to see if I can stand. Gimme a few minutes."

Emma began to cry. "I'm sorry, Henny. It's all my fault. I shouldn't have talked you into climbing that tree. Just to get some old crow's eggs."

"It's OK, Emmie. Don't cry. Looks like I ripped up this leg of my overalls. Mama's gonna be mad." Henrik pulled the torn cloth aside to reveal bloody abrasions along his right leg. "Ripped my leg up a little too."

"Does it hurt? Can you walk? We got to get you back to the house and cleaned up."

Henrik struggled to his feet and then cried out. "Oh, shit!"

"Is it broke?"

"I don't think so, but it sure hurts when I stand on it."

They made their way from the woods back to the farmstead. Henrik leaned on Emma and limped painfully. How strange it was to support her big, strong blond brother, fully a head taller, the brother on whom she had leaned—figuratively at least—for years. She was filled with tenderness.

"What happened? How'd you hurt yourself?" their mother demanded when they crept into the farm house.

Henrik hung his head and remained silent, but Emma spoke up.

"He fell out of a tree. We think it's just a sprain or a bruise. It isn't broken."

"What the Sam Hill was he doing up a tree?" Papa asked.

"He was fetching some crow's eggs for my collection. It's my fault. I put him up to it."

"That's just enough of this foolishness," her mother cried. "I want you to get rid of them damned eggs. Throw 'em out and stay out of trees."

"Mama, no!"

"Yes. Now. A girl has no business fooling around with such things in the first place."

"Mama, please let her keep the eggs," Henrik pleaded. "I'll promise not to climb no more trees."

Their mother shook her head. Emma and Henrik turned their eyes to their father in appeal. His word would be final.

He ran his fingers through his graying hair, avoided his wife's glare. "Well, all right. She can keep 'em so long's you both promise not to climb no more trees."

"We promise," they chorused, but Henrik winked at Emma.

She led him to the kitchen and dabbed the wounds to his leg with a clean rag and warm water from the teakettle on the stove. He tried not to wince as she painted the abrasions with tincture of iodine.

"Don't forget to blow out them crow's eggs," he whispered. "They're beauties."

TWO WEEKS LATER on a Friday afternoon after all the other pupils were dismissed and ran shouting out of the schoolhouse, Emma was surprised when Miss Conner asked her to remain behind.

"You can clean the blackboards and help me tidy up. Then I'll take you home with me. I need to talk to your parents." What on earth was this about? Surely she was not in trouble. Miss Conner used a horse and buggy to travel between Stanton Mills and Hamilton Grove School when the roads were passable. The horse was kept in a little barn next to the boys' outhouse. Emma helped Miss Connor hitch up the horse and the two set off for the Hansen farm.

"For Heaven's sakes, it's the school teacher, Miss Connor," Emma's mother exclaimed when she saw her and Emma dismount the buggy. "What on earth does she want? Does you suppose Emma's sick?"

She pulled off her apron and moved quickly from the house to greet Miss Connor. Emma trailed behind her teacher.

"Miss Connor. This is a surprise. Can you stay for dinner?"

"Oh, no, thank you. I can't stay. I wonder if I might have a word with you and Mr. Hansen about Emma."

"What's she done?"

Miss Connor laughed. "Oh, it's nothing like that. You can be very proud of Emma. I want to talk about her going to high school next year."

Papa Hansen was summoned from the barn, and Emma's parents sat down at the kitchen table opposite Miss Connor. Emma looked inquiringly at her parents, then Miss Connor.

"Emma, stay here. This concerns you," Miss Connor said. "Mr. and Mrs. Hansen, as you know, Emma will be going to high school in Stanton Mills this fall."

"Well, I don't know," Papa muttered. "None of the other ones went to high school."

"Oh, but, Mr. Hansen, there's a new law now. Graduation for eighth grade is no longer the end of required education in Illinois. She has to go to school until she's sixteen, and she's only just turned thirteen. Besides, she really must go. Emma is without question the brightest pupil I have taught in fifteen years."

"Well, I don't see how it's gonna work," Papa replied. "Stanton Mills is twelve miles from here. I can't let her have a horse and wagon all day every day. Besides, in winter sometimes you can't hardly get through them roads for the snow. And springtime they're nothin' but mud. We can't send a little snip of a girl out into that."

"I agree," Miss Connor replied calmly. "I've been thinking about that, and I believe I have come up with a solution. Emma can board in town."

"Board in town," Mama cried. "We can't afford that."

"I've talked to the Oosterfelds, the folks who operate the grocery store on Center Street in Stanton Mills. They would be willing to provide room and board for Emma in exchange for her working in the store in evenings and weekends. They have no children and they could use the help. I've known them for years. They're good Christian folks.

I'm sure they'd be good to Emma. And Emma would do a good job for them."

Papa Hansen rubbed his chin. "What do you think, Emma?"

"Oh, Papa, it's a wonderful idea. Please, may I do it?"

"Not so darned fast," Mama Hansen cried. "What about gettin' the work done here? I've got this little one here and Kirstin is off at the Reinhardts. There's cows to milk, and *you*"—she glared at her husband— "want to get a whole bunch more. There's the garden to put out and hoe and harvest, the canning to be done, and laundry and cooking and God knows what all. I need her right here at home. Not off at some fancy high school and workin' for somebody else."

"I understand, Mrs. Hansen," Miss Connor replied softly. "It would be . . . a . . . strain for you. But Emma really must stay in school until she is sixteen. But, what's more important is that this is the greatest possible gift that you can give her. I have never known a child who has more potential to benefit from further education. If she completes high school and passes the state examination—and I have no doubt that she would—she could become a teacher. Teachers are earning thirty dollars a month nowadays. Emma is already doing high school work and helping me teach the first and second graders. She has gone beyond what I can teach her. She's been doing algebra and Latin on her own all year."

"That's all well and good, but high school is four years, ain't it? A long time until she gets a job. In the meantime, what about my work? Algebra and Latin don't get the milkin' done."

"She would be home during the three months of summer when the garden work and canning is heaviest," Miss Connor replied. "Is there any chance that her sister could return home?"

"We need the money."

"Well, maybe with the extra income from sellin' the milk from the new cows, she could come back," Papa offered. "The barn addition will be done by fall and we can increase the herd by then."

"But there'll be the bank loan to pay off. And what if Kirsten wants to get married? She says that Reinhardt's younger brother has been courtin' her."

"Guess we'll cross that bridge when we come to it."

The table fell silent. Finally Miss Connor spoke. "Well, please give it serious consideration. Emma is an exceptional pupil. It's worth some sacrifice to provide her with a good education."

"Ya," Papa Hansen replied. "We'll think about it."

Mama was silent, unsmiling.

Please, oh, please, Emma thought, set me free. Let me fly.

CHAPTER 3
1916

EMMA SLID THE brass weight across the scale's balance beam to the 10 lb mark, then poured beans from a large metal scoop into the pan, briskly at first, then slowly until the beam rose and hovered at the midline. She poured the contents of the pan into a paper sack.

"That's ten pounds of navy beans at eleven cents a pound for a dollar ten, plus ten pounds of flour, fifty cents, for one sixty, five pounds of sugar at nine cents, forty-five; that's two oh five, and thirty cents for the coffee. Two dollars and thirty-five cents. Will that be all, Mrs. Schultheiss?"

"Ja, tanks. You iss zo fast wiss tze numbers, Emma. I can't do tzat in English, but I trust you godt it right." Emma punched the keys on the big brass cash register so that white tabs reading $2, 30c and 5c popped up in the little glass window. Mrs. Schultheiss had difficulty when she heard numbers spoken in English, but she understood them readily if she saw them. She sat her infant on the counter and fumbled with her pocketbook with her free hand.

"Here, I'll hold the little one," Emma said.

Mrs. Schultheiss pulled a small cloth purse out of her pocketbook and carefully counted out the correct amount in coins. "Tze prices, tzey always goink up."

"I know. Quite a lot since I started working here. It's the Great War driving them up, I think." Emma wondered if she should have said that.

"Ja."

The war, already churning in Europe for two years, was a sensitive topic with the Schultheiss family. German immigrants were often treated with hostility or suspicion. There was much wild talk of America entering the war against the Central Powers, of the vile acts of the "Huns," stories of atrocities in Belgium.

"Let me help you carry the groceries out. You've got your hands full with the baby."

The Schultheiss' team and buggy stood in front of the Oosterfeld's grocery alongside two Model T Fords. Emma knew that Mrs. Schultheiss would have to trudge up the street with her infant on her hip to retrieve her husband from the tavern.

When Emma returned to the store, Piet Oosterfeld smiled from the stool where he was stacking cans on shelves flanked with barrels and sacks. He didn't speak; it wasn't necessary. Emma had readily mastered every task there was to operating the store. Moreover, she was efficient and courteous with the customers, remembered their names, asked about their families, anticipated their needs.

Emma had become comfortable with the Oosterfelds, a gentle and reserved childless couple. Indeed, she would have been ashamed to admit that she was happier with them than she was at home on the Hansen farm. She had become a surrogate daughter to the Oosterfelds, she enjoyed working in the store in the evenings and weekends, she very much appreciated the comfort of living in the village, where rooms were well heated and electric lights glowed at night.

But the greatest source of her happiness was attending Stanton Mills High School. How quickly the four years had gone by. She had loved her courses and earned high marks. She was in line to graduate as the class valedictorian in two months.

The thought filled her with pride, but also unease. What lay ahead? She would take the state examination to qualify for an elementary teaching certificate next month, so teaching in a one-room country school was a possibility, but that plan had been displaced by a newer, more unreachable dream—college, four years of college and a Bachelor's Degree.

Biology was driving her there. Biology. How she loved it. During her junior year she had gained an overview of the living world, the tree of life so carefully organized in the Linnaean system from the simplest unicellular organisms through sponges, coelenterates, and echinoderms to the majestic kingdoms of higher plants and animals.

Emma's knowledge of Latin made it easy for her to learn the formal Linnaean names of the phyla, orders, families, and species as well as body parts from textbook drawings and dissections. She had gathered the leaves of seventy-three species of local trees and presented them, carefully pressed and labeled, to the class, and followed that with an equally impressive collection of insects, killed with chloroform, dried and mounted on pins in boxes. Henrik had helped her with both collections during her visits and summers at the home farm.

But it was Emma's studies of human physiology and hygiene during her senior year that had blown the glowing coals of her enthusiasm into a bright flame, for here she was brought face-to-face with the most fundamental question of biology, which was not taxonomy or anatomy as stressed in last year's course, but a more profound question: how does it work?

Her puzzlement began with the "germ theory" of disease. Her textbook described the work of Robert Koch, who had shown that anthrax and tuberculosis were caused by germs—properly called "bacteria." His work was so beautifully logical. Koch always found this particular germ in the lungs or sputum of tuberculosis patients. He could grow the germ in pure cultures in the laboratory, and it caused tuberculosis when he introduced it back into animals.

But what were bacteria? The textbook said they were tiny plants, but that didn't seem right to Emma, because the drawings in the textbook certainly didn't look like plants and they weren't green. How did this miniscule creature cause disease and why did some people recover while others sickened and died?

The high school had no microscopes that would permit Emma to see bacteria for herself, yet the textbook insisted that they were everywhere—in milk, water, and food, in the air. Why didn't everyone get sick? Then came the section on smallpox vaccination. How did that work? No one could find the smallpox germ—why not? Emma pestered Mr. Witherspoon with questions, which he could not answer.

"I'm afraid I do not know, Miss Hansen," he said. "Perhaps no one knows as of yet. You will have to go to a college or university if you want to pursue it."

So indeed she would.

There was a particular poignancy to Emma's questions because little Aaron had died of diphtheria just a month after his second birthday. Her family had watched in agony as the pale little boy gasped and choked, his neck swollen to twice its normal thickness. Mama and Papa had assumed that it was "just croup" and delayed summoning a doctor until it was too late; their grief was compounded with guilt.

Mama was engulfed with depression, which persisted even now, two years later. Papa's silences and fierce involvement with farm work deepened. Emma had been living in Stanton Mills when baby Aaron died, so she had been spared the agony of witnessing his asphyxiating death, but the recollection of his miniature coffin being lowered into the barren ground still brought tears to her eyes. Why was such suffering visited on the innocent child she had so often rocked to sleep?

Diphtheria was caused by a bacterium, Emma learned from her textbook. Why had little Aaron been infected, but no other members of the family? Why was there no vaccine for diphtheria as there was for smallpox? The doctor had injected an "antitoxin," but it had not saved the baby. Why not? Mr. Witherspoon could not tell Emma what an antitoxin was or how it differed from a vaccine. So many questions.

There was one area of human physiology that was completely absent from her textbook, however, and it was one in which Emma would have been embarrassed to admit, she had done a bit of research on her own: human reproductive biology. Her friend and classmate Victor Midlothian had been her willing partner in these investigations.

Victor was the son of a bank officer in Stanton Mills and lived with his parents just a few blocks from the Oosterfeld's grocery store. He was less intimidated by Emma's intelligence and outspoken questions than most of the farm boys in their high school classes, and the two occasionally studied together. Indeed, Victor admitted that he would not have passed geometry without Emma's tutoring. Rumors went around the school that Victor was "sweet" on Emma, and she supposed it was true because of his attentiveness. He was a nice-looking boy with large blue eyes and dark brown hair fashionably parted down the middle. Emma enjoyed his companionship, but she thought of him more as a brother—like Henrik—than as beau. Her plans for the future did not include a beau.

Emma had created an embarrassment in the senior human physiology class when she asked Mr. Witherspoon why there was nothing in their textbook about reproduction.

He had flushed and shuffled uncomfortably. "Well, those are, um, delicate matters best explained by your parents, Miss Hansen," he replied. "Besides, surely you know the, er, basic facts."

"Of course. Anyone who grew up on a farm knows that, but there's a lot about how the body works that we don't know." Emma, like the few other girls in the class, had reasons to want to know more. She had experienced the changes in her body wrought by puberty. The blossoming of her breasts prepared them to nurse future babies, that seemed obvious, but what on earth did the sprouting of hair between her legs and the flow of blood from her nether regions every month have to do with it? She couldn't ask these questions of Mr. Witherspoon, and her mother's answers had been vague.

"It just means you can have a baby now if you lie with a man," she said. Mrs. Oosterfeld was quiet and motherly, but Emma didn't feel free to ask her about such personal matters.

There had been some rather unchaste explorations with Victor while the two of them were alone on an April Sunday afternoon searching for mushrooms in Wilson's Woods, which lay at the edge of Stanton Mills. What Victor had revealed to her not only answered some of Emma's questions about human reproductive anatomy, but they awakened new feelings that were both pleasurable and troubling. There was so much she needed to understand. Victor coaxed for more walks in the woods, but Emma declined. "C'mon, Vic, let's just be friends."

HENRIK LIFTED THE wooden orange crate filled with groceries into the back of the truck, then flipped a fifty pound flour sack off of his shoulder and laid it next to the crate. As big and strong as a man, Emma thought, just turned nineteen. He opened the door to the cab for Emma.

"Get in and sit behind the wheel, Emmie. Pull the choke out—that knob there—while I crank 'er. Push it in when she starts up. Pull the throttle lever down—this one—so it's not racing, but not all the way down. Then I'll hop in and off we go."

The Model T Ford truck was unfamiliar to Emma. The Hansens had bought it last year while she was living in Stanton Mills. There were two handles on either side of the steering post, the knob Henrik called a choke, three pedals on the floor, and a lever coming up from the floor beside the driver, as well as three small glass-covered dials on the dashboard.

Emma had no idea what any of them did, but she was keen to learn, and she knew that Henrik would be proud to teach her. After a couple of quick twists of the crank at the front of the vehicle, the engine sputtered into a rhythmic chugging, and Henrik jumped onto the seat, nudged Emma aside, adjusted the spark lever, and settled behind the steering wheel.

"She starts good," he said, as he depressed the middle pedal, pulled down the hand throttle, and twisted his head to see as he backed the truck out into the street. "The roads were so bad this spring, we couldn't drive it, but now the ruts have dried out. Rough as hell, though. Hang on."

"I remember you and Papa had to bring me back home on the bobsled for Christmas, the snow was so deep."

"Yeah, this thing can't get through deep snow like a team of horses. Gee, Emmie, here it is Easter and I haven't seen you since New Year's." Henrik glanced at Emma, then turned his eyes back to the rough dirt road. "I've missed ya, kiddo."

"Me too, Hennie." Than after a long pause. "How're things at home?"

"Well, I gotta be honest with you. They ain't so good."

"What's wrong? Is Mama still poorly? Seems like she never got over it when Aaron died."

"That's part of it. But she and Susan don't get along, always barkin' at one another. Mama's the boss of the house and garden, you know, but Susan's got her own ideas, and she can't keep her trap shut."

"Oh, that's not fair. You know how cross Mama can be, and it can't be easy, a new daughter-in-law and all, moving in right after they got married."

"Well, Bjorn told me they'd move out except for they want to take over the farm someday. And Papa ain't ready for that. The farm's all he gives a damn about."

"How about you? Do you want to stay on the farm?"

"Oh, hell no. Bjorn's the oldest; he's gonna inherit it all anyway. Soon's we get into the Big War, I'm gonna sign up." Henrik flashed a grin. "Can't you see me as a soldier boy? Take a big ship across the ocean. March across France. Kick the Huns all the way back to Berlin."

"Oh, Hennie. Don't do it. Haven't you read in the papers? All those boys, thousands and thousands of them, piled up dead in the trenches. And poison gas. It's horrible. No, please, no. What's wrong with you boys? Victor's been talking that way too. Says he wants to fly one of those fighting aeroplanes."

"Who's Victor?"

"Oh, he's a boy I go to school with. Victor Midlothian."

"Is he your beau, Emmie? You sweet on him, huh?" Henrik teased.

"No," Emma shot back. What was Victor? Something more than a friend, surely. "He's just a nice boy, a senior like me. We study together sometimes."

"Uh-huh." The truck lurched roughly, and Henrik wrestled the steering wheel, shifted back into low gear with his feet.

"Besides, you're changing the subject, Henrik. Please don't go off to the army. If something happened to you, well, we . . . I . . . just couldn't stand it. Think of poor Mama. After baby Aaron and everything. Besides America isn't going to get into the war. President Wilson said so."

"Well, we'll see. If the Germans start sinkin' our ships with their U-boats again . . ."

WHATEVER TROUBLES WRITHED beneath the surface in the Hansen farmhouse, they were ignored for the family Easter dinner. Papa and Mama sat side by side at one end of the expanded table in the front room and Bjorn and Susan at the other end, Emma and Henrik at one side, and Kurt and Kirsten, who had come all the way from Greene County for Easter, opposite. Kirsten was obviously pregnant, although she and Kurt had only married three months previously—the topic was not discussed.

The family had completed a heavy meal of ham, scalloped potatoes, peas fresh from the garden, and bread baked the day before, with both cherry and apple pie and were so satiated that conversation, which had been sporadic during the meal, died out completely.

Emma caught the sleepy eyes of her sister-in-law and her sister—how odd to see her with her belly so swollen. She had tried to imagine the events that had led up to that: Kurt in a state like Victor's, her sister yielding to penetration.

"Why don't you all take a rest?" she said. "Susan, you worked all morning, and Kirsten you've had a long ride. I'll help Mama with the dishes."

The young women protested, but feebly, and remained seated—as did the men—when Emma left the room. Emma was rewarded with a rare smile from Mama.

Cleaning up and washing dishes in the kitchen were familiar tasks: scraps saved for the pigs, hot water carried from the reservoir at the side of the kitchen range to the dry sink with a second large metal pan for rinsing. Familiar, yet a bit strange, because Emma had lived with the Oosterfelds in their apartment over the store for much of the past four years. How primitive living conditions were for her family—for nearly all farm families—as compared to those who dwelt in town.

The Hansen farm had no electricity, no telephone, no central heat, no indoor plumbing, no toilet, or bathtub—all comforts she had come to enjoy in Stanton Mills. Life was so much harder and more uncomfortable for her mother than it was for Mrs. Oosterfeld. Did Mama realize this and resent it, or did her evident unhappiness have deeper, less material roots?

"I'll be graduating in June," Emma said. "I hope you and Papa and Bjorn and Henrik can come to the ceremony. It's not official yet, but I expect to be named valedictorian and will have to make a speech."

"Valedictorian, what's that?"

"It's the person who makes a farewell speech at graduation—*vale dictum*, to say goodbye—and it's usually the pupil with the highest marks in the class," Emma replied, then felt a twinge of shame at the pridefulness of her statement and parading of her knowledge of Latin.

"Then you'll be coming home this summer, home to stay?" Mama washed the dinner plates with such speed that Emma could barely keep up with rinsing and drying them.

"Yes, but I will probably have to go to the normal college in DeKalb for six weeks this summer. If I pass the state examination, I will still have to take the teaching course to get my teacher's certificate."

"Six weeks? How are we going to pay for that?"

"I'm not sure. Maybe I can borrow it from the bank and pay them back from my salary this fall."

"So you're going to be a schoolteacher? Live at home then and go to the school? I hope so. I could use the help, what with Kirstin gone and Susan refusing to help in the barn with the milking and all."

"I don't know, Mama. It depends on where I can get a job. If the school is too far from here, I'll have to board somewhere close. You know how it gets in winter." Then Emma took a deep breath. Might as well get it over with, tell her the rest of it. "I'm only going to teach for a year or two, Mama. Save enough money to go to college. I want to study biology."

"College? Where to?"

"I don't know yet, Mama. But it won't be close to here. I may not be living at home much longer."

"Oh, so you're going to run off too, are you?" Mama said bitterly. She threw her dishrag into the sink, wiped her hands on her apron, and sat down at the kitchen table, her body crumpled in misery. "I just don't know. What does it all come to, Emma? You work all day, every day, summer and winter. Five children and they all go off. Little Aaron dead. Kirsten and Kurt clear over in Greene County. Henrik says he wants to join the Army. Bjorn, well, he might as well not be here. I know he and Susan ain't happy. Now, you wantin' go off to college."

"But, Mama, you still have Papa."

She waved her hand dismissively. "Oh, he doesn't care about me. All he cares about is the farm. This house is so cold in the winter, but do you think he will put on some storm windows? Maybe put in a furnace like they do in town? He can put an addition the barn, buy a dozen cows, but something for the house . . . ?"

"Oh, Mama."

"It's true, girl. You work and work all your life and what do you get? You get old and alone. That's what it all comes down to."

She folded back in on herself, tucked her arms in to her sides, as though to make herself so small that she might disappear. Her eyes were vacant with despair, but dry.

Emma felt a wave of pity, started to reach her hand out to caress her mother's shoulder, but stopped. She sensed that the gesture would make them both uncomfortable. Words wouldn't form, turned to glue in her throat. Her sympathy and sadness were interwoven with a fierce, but guilty determination: not this path. No, whatever hardships and uncertainties she might face, she would not follow her mother's path, no, not ever.

"MISS HANSEN, WOULD you step into my office, please?" Mr. Ramsey, the principal of Stanton Mills High School, stood unsmiling as usual, in the doorway of his office.

A tall, stiff man with thinning gray hair, a narrow face and wire-rimmed glasses, Ramsey, who was known behind his back as "Ramrod Ramsey," had been the principal of a parochial all-boys high school before coming to Stanton Mills, and he brought with him the humorless strictness for which he was notorious.

A summons to his office was dreaded by the pupils, but nothing could dampen Emma's high spirits today. She was not in trouble; he presumably simply intended to return to her the draft of her valedictory address, which he had demanded to approve in advance of its delivery on the coming Friday evening.

Two weeks earlier Emma had been notified of her selection as valedictorian of the Class of 1916. It was hardly a surprise, but Emma took pleasure in receiving a secretly long-desired recognition. Nor was this the only good news. Emma had received a letter from the state education department informing her that she had passed the primary teacher's qualifying examination with high scores and that "upon completion of the required teacher's training at a state normal school, a certificate qualifying you to teach Grades 1 through 8 in this state will be issued." Her plans for the coming year were falling into place.

An even more exciting prospect had arrived unexpectedly. Hancock College, a small Lutheran college in western Illinois, had offered her admission and waiver of the first year's tuition and fees on the strength of her "outstanding promise as evidenced by your graduation as valedictorian of your high school class." Emma had written the college asking to defer acceptance for one year. She was determined to save enough from her teacher's salary to pay for the cost of lodging, books, and transportation for her first year of college. How she would manage the remaining three years of college, she did not know. Perhaps she would have to alternate years of teaching with college years, but she *was* going to college. And biology would be her chosen major.

Ramsey led Emma into his office, waved her toward a seat, and settled behind his desk. He frowned and pushed a sheaf of handwritten pages toward her. It was Emma's speech, and the final page had been crossed out in red ink.

"Miss Hansen, I cannot permit you to include this paragraph. It is highly inappropriate for a girl of sixteen to lecture her elders on world affairs."

So that was it. Most of Emma's address covered well-trodden paths for valedictory addresses. She congratulated her classmates on reaching this important milestone, she fulsomely thanked their teachers and parents for supporting their education, and she listed several "challenges we face," which was the title of her address. These, too, were predictable: to find productive work that contributed to society at large, to continue to learn and expand understanding of a rapidly changing world, to honor and protect their families, to care for the less fortunate, to maintain the highest standards of personal integrity. But, it was her last "challenge" that had offended the principal. It read:

We must maintain cool heads and rational minds in the face of growing pressures for our nation to enter the terrible war that has engulfed Europe. So often we hear cries that enflame our hearts and urge us onto the fields of battle. But have we not seen the awful and futile slaughter in the trenches of France? Must we spill the blood of the flower of our youth in this senseless conflict? Must America involve her lives and fortune in the conflicting imperial ambitions and hereditary quarrels of the crowned heads of Europe? Are we not wiser to heed the advice of President Washington—and of President

Wilson—and remain neutral? War is a terrible, terrible thing; only the gravest of dangers can justify taking a nation to war. Let us resist the calls of adventurers and those seeking to profit from war. Let us remain a proud independent nation, slow to anger, loving peace and security.

"This paragraph must be excised, Miss Hansen. It is pacifist propaganda."

"But it is my strongly held view, Mr. Ramsey. The boys in our class will be called upon to die if we enter the war. Surely it is a challenge to them and worthy of discussion."

"Not by an arrogant snip of a girl, it isn't. Politics is not appropriate for this address. Girls do not presume to instruct their betters on such matters. Next I suppose you will be telling me that you are one those suffragettes and will lecture me on that."

"I do believe that women should have the right to vote, yes."

"Nonsense. Women are not equipped to deal with such weighty matters. They will simply vote as their fathers or husbands instruct them. A waste of time."

"With respect, sir, there is a contradiction in your argument. You say that women are incapable of thinking about world affairs, but you also seek to prevent me from doing just that."

"That's enough insolence. I am directing to you remove this paragraph."

"And if I do not?"

"Then I shall withdraw your designation as valedictorian and appoint the salutatorian, Mr. Midlothian, in your place. Either way, this"—he smirked and tapped the offending page—"will not be read."

"But that's unfair. Victor's marks were not as high as mine."

"Miss Hansen, I will brook no further discussion of this matter. Either comply or be replaced." Ramsey set his mouth and stared coldly at Emma, who stared back. Her cheeks grew hot; her fists were knots. A long silence followed.

"Your decision, Miss Hansen?"

"Very well. I will remove the paragraph." Emma was angry, humiliated, but the loss of her well-earned recognition was too high a price.

I'll fix you, Mr. Ramrod Ramsey, she thought. After graduation I will send that paragraph as a letter to the editor of the *Stanton Mills Gazette*.

And so she did. She considered including a note saying that she had been forced to excise it from her valedictory address, but decided not to do that.

Even though her sentiments were widely shared in the area, Emma's letter was never published.

CHAPTER 4
1919 - 1920

"WHAT SHALL WE call it, Emma, your *novum species?*" Professor Lucinda Weatherbee peered over her wire-rimmed glasses with characteristic directness, her motherliness masked with severity, her voice deep and throaty with authority. Her dark brown hair was pulled back into a bun, and she wore her usual shapeless lavender dress.

"I have thought about that a little, Dr. Weatherbee," Emma replied. "How about *Copris ereptor.* dung beetle thief? *Copris latrocinius* would fit too, but I prefer the shorter one."

"So it shall be. *Copris ereptor.* I must say, I am pleased, Emma. You are developing the intellectual habits of a fine naturalist. Your field observations were most interesting, of course, but I was skeptical that you had identified a new species. Your arguments on the basis of anatomical differences between the new beetle and the known scarab beetle species now have me convinced. I want you to submit your findings to an entomological journal for publication. Let's see if an expert agrees with you."

Emma flushed with pleasure. Her admiration for Dr. Weatherbee, one of only two professors of biology at Hancock College and the only female professor on the faculty, was intense, bordering on hero worship. Dr. Weatherbee was one of the first women in America to earn a Ph.D., a Ph.D. in biology from Cornell University in 1901. She was a popular, if somewhat eccentric and formidable, figure on campus. Emma glowed under the respect and encouragement that her teacher now paid to her fledgling biological studies.

"Oh, Dr. Weatherbee, I have no idea how to write a scientific paper."

"Don't worry. I'll help you. It is most unusual for a sophomore in college—and a woman at that—to publish a scientific paper. I suggest that we simply list the author as 'E. Hansen, from the Biology Department of Hancock College.' That way they won't trip over their prejudices." Dr. Weatherbee rarely smiled, but a look of mischief flashed across her face. Then she stood up from her desk. "Oh, I have a lecture in five minutes. Come back tomorrow at four and I'll help you get started."

As she passed Emma on her way out of the office, her hand lingered on Emma's shoulder, an unusual gesture of warmth.

EMMA'S OBSERVATIONS OF the new thieving dung beetles had been made during the previous summer, 1919, after her freshman year at Hancock, while she was living at home on the Hansen farm. Even as a child she had been fascinated with these diligent little insects. She occasionally spotted them on the dusty paths worn in a narrow lane by the farm's cows as they traipsed along, single file, year after year, to and from a pasture at the rear of the farm.

While driving the cows to the barn for milking, Emma occasionally saw a shiny black beetle, about the size of a thimble, laboriously rolling a perfectly spherical ball of dung, freshly harvested from a wet cow flop, a ball nearly as big as the beetle itself, through the powdery dirt. Now, as a student of biology in college, Emma set about seeking answers to her questions. What was the value of the dung balls to the beetles? Did they serve as a food reserve? Did the beetles lay eggs in them? If so, when? Where did they go with their little round prizes? Was it males or females that did the work—she might be able to decide which was which if she could capture a mating pair.

During her observations Emma had noticed a surprising event: a slightly larger black beetle flew up to a dung beetle busy rolling a brownish ball, landed, and attacked the smaller beetle. After a brief struggle the small beetle retreated and surrendered its prize to the aggressor, which clasped it in its legs and flew a short distance to a spot where it shoved the dung ball into a hole in a little dirt bank and crawled in after it.

After Emma observed similar acts two more times, she shifted her attention to the phenomenon of dung ball robbery. She captured and preserved specimens of both beetles; she collected dung balls, intending to examine their contents for eggs with a dissecting microscope when she returned to college. She even carefully excavated two of the burrows of the larger beetle and saved the dung balls she found stored within.

Emma's family greeted her fascination with dung beetles with teasing and annoyance.

"I see you spent another whole afternoon out studyin' them shit-ball roller bugs again, Emma," Bjorn groused at supper. "Dunno what's so darn interesting about 'em."

By then Emma's irritation with her family's jibes had mellowed to quiet tolerance. "Bjorn, I've told you before, they're called scarab beetles. They use the dung balls for food storage, and I think they lay their eggs in them."

"Ugh. Disgusting. I'd think you could find something better to study. Is that the kind of thing they teach at that college?" Mama grumbled.

"No, but they teach us to observe nature closely. Ask questions. How to find the answers. I've noticed something really interesting. Some other beetle flies in and steals the dung balls. It's an example of natural opportunism, a kind of parasitism. Like when a cowbird lays its eggs in another bird's nest. We used to find that sometimes, didn't we, Henrik?"

Henrik mumbled, "uh-huh," without interest. He avoided Emma's eyes and his hands trembled.

Henrik, oh, her dear brother Henrik! Emma's heart ached for him. He'd gone to war in June of 1917 and was wounded in France at Chateau-Thierry in 1918, but he had not returned home until after the Armistice, more or less physically healed, but broken in spirit by what was called "shell shock." His boyish playfulness was gone, displaced by moody silences. He suffered from terrible nightmares from which he could only be comforted by Mama or Emma. Worse, he had taken to driving the Ford truck into Stanton Mills and returning stumbling drunk. He worked steadily, joylessly, with his father and brother on the farm and rarely spoke of his experiences of war.

Occasionally he sat without speaking beside Emma on the porch steps in the evening. She was careful not to embrace him on such occasions, because this display of tenderness had caused him to weep without consolation. Emma wondered what had caused such devastation. He had been wounded in his right leg and shoulder by shrapnel; there had been no head injuries. Yet his mind was damaged as surely as if shards of metal had sliced into his brain. How could one understand what had happened to Henrik and how could he be healed?

"Well, I just don't see the use of it," Papa grumbled. "Them roller bugs don't amount to anything. Why waste time with 'em? If you have to look at bugs, how about something practical like the borers that get in my corn? Or them flies that bite the cows and make grubs under their hides? Something like that?"

"I'm just trying to learn how to be a good biologist, Papa. Maybe someday I can use my skills for practical problems. Besides, don't you think there is value in studying nature just out of curiosity?"

The question hung in the air. Mama had complained frequently that Emma's time would be better spent helping in the house and garden.

Emma had learned to avoid arguing, to work diligently with her mother and sister-in-law Susan, but insisted on a few hours a week with her beetles on the cow path. They had arrived at an unspoken truce—not peace, but a cease-fire.

THE SUMMER OF 1919 was Emma's fourth summer living and working at home since graduating from high school. The first summer has been interrupted by her six weeks of teacher training at the normal school in DeKalb. For the next two years she had taught grades one through eight at a one-room country school sixteen miles west of Stanton Mills. Because that school was located too far from the Hansen farm, she was forced to board with a nearby farm family, which reduced her earnings. It had taken two years for her to accumulate sufficient money to begin her college studies at Hancock.

The tuition waiver had been granted by the college for her first year only. She supplemented her meager funds for her sophomore year by taking a job in the dormitory kitchen to earn her meals and with a small loan from the Stanton Mills State Bank, but Emma feared that she would have to interrupt her studies again and return to teaching to earn her junior and senior years. There was no question of asking her family for financial help. The Hansens were struggling to pay off a loan—taken out over Mama's bitter objections—that had permitted them to purchase cows and enlarge their barn four years earlier.

Each summer Emma felt a bit more estranged from her own family, and the feeling grew more intense after her years in college. She was so excited and happy at Hancock, despite her poverty, especially now that Dr. Weatherbee had recognized her ability and had taken her on as a protégée. She spent all of her free time during the summer on the farm studying the biology books she had brought home and thinking about the natural world around her. It was as though a film had been lifted from her eyes and every living thing was seen sharply in full color and dramatic motion for the first time.

Her family expressed no interest in her preoccupations. Her mother scolded her for daydreaming and isolating herself in her bedroom to read. In fairness, Emma knew that none of them had been exposed to the facts and ideas that now beguiled her and they hardly knew how to discuss them. She would have been too self-conscious to lecture them about what she learned. She yearned for someone to share her fascinations. Henrik would have been her natural companion. He had enjoyed sharing her youthful collections of wild bird eggs, plants, and insects. But Henrik had gone to war and returned hollow-eyed and slack-jawed, preoccupied with private pain.

One evening as they were sitting silently on the porch as the hot air of the day cooled and thrummed with cicada song, Emma dared to draw him out. Henrik had begun shifting restlessly, which Emma recognized as a sign that he would soon climb into the truck and head for Stanton Mills.

She placed her hand on his arm. "We used to be more happy, Hennie. Now I feel kind of like a stranger living here. Mama and I don't argue much anymore, but . . . well . . . I don't know. I feel like my heart's somewhere else."

"Yeah, me too. Except everywhere else is worse."

"It's what happened in the war, isn't it?"

"Yeah."

"Do you ever want to talk about it? I mean, you don't have to . . . if . . ."

He began to tremble. "I . . . I can't let go of it. I don't know why."

"You must have seen terrible things."

"Oh, God!" His speech became rapid, high-pitched with fear and confusion. "I saw men blown to bits. Their guts hanging out. Screaming. Begging us to shoot them. I killed a German. He came jumping into our trench. I think he got mixed up and thought we were Germans too. And I shot him. But it didn't kill him. He was just a kid like me. He was crying and saying stuff in German. I couldn't understand, but I knew there were words like 'God' and 'Mama.' The sergeant just came up and shot him in the head with his pistol to shut him up." Henrik covered his face with his hands and wept.

Emma caressed his shoulder and repeated over and over, "It's all right now. It's over."

"No. It's not. I couldn't take it. I always wanted to run away. I'm a coward. I was glad when I was wounded and got to leave the front."

"No, Hennie, no. Anybody would run away. I would have too."

"You're a girl. It's different. A man can't run away. I was so scared."

They sat in a clumsy embrace until Henrik's weeping calmed.

"It doesn't matter now," Emma whispered. "Please try not to think about it. I want you back the way you used to be. I'm so lonely here. No one has any interest in the things I care about. Like you used to. Remember? How we used to hunt bird's eggs?"

Henrik stared at her, eyes wide with incomprehension. His mouth moved, but no words emerged. He jumped up, strode over to the truck, cranked the engine, and drove out the lane.

EMMA STOOD WITH the rest of the student congregation and joined in singing the closing hymn, "A Mighty Fortress is Our God." (Before the Great War the Hancock College chapel had sung the hymn in Luther's original words: "*Ein feste Burg ist unser Gott,*" but no longer.) Like all students at Hancock, Emma was required to attend chapel on Sundays and to take two courses on biblical teachings: New Testament, followed by Old Testament.

Emma had come to love religious music—the college had an excellent chapel choir and the chapel was equipped with a fine organ—and she found the familiar repeated rituals of liturgical worship comforting in ways that she could not have articulated. But the habits of questioning and skeptical seeking for evidence that she was acquiring in her science courses had made it difficult for her to accept the Church's teachings as the literal truth. Dr. Bauermeister, who as professor of theology and an ordained minister had taught the required Bible courses, had insisted in answer to her questions that the Virgin Birth and the Resurrection were not metaphors, but real historical events that confirmed the uniqueness of Christ as "God on earth" and His mission to rescue humanity from sin.

Dr. Weatherbee had shrugged impatiently. "In my opinion, Emma, the Bible is not a reliable source of information about natural phenomena. We must rely on observation and experiment."

"But if God created Nature and its laws, couldn't He break them?"

"Perhaps, but an alternative explanation is that these reported miracles were invented stories, stories made up by a gullible and superstitious people almost two thousand years ago."

"How can we tell which is the truth?"

"I doubt that we can, dear. I've long felt that it was a waste of time trying. Mind you, this is a church-supported college. I try not to bite the hand that feeds me."

For the moment, though, caught up the surging hymn borne on hundreds of youthful voices and a thundering pipe organ, Emma shivered with pleasure and ignored her doubts—did it even matter whether it was true or not?

As the students filed out of the chapel after the Benediction, Max Swerdt, who had been coming to chapel with Emma for the past few months, leaned close to her and said, "You seemed especially radiant this morning, Emma, filled with the Holy Spirit."

"Oh, Max, you make me too saintly. I just love the music."

Max was a senior, son of a Lutheran minister, and planning to follow his father's path to seminary and the ministry. He had begun paying attention to Emma during the fall of her sophomore year, and they had had a few "dates," if that's what they could be called. Emma had little free time, and there was not much to do around the college or in the surrounding town other than some college sporting events and infrequent musical and theatrical performances.

Max did not approve of drinking, dancing, or the picture shows in town. They took walks on shady campus paths. On one of these walks he had embraced her and kissed her very quickly and gently, then walked on in embarrassed silence. Emma had felt none of the strange electricity that she recalled from her episode in the woods with Victor. Max's wooing—was it wooing?—was not unwelcome. He was tall and blond, attractive in a way that reminded her of Henrik. He was unfailingly courteous and never teased her about her background as a farm girl. He listened politely, but without real interest, to her enthusiastic chatter about biology and her discovery of thieving dung beetles.

"Would you walk with me for a while, Emma?" Max asked.

"OK, we can take the long way to Winston Hall. I have to go to work in the kitchen at eleven thirty."

After a few minutes Max cleared his throat. "Do you think much about the future?"

"Well, of course. All the time. I've got to figure out how I can pay for the next two years of college."

"Yes, but I mean . . . uh . . . beyond that."

"Well, my idea was to become a high school biology teacher after I graduate. But I've begun to think—daydream, really—about becoming a real scientist, maybe a professor like Dr. Weatherbee. I'd have to go to post-graduate school. I would love to be able to do that. It seems almost beyond my reach, but . . ."

"What about marrying . . . some day?"

"Oh, I don't see where that fits in. Not yet." She almost said that she hadn't met anyone she wanted to marry, but stopped herself. Was Max hinting at his interest in marrying her? Would she consider marrying him?

"Surely you don't want to spend your life as a spinster? Like Dr. Weatherbee?"

"No. I think I'd like to be married someday. Have a family. But wouldn't a husband expect me to stay home? Give up science?"

"Well, naturally, yes. A wife and mother's place is in the home. If I were married, it wouldn't do for a pastor's wife to . . . well . . . be teaching and working in a laboratory all the time . . . it wouldn't look right. There are so many duties a pastor's wife must do for the church. And the home and children to take care of. I don't think any man would stand for that."

"Well then, maybe I will never marry after all." Emma's words carried a greater tone of anger than she wished. Most men felt as Max did. She didn't wish to drive him away, but hurt and disappointment clouded his face.

"I just don't see why it matters that much. I mean, staring in microscopes and dissecting dung beetles."

"Max," Emma said hotly. "The man I marry—if I do ever marry—will understand why it matters that much."

Max raised his eyebrows and turned away. They walked in unhappy silence the rest of the way through the campus to Winston Hall.

"WHAT ON EARTH has happened, Emma? You're always so cheerful. I've never seen you crying before." Dr. Weatherbee pulled up a lab stool and sat opposite Emma.

"Oh, I'm sorry to be such a crybaby." Emma sniffled and wiped her face with the back of her hand. Dr. Weatherbee handed her a handkerchief and sat quietly, then gently, very tentatively, patted the back of Emma's hand.

"Come now. What is it? I'd have thought you'd be especially happy after getting word that your paper has been accepted. I was worried that you would have to go to the Field Museum to look at their beetle collection to rule out those other *Copris* species, but fortunately they relented when we pointed out that the collection will be unavailable until the new building is opened next year, or whenever it is finally finished."

"I am happy about that, and I'm so grateful that you helped me with that letter to the editor. I'm . . . I'm . . . being silly, I guess."

"No. Silly does not describe you. What's wrong?"

"I was called into the Registrar's office just now and scolded because I still haven't paid the balance on my dorm bill. She said that if it isn't paid at once, my grades for the spring semester will be withheld and I will not be allowed to continue at Hancock. Oh, I don't know what to do. I haven't got the money. Even if I gave them every penny I have left, it wouldn't be enough. And I wouldn't have anything for train fare to get back home this summer." Emma's voice quavered, but she successfully fought back more tears.

"How much is owing, dear?"

"Seventy eight dollars."

"Well, how about if I lend it to you?"

"Oh, that's not right. I couldn't take money from you. Not after all you've done for me."

"Nonsense. You can repay me in the fall when you start your junior year."

"No, I can't." Emma's tears regained the upper hand. "I won't be coming back in the fall. I'm going to have to go back to teaching again until I can earn enough to pay my tuition and board. It'll take me two years. It's taking me forever to complete my studies. And, Dr. Weatherbee, I've begun to dream of graduate study, of getting a Ph.D. and becoming a real scientist . . . like you."

"As well you should."

"But I'll never be able to pay for it. What is it: Three, four more years? How ever did you manage it?"

"Oh, I had the good fortune to be born into a well-off family. My grandfather made his fortune in lumber and iron mining. My education was paid for by my family."

"Oh."

"Emma, you are so bright, so gifted. You *must* continue. Please don't become discouraged."

"I'll try. I'll just have to take it a year at a time, I guess. The next two years feel like a prison sentence, but I'll be back."

"Yes, and I'll be waiting for you. You're going to be Dr. Emma Hansen someday, yes, you are."

CHAPTER 5
1920

CHANGE COMES SLOWLY to small rural towns. Oosterfeld's Grocery was the same as it had been in the days when Emma lived and worked there four years earlier. The shelves lined with cans and jars, kegs of dried beans, corn meal and oatmeal, warm, dusty air, the creaking wooden floors, the patter of the ceiling fans was welcoming, like returning home—no, better. Piet and Hannah Oosterfeld greeted her, taking her hand in both of theirs, a gesture of unusual warmth for this reserved Dutch couple.

"Emma, you've come back to us. The store is closing in five minutes. Can you come upstairs and visit a little?"

"Yes, please, I'd like that."

Upstairs in the apartment Emma had shared with Piet and Hannah, the three of them followed the usual ritual of asking after one another's health, news of her family—she omitted her concern about Henrik, who had driven her into town this evening and now sat drinking in a speakeasy off an alley behind the main street—recent events in Stanton Mills, and commenting on the weather and prospects for the year's crops. The apartment was exactly as Emma remembered it—even the embroidered cloths covering the chair arms and backs were the same—but Piet and Hannah seemed older, grayer, and slow moving. Hannah's hands trembled slightly, and Piet had gently guided her to a chair.

"Now, tell us about college, dear. Are you happy there?" Hannah asked.

"Oh, yes. I love it. And I'm learning so much. There's a wonderful biology professor, Dr. Weatherbee, and she helped me to publish my first research paper."

"Is that something quite special?"

"It is. Dr. Weatherbee has only ever had three students do that. And none were sophomores, but me."

"That's wonderful. You must be so excited to be going back in the fall."

"Ah, that's the sad part that I need to talk to you about. I can't go back in the fall."

"Why ever not?"

"I'm completely out of money. In fact, I'm in debt. I'm going to have to teach again for a couple of years to replenish my savings." Emma had not intended to blurt out her request so quickly, but it spilled out. "I . . . I wondered if . . . if I can get a teaching position here in Stanton Mills . . . if I could live with you again and work in the store for my board. Like I did in high school. It would help me to build up funds for college so much quicker. Oh, if it's not . . . if it's an imposition . . . I understand. I hope you don't mind my asking."

"We'd love to have you, and we could use the help. We're not getting any younger. Do you think you can find a teaching job nearby?"

"I'll start looking right away. Oh, it would be so good to . . . to . . . be with you again."

WHEN EMMA SAID good-bye to the Osterfelds and left the store, she suppressed an urge to hug them. No, that would embarrass them. But now she had to persuade Henrik to drive home with her. With the coming of Prohibition this year, Stanton Mills' taverns had been shut down, but one of them had simply relocated to the rear of Schneider's hardware store and operated as a speakeasy that could only be entered from a back alley. Henrik had told her to find him there. Emma made her way through the dark alley, littered with trashcans and discarded rubbish, until she found a closed, solid door that she guessed lay behind the hardware store. Muffled sounds of gruff male voices and laughter emerged. She knocked—two beats, two beats, three beats, as Henrik had instructed her. The door opened an inch or two. A rich warm brew of smells greeted her—the sharpness of unwashed male bodies, stale beer, bootleg whiskey, and tobacco smoke.

"Yeah?"

"Is Henrik Hansen here? Please send him out."

"Who're you, girlie?"

"I'm his sister."

The man turned and shouted into the room. "Henrik, there's a girl here. Says she's your sister. Sure it ain't your piece of ass?"

"Long's it's not my fuckin' wife," an unfamiliar voice called out. Laughter.

After a few minutes Henrik appeared at the door. "Wha'? You wanna go home already? Da night'sh young, Emma." His voice was slushy, and he avoided her eyes.

"Come, please, Henrik. I need you to drive me home, and you've had enough"

"Aw."

"Please?"

"Oh, all right." Henrik leaned on Emma and he stumbled twice as they left the alley and tottered toward the Ford. He bent down in front of the vehicle to crank it and the engine backfired. He fell onto his rump in the street. "Christ! Retard da shpark. Like to broke my arm!" He remained sitting in the street.

Emma looked around. Who was witnessing this sad scene? The story would be all over the county.

"Hennie, get in the truck. I'll crank it myself. And I'm going to drive it home. In your condition, you'll run us off the road." Henrik had taught Emma how to drive the truck over the past two summers, although he was the only male in the Hansen family who ever permitted her to do so, and then only infrequently.

"Nah, you can't drive 'er."

Emma climbed out of the truck's seat, roughly pulled Henrik to a standing position by his suspenders, and hissed, "Get up, damn it. Get in the truck. On the right side. Now."

Fortunately, he complied without a word. It took three tries to get the engine started, but soon she was puttering down the street toward home.

When they left downtown area that was illuminated by streetlamps, she called out, "How do you turn on the headlamps?"

She had never driven at night. Henrik pointed to the switch, then slumped in his seat. The country road was very rough and poorly lit by their feeble headlamps. Even though Emma drove slowly, the truck jerked from side to side as it jounced over ruts and potholes. Henrik groaned with each violent jolt.

About two miles from home, he cried out, "Oh, God, stop. I'm gonna . . . I gotta puke."

Emma crammed her foot on the brake and stopped abruptly.

Henrik half-climbed, half-fell out of the truck's right side door, dropped to his knees at the side of the road, and vomited.

The sounds of his violent retching twisted Emma's belly and she began to cry. Leaving the engine running and the headlamps on, she climbed out of the truck and knelt beside him with her arm over his heaving shoulders. He finally calmed, and she pulled him to his feet.

They sat side-by-side on the running board while he wiped his mouth and eyes with the back of his hand.

"Hennie, Hennie, this has got to stop. You're killing yourself."

"Who cares? I'm no good any more. I'm so screwed up."

"I care." Tears poured down Emma's face. "I care so much. I can't lose you. You're the only one in the whole family that . . . that . . . understands me. Mama and Susan think I've gone high hat. Everything I care about is useless to them. Papa and Bjorn don't care either. As long as I help with the milking and cooking and gardening and canning and the laundry. I'm just a hired girl. You're all I've got. You loved me, I know you did. At least until that damned war. And I love you too. I still do. Hennie, I want you back."

She wrapped both arms around his neck and sobbed. She had never spoken the words of love before. Never. Not to anyone. Nor had she ever heard them.

Henrik didn't reply. They sat together, sniffling and breathing irregularly. Finally, Henrik embraced her awkwardly. Emma helped him back into the passenger seat, and they drove the rest of the way back to the Hansen farm in silence.

FOUR WEEKS LATER Emma returned to the Oosterfeld's store, her head down in despair. Her search for a teaching job—any teaching job—in the Stanton Mills area had been futile. No positions were open at the city's elementary school or at any of the nearby one-room country schools. She was not credentialed to teach in high school. Just this Friday the County Superintendent of Schools had bluntly told her that he foresaw no possibility of a vacant teaching position anywhere in the county.

Now she had accompanied Henrik into town in the family truck—after extracting a promise that he would permit her to drive home—and needed to share the bad news with Piet and Hannah: she would not be staying with them in the coming year. She would have to search for a position in a distant county and board near the school that hired her, if she could find one. Staying at home on the farm without a job was not a choice she would ever accept.

The Oosterfelds saw the disappointment in Emma's face at once, and, as there were no customers at the moment, sat down with her at the back of the store.

"It's no good," Emma said softly. "I just can't find a job close enough to Stanton Mills to stay with you. In fact, I haven't found a job anywhere yet."

"Oh, we're so sorry. We were looking forward to having you back with us," Hannah said.

"So was I. More than you know. And, if I have to pay room and board, it's going to take even longer to accumulate enough to go back to college." Emma bit her lip, determined not to cry.

Piet rose and put a hand on her shoulder. "Emma, Hannah and I have been talking about this. It's not right, you having to interrupt your education for so long. Maybe, maybe we can help you."

Hannah nodded vigorously.

"What do you say, we lend you the money for the next two years?" Piet asked.

"Oh, that would be wonderful, but I can't ask you to do that. It's too much. And who knows how long it would take me to pay you back. You're so kind, but I . . . just . . . I couldn't take so much from you."

"Now, why not? You've been like a daughter to us, Emma. We haven't any children of our own. It would give us pleasure to help you. And don't worry about paying us back. We'll work out a schedule so you can do that after you graduate."

The Oosterfeld's offer was a splendid, unexpected gift. Emma yearned to accept it. But her family would be humiliated, furious that she had taken charity from the elderly couple. And, if she pursued her dream of earning a Ph.D., she wouldn't be able to repay the loan for many years. In fact, she would go deeper into debt in graduate school.

Still, shouldn't she solve one problem at a time, rather than becoming overwhelmed by the obstacles further down the path? Perhaps, two years from now she could teach in a high school for a couple of years to earn money to repay the Oosterfelds and for graduate school? Did her parents really have to know about the loan?

"It's such a generous, kind offer. I can't say no. Oh, thank you, thank you from the bottom of my heart." Tears filled her eyes.

Piet and Hannah looked down in embarrassment.

"There, there, Emma. It makes us happy too. I'll have the bank draw up the papers," Piet said. "Now, come, have some coffee with us. You do drink coffee now that you go to college, don't you?"

When Emma left the darkened grocery store, her emotions were fragile, confused. Relief and happiness mingled with worry for the future and the strange vulnerability and sadness that come with an undeserved gift. On the street, she breathed the cooling night air deeply to clear her head. The cries of night birds hunting insects attracted by the town's streetlights pulsed, along with the occasional muttering of an automobile.

I'd better go get Henrik before he's too drunk, she thought, and started up the street.

"Emma!"

She swiveled her head to see a young man trotting toward her. "Victor. Victor Midlothian," she cried.

He stood before her grinning. His long brown hair was no longer parted down the middle, but fell rakishly across his brow. His face, still smooth, but no longer boyish, had become leaner and more sharply defined, and he sported a thin mustache. His chest had broadened, his arms were thicker than in high school days. He was wearing a short-sleeved white shirt with a blue kerchief at the open neck—much more stylish than the young men of Stanton Mills.

Emma's mouth fell open.

He stepped forward, wrapped his arms around her, and kissed her, first on one cheek, then the other. "There," he announced, "That's how the French do it. Emma, you are so pretty. Even prettier than I remembered. I am so glad to see you. I heard you were off at college. So smart—of course you'd be at college."

"Yes, Hancock College. But I'm home for the summer. How about you? What are you doing? I heard that you were flying aeroplanes in the War. I'm so happy that you weren't . . . hurt."

"Oh, I love flying. And I was lucky I guess. I didn't get back from France until 1919. Since then, I've been flying mail for the government. I've got a month's leave. Visiting my folks." He swept both of her hands into his, so much more bold and self-confident than Emma remembered him. "I've thought of you so many times. Emma, may I call on you while I'm here? We could use my father's Buick, go to the picture show. Oh, please, say yes. You don't have a sweetheart, do you? A special beau?"

"No, no. No one special." Emma's face had grown warm, her breathing quicker.

"All right. Tomorrow night? Seven o'clock? I'll drive out to your farm."

"Yes, Vic. Yes, I'd like that."

"Swell! I'll see you then. We can talk and talk."

In the coming days Victor's courtship of Emma—could it be called that, she wondered—proved to be lighthearted, but surprisingly ardent. Every second or third evening the Midlothian's big Buick sedan chugged into the Hansen's farmyard, and he escorted Emma to the car after exchanging pleasantries with her mother and father. Victor related tales—probably embellished—of his adventures flying in France in the closing months of the war, views of the battlefields from the air, the wonders of Paris after the war, and the sophistication of the French people. How different his experiences were from Henrik's. Henrik's soul had been crushed; Victor was invigorated, even cocky.

Their companionship was a welcome relief from the farm's domestic chores, her mother's depression, and Emma's worries about paying for college. Much as she liked him, Emma did not wish to marry Victor. She didn't want to marry anyone, not any time soon. But, he soon made clear, Victor wasn't interested in marriage either. He explained that he had adopted the sophisticated French attitude toward sexual morality, and he gently invited Emma to share his views.

She was tempted. An attractive man who didn't demand or offer commitment? It was just as well that she had to return to Hancock College in September.

CHAPTER 6
1922

TINY BALLET SLIPPERS, they dip and glide, twist and turn, gracefully swimming with the ease of silvery fish, pausing, speeding, reversing, brushing affectionately against one another in their miniscule pond under the objective lens of Emma's microscope. How do they know where they are going, what they are seeking?

Emma had been studying paramecium for months now, and, although she still had to be certain that her observations were reproducible, she now believed that she had strong evidence to support her hypothesis. But her data presented new puzzles, raised new questions. Complete understanding seemed to recede before her like the terminus of a rainbow.

Emma's view of the world of biology had begun to shift from the macroscopically accessible universe of plants and animals, their anatomy and phylogenetic relationships, to the unseen world of protozoa and bacteria. She had mastered her classes in botany, vertebrate and invertebrate zoology and embryology, but studies in her junior year of microbiology and genetics challenged her previous ideas about living systems.

The world teems with diminutive single-celled organisms that have all the fundamental properties of larger, multi-celled creatures. They can only be observed under a microscope, and often inadequately at that. Anatomical features of the protozoa can be seen, but the true bacteria are so tiny that little can be discerned other than the overall shape of their cells. Rather, the bacteria were characterized by indirect means, such as the differential staining of their cells with the Gram stain, determination of the sugars that support their growth, whether they could grow without oxygen, or the products—acids and gases—they produce. This knowledge forced Emma to realize that she knew woefully little of chemistry, and in her senior year she enrolled in a general chemistry class.

The other discipline that unsettled Emma's previous ideas about biology was genetics, the science of heredity. The elegance of Mendelian patterns of inheritance that could be predicted with mathematical precision appealed to her orderly mind. They implied an underlying regularity to the structure of the apparatus of inheritance—whatever that was—that called out for understanding, that harkened to Emma's old question: *how does it work?* What were genes and how did they carry and convey genetic information? There was recent evidence that genes were somehow carried on tiny subcellular bodies, called chromosomes, that could be made microscopically visible with stains, but no one knew how.

Her studies of genetics required Emma to overcome her dislike of Professor Thomas Gillespie, Hancock College's only professor of biology other than her admired mentor, Dr. Weatherbee. A small, sour man with a pointed Van Dyke beard, Gillespie was overtly hostile to female students. In his first class meeting, he asked the few women students present to cross their legs. Puzzled, they complied.

Then he announced, "Now that the Gates of Hell are closed, we can proceed."

The male students laughed, but Emma fumed. He only called on the male students in his classes and answered Emma's many questions disdainfully. When she suspected that he did not know an answer, he would announce, "That's beyond the scope of this course, Miss Hansen. I suggest that you research it in the library, rather than consume class time with it."

Gillespie was not particularly curious about the fundamental mechanisms of inheritance. He was more interested in the practical applications of genetics and provided the class with many fascinating examples of studies of inheritance with plants and animals, stressing dominant and recessive genes, the formation of genetic hybrids and their use in agriculture.

Emma seized upon the idea that she might combine her newly found enthusiasms. Could not genetics be studied with microbes? They could be grown readily in the laboratory, and they reproduced within hours, not the months or year needed for a new generation of animals and plants. When she broached the idea with Professor Gillespie, he scoffed.

"Nonsense, Miss Hansen, bacteria reproduce asexually, by binary fission. There's no genetics to study. Besides, they have no chromosomes. What a silly idea."

"But," she protested, "they must pass on inherited information, because the daughter cells are identical to their parents."

"Perhaps so, but if you can't mate strains with different genotypes, you can't do genetic analysis."

Emma conceded his argument. But she persisted. "How about the protozoa? Some species are thought to reproduce sexually."

Gillespie shrugged. "What could possibly be the practical use of studying that?"

Emma repeated the conversation to Dr. Weatherbee, who smiled and said, "Gillespie can be an unpleasant man, I'm afraid. But you have an interesting idea. This is an area outside of my expertise, but I do recall reading a paper about sexual reproduction of Paramecium. We cultivate them for our biology classes, mostly, I confess, because they are so lovely to observe under the microscope. Perhaps you should read up on that and see if you can identify a project that you have a good chance to complete this year."

From her reading and hours of observing her graceful little "slippers" under the microscope, Emma formulated the question that she now felt she had answered. When they are well fed, paramecium cells divide frequently by asexual binary fission, giving rise to identical daughter cells, but when they are starved, one cell is occasionally observed to fuse with another cell and both undergo changes in their macro- and micronuclei that suggest mating.

But, she learned from her reading, no one had directly demonstrated the transmission of an inherited trait after these putative mating events. The possibility of doing this occurred to her when, by chance, she found a peculiar, paralyzed paramecium cell, unable to swim, but merely flopping about in an uncoordinated manner. Had the cell been injured? Would it recover the ability to swim if it was cultivated in nutritious medium?

She carefully isolated the helpless cell with a tiny pipette and grew it in a separate rich culture. To her delight, it divided regularly and gave rise to hundreds of progeny—*all of them similarly paralyzed.* The swimming defect was inherited. She had isolated a genetic variant, a mutant strain. Now, she thought with growing excitement, I can mate them with the normal strain and determine whether the progeny can swim or not. And I can mate the progeny and see if they obey Mendel's law.

The execution of her simple idea proved more difficult than she anticipated. Finding conditions of starvation that regularly led to mating events required much trial and error. When that was finally accomplished, Emma found that some cultures of paramecium never mated with her variant strain, but that others did.

She did not understand why, but eventually decided to proceed with the strains with which she could observe mating pairs—although they were infrequent and required much patient and eye-straining screening of cultures under the microscope. Mating pairs had to be tediously isolated and the properties of their offspring recorded. It was the spring of her senior year before Emma had collected sufficient observations to be confident of her conclusions.

AS EMMA SPENT more and more time in the laboratory, she had to reserve time carefully for the demands of her classes and her meal job at the college dining hall. No free time remained for social activities, and she acquired a reputation among her classmates as a bookish grind and a hermit.

She declined the few invitations from male students that came her way. Max Swerdt had lost interest in her already two years ago and had noised it about that she was "more interested in beetles than men." That was untrue, of course. She was just insistent upon finishing her education first. And she wanted the independence that she would likely lose in marriage.

There had been a man in her life: Victor Midlothian. She had even been intimate with him on a few occasions. It was a secret she could share with no one. She knew how harshly she would be condemned. But she felt no shame, no guilt. They had been completely honest with one another. A door had been opened for Emma, a door to rooms that she hoped to explore more fully some day. But not with Victor. There were other women in his life. He flew—literally—like a bird across America. He sent her penny postcards from the cities he visited inscribed with cheerful messages. "Flew nonstop from Florida to New York!" one crowed. No, even if she were ready for marriage, she wouldn't marry a man so restless, so reckless as that.

THE TABULATED DATA in her notebooks all supported her conclusions, Emma had decided, and she now began to think of writing a research report for publication. Most importantly, she had demonstrated that the physical conjugation of paramecium cells, which had been presumed by previous authors to result in sexual reproduction, did indeed result in the transmission of hereditable characteristics. When her paralyzed mutant cells were mated with motile wild type cells, all of the progeny were able to swim like their motile parent, generation after generation. This indicated that the non-swimmers carried a loss-of-function mutation that was recessive to the dominant swimming genotype. The swimmers had the genetic information needed to correct the defect inherited by the non-swimmers. But the pattern of inheritance did not obey Mendel's law.

When Emma mated the first generation of descendants with non-swimmers, the proportion of swimming and non-swimming progeny did not fit the predicted pattern. Only very rarely did a non-swimmer result. Emma could not explain this. She suspected that it had something to do with the fact that Paramecium usually has more than one micronucleus, but she had not been able to test that conjecture.

Emma needed to discuss her results with Dr. Weatherbee, and—this she dreaded—with Professor Gillespie. Did they agree that her findings were sufficiently well documented to write up in a paper and submit for publication? First, Dr. Weatherbee.

Emma gathered up her notebooks and a sheet on which she had written out her conclusions and summarized the supporting evidence and strode excitedly down the hall to her mentor's office. The door was closed, but she burst in.

"Dr. Weatherbee, I think I have enough evidence now . . ." She stopped, immobilized by the sight of her mentor in an intimate embrace with another woman, whom she recognized as the secretary to the Dean of the college. "Oh!" she mumbled. "I'm sorry. I . . . I should have knocked."

She backed out quickly and pulled the office door closed behind her. Trembling, she retreated to her desk in the lab. Embarrassment was overcome with anxiety about the consequences of her foolish intrusion. Would her beloved professor be angry with her? Would she turn cold and avoid her? Emma had occasionally heard whispers that Professor Weatherbee was an "old maid" and "not a natural woman," but she had always discounted them as the usual intolerance for independently minded single women. Perhaps there was some truth to the rumors after all.

Emma didn't care whether they were true or not. How could she discreetly assure Dr. Weatherbee that she didn't condemn her for her private life? Affection and pleasure, she knew full well, were to be found outside the bounds of conventional marriage. But the two of them had never discussed such intimate things. How could all this be set right?

After what seemed an agonizingly long time, but what was actually less than fifteen minutes, Dr. Weatherbee softly approached Emma, placed a hand on her shoulder and said, "Emma, would you please come into my office for a moment?"

"Dr. Weatherbee, I'm so sorry. I should not have . . ."

"Hush. We'll talk about it in a minute." In the neat little office with the door closed behind them, Dr. Weatherbee waved Emma to a seat and cleared her throat. "My dear, about what you witnessed just now. I must ask for both your discretion and your understanding."

Emma blushed deeply and fighting tears, did not reply.

"Miss Hudson and I have . . . maintained . . . a special friendship for some time now. I hardly need explain to you that any . . . unfortunate . . . rumors . . . could have . . . serious consequences. She could lose her job. Indeed, so could I. Even with tenure. This is a church-supported college. I trust you understand."

"Of course," Emma cried. "I would never . . . I will *never* speak of it. Ever. To anyone."

"Thank you. I felt certain I could rely on you."

"It's none of my business. I'm so ashamed that I just barged in like that."

"It was a simple mistake. We . . . were . . . not thinking either." Professor Weatherbee paused, as if considering what to say next. "I hope you won't think less of me. I don't think one has much choice in such matters, but it corrodes the soul to be absolutely alone." Her eyes shone in appeal. "A woman who wishes to achieve at the highest levels must give up a great deal. Marriage, children, the comforts of domesticity, even respectability. She should not also have to give up love."

Emma shivered. Would these sacrifices really be required of her too? "No," she replied with surprising heat. "She should not. Please, don't worry, Dr. Weatherbee. I'm no angel myself, not good enough to judge you."

"Thank you. Now, Emma, tell me about your research. That's what you wanted to discuss, wasn't it?"

AT THE END of his course on genetics Professor Gillespie devoted several lectures to the subject of eugenics, which he described as "the application of the laws of heredity to the improvement of the human race." An enthusiastic supporter of the eugenics movement, Gillespie summarized the evidence that the laws of heredity applied to humans.

He followed this with a long list of diseases that were known and suspected of being genetically transmitted. He traced the occurrence of hemophilia, an acute bleeding disorder, in the royal families of Europe. The students were required to read Charles B. Davenport's well-known book, *Heredity in Relation to Eugenics*, and Gillespie read with relish aloud to the class, Davenport's description of the wretched "Jukes" family:

> On the other hand, we have the striking cases of families of defectives and criminals that can be traced back to a single ancestor. The case of the "Jukes" is well known. We are first introduced to a man known in literature as Max, living as a backwoodsman in New York State and a descendant of the early Dutch settlers; a good-natured, lazy sot, without doubt of defective mentality. He has two sons who marry two of six sisters whose ancestry is uncertain but of such a nature as to lead to the suspicion that they are not full sisters. One of these sisters is known as "Ada Juke," also as "Margaret, the mother of criminals." She was indolent and a harlot before marriage. Besides an illegitimate son she had four legitimate children. The first, a son, was indolent, licentious and syphilitic; he married a cousin and had eight children all syphilitic from birth. Of the 7 daughters 5 were harlots and of the others one was an idiot and one of good reputation. Their descendants show a preponderance of harlotry in the females and much consanguineous marriage. The second son was a farm laborer, was industrious and saved enough to buy 14 acres of land. He married a cousin and the product was 3 stillborn children, a harlot, an insane daughter who committed suicide, an industrious son, who, however, was licentious, and a pauper son. The first daughter of "Ada" was an indolent harlot who later married a lazy mulatto and produced 9 children, harlots and paupers, who produced in turn a licentious progeny. Ada had an illegitimate son who was an industrious and honest laborer and married a cousin. Two of the three sons were licentious and criminalistic in tendency and the third, while capable, drank and received outdoor relief. All of the three daughters were harlots or prostitutes and two married criminals. The third generation shows the

eruption of criminality. Excepting the children of the third son, none of whom were criminalistic, we find among the males 12 criminals, 1 licentious, 5 paupers, 1 alcoholic and 1 unknown; none were normal citizens. Among the females 3 were harlots, 1 pauper, 1 a vagrant and 2 unknown; none were known to be reputable. Thus it appears that criminality lies in the illegitimate line from Ada and not at all in the legitimate—doubtless because of a difference in germ plasm of the fathers.

Gillespie continued this recitation of the woeful Jukes family history through two more generations, well aware of the shocked reactions of the students. The story of the Jukes was followed by an elaborate family tree tracing the line of descent of the "Kallikaks," supposedly the result of an illicit union between a normal man and a feeble-minded servant girl. The subsequent generations were described as overwhelmingly mentally defective; of 480 descendants, 143 were said to be feeble-minded, 80 had died in infancy, and only 46 were described as "apparently normal."

These sensational descriptions soon gave rise to many jokes about the Jukes and the Kallikaks among the Hancock College students, but Gillespie was serious in his advocacy of eugenics. Many states already mandated the sterilization of "imbeciles," he said, and he argued that the betterment of the human race could be much advanced by restricting the reproduction of persons who carried the genetic traits for disease, feeble-mindedness, and physical disability.

Most of Emma's classmates seemed to feel that Gillespie's ideas were reasonable, but she was uneasy. She wasn't sure whether her feelings resulted from her growing dislike of the professor or from distaste for his rash prescriptions. She was troubled by the censorious tone of Davenport's writing, his frequent use of the term "harlot" to describe female descendants of the Jukes family. Harlots were sexually promiscuous women. Could not such a term be applied to her because of the pleasure she took from her infrequent couplings with Victor? Many would do so, she knew. She was shamed and angered to see such behavior lumped together with feeble-mindedness, drunkenness, and idleness as inherited defects.

When she raised the topic of eugenics with Dr. Weatherbee, she sniffed. "Oh, that disgusting little man. Going on again about eugenics, was he?"

"Yes. But what do you think? Some of the genetic arguments seem sound to me."

"Well, I suppose there is some rational biology there. The evidence that some diseases are inherited is very strong, so probably some feeble-mindedness is inherited too. But these studies of families—these Jukes and Kallikaks—overlook the effects of growing up in a poor family environment. If a mother is feeble-minded or alcoholic or a pauper or whatever, the child cannot develop normally. That's not in the genes. Besides, humans are not cattle or dogs that can be bred to create whatever characteristics we want. The whole idea is morally repugnant."

"Perhaps I should raise these questions in class?"

"Waste of time, my dear. Now, let's go over your paper again. I would change the title to 'Demonstration of Transmission of a Hereditable Trait During Sexual Reproduction in Paramecium.' You want to stress your most important findings. I'd reserve mention of motility to the main text. And, here in Table 2, I'd reorganize it so that the reader scans across rather than down. Otherwise, it's nearly ready to submit. Your Results and Discussion sections are very clear and concise."

"Thank you. And thank you for all your help. Dr. Gillespie said he didn't have time to read it."

"Too bad. If he could get over his biases, he might have had some useful suggestions. But, never mind that. There's something else we must get to. You need to start making applications to graduate schools."

"Oh my, already?"

"Yes. Now let's think about where to apply. Unfortunately, some of the best universities won't take women, and some of the others say they do, but in fact rarely accept any. We won't waste your time with those."

"You know which ones they are?"

"I'm afraid I do. It will also be a bit more difficult because Hancock is a small Midwestern church college, not so well regarded out east. I want you to apply to my alma mater, Cornell. I think that, with my strong support, you can be admitted there, perhaps even obtain a small scholarship to help with expenses."

"That's a terrible source of worry, Dr. Weatherbee. I'm already deeply in debt to the Oosterfelds. I have no idea how I'm going to pay for graduate school. I expect I will have to teach for two or three years to save up the money."

"Too bad. A dream postponed often becomes a dream extinguished."

CHAPTER 7
1924

THE CORNELL UNIVERSITY campus lay before her, a park-like city of higher learning, so much larger than Hancock College, thrilling in its peaceful beauty on this early fall day, and yet, intimidating. The hilly campus was divided into quadrangles, each surrounded with formal academic buildings; Emma's undergraduate college would have fit into just one of the "quads." The multiple lawns and clusters of buildings sloped gently toward Beebe Lake, fed by a creek that flowed through the campus. McGraw Tower, a tall bell and clock tower topped with a pyramidal cap, presided over the graceful landscape. The rugged hills and woods surrounding the campus, while scenic, contrasted to the gently undulating open fields and treeless prairies of Emma's Illinois years and was somehow strange, unsettling.

Emma should have been exhilarated, triumphant in the realization of a fiercely sought dream—she had arrived in Ithaca three days ago to begin studies toward a Ph.D. in biology—but she seethed with anxiety, uncertainty, and anger. This was going to be so strange, so difficult, so unfamiliar, and she was going to have to face it alone. Would all of the faculty be as indifferent or hostile as her just-completed conversation with Professor Osborne had been? Was she strong enough to do this without the warmth and encouragement she had received from Dr. Weatherbee? By God, she would have to be strong enough; there was no going back to Stanton Mills.

When Emma entered his office for her first interview with a Cornell advisor to discuss her academic program, Professor Osborne, a corpulent, bald man in a dark three-piece suit with a gold watch chain drooping from his vest pocket, did not rise from his office chair. He waved her to a chair and scanned the papers in her file, emitting an occasional humpf or grunt as he did so.

"So, Miss Hansen, what are your intentions in enrolling in graduate study?"

"I wish to pursue a doctorate in biology, sir."

"Um, yes. The few women graduate students we have had did not continue past the Master's degree."

"Oh, but I intend to go on to the Ph.D."

"Why?"

"It is my ambition to become a college professor, to teach and conduct research."

Osborne's eyes widened with incredulity. "At a university? Like this one?"

"Possibly. Why not?"

"Forget it. It's simply not done. There are no lady professors at research universities. A few instructors and research assistants, but professors? No. Perhaps at a lady's academy . . ."

"I would be happy on the faculty of a smaller college. Like Hancock, where I took my Bachelor's degree."

"Never heard of it. Where is it?"

"Hancock, Illinois. It's a small town in western Illinois."

"Is it a church school?"

"Yes, sir. Lutheran."

"Hmm. Do they permit the teaching of Darwinism? Do you know about evolution?"

Emma felt warm, tension slowly twisted her arms. "Of course. There was no interference in the teaching of modern biology. You will see from my record that I have a thorough background."

"I see course titles, but that tells me little about content. About rigor."

"Well, I propose that I enroll in the usual graduate-level courses. We'll soon see if I am adequately prepared."

Osborne stared at Emma for a moment over his glasses. "Um, yes. You should take a wide range of advanced biology courses if you intend to teach. I see that you taught in high school for two years. Why did you not enroll right after graduating?"

"I had to earn sufficient funds for my expenses, sir."

"Oh. Most of our students are supported by their families."

"That's not possible in my case. In fact, I want to apply for a position as a teaching or laboratory assistant as soon as I can."

"Well, we might consider that after you've been here for a year or so. After we've had a look at you. A lab assistant would be out of the question. Do you even know what research is?"

"I certainly do," Emma replied hotly. "I have published three research papers. There are offprints in my file. Didn't you see them?"

Osborne shuffled through the papers in Emma's file. Emma suppressed a slight trembling in her hands during his long silence. She had not expected such hostility.

"Well, you might wish to show these to prospective Ph.D. thesis advisors, if you can find any." He scraped his chair back, leaned forward, and fixed his gaze on Emma. "I'll be frank with you, Miss Hansen. I, and many of my colleagues, are not enthusiastic about women in the Ph.D. program. Cornell prides itself on co-education. That's all right for undergraduates, perhaps, but many of us feel that the limited resources for graduate education should be reserved for men, who have families to support. Women generally drop out, marry, have children. They don't pursue serious professional careers. It's a waste of our efforts. I'd suggest that you take courses toward the Master's, then return to teaching. The smaller colleges will accept faculty with Master's degrees. Alternatively, if you prove to have any capacity for research, you might attach yourself to a professor somewhere. A husband, perhaps."

Emma glared at him. "With respect, sir, I ask that you not question my seriousness without giving me a chance to demonstrate it. I will certainly take an intensive course program, but I intend to seek a research director. I have become quite interested in genetics, as you can see from my last two publications. Can you suggest some professors— professors who don't share your prejudices?" It was a mistake to make an enemy so early in her graduate career, she would reflect after her anger cooled.

Osborne merely shrugged. "You might talk to C. B. Hutchison. He works on genetics of maize—what you Midwesterners call corn. I believe he has females in his group. Maize genetics has obvious practical consequences—unlike these, uh, paramecia. This *is* the College of Agriculture, Miss Hansen."

NOW, AS EMMA stood outside, looking out over the Ag Quad and trying to settle her nerves, to quiet her anger, she thought, so, that's how it will be. Fight for it. No coddling by Dr. Weatherbee here.

It had taken two long years since she graduated from Hancock College in 1922 to get to Cornell, two years of frustrated waiting, years in which Emma was ashamed that she had grown away from her family. The grinding labor of farm life and the gradual disintegration of the Hansen family consumed all of their emotional energy. To these miseries had been added poverty, brought on by the severe and persistent depression in farm prices that followed the end of the Great War.

And Henrik—her beloved brother Henrik—lost to her now too. He had simply disappeared over a year ago. The family truck was found parked on Main Street in Stanton Mills, but no one knew where Henrik was. Papa had held his nose and entered the speakeasy behind the hardware store to quiz the regulars, but none of them could offer an explanation for Henrik's disappearance or had any idea where he was.

"He might of hit the rails," one man offered. "He used to talk about getting out of here."

Was that it? Had Henrik jumped into an open freight car down at the railroad tracks and ridden it to wherever it was headed? Emma had heard stories of such hobos who rode rail cars, lived in shanties—or worse—by open fires, begged or stole food, dogged by railway officials and local police. Drunkards, many of them, and slightly mad: a description that sadly fit Henrik as he was now. Lost to his family, lost to her. Would she ever see him again?

No one from her family came to Hancock College for the graduation ceremonies when Emma received her Bachelor of Science degree in 1922; they couldn't get away from the farm, they said, and there was the expense to consider. Emma had coaxed Mama and Papa to come, arguing that Bjorn, Henrik, and Susan could milk the cows for three days. And she had offered to pay their train fare, but they declined. Eventually—and this filled her with sadness—she realized that they were embarrassed, intimidated by the thought of mingling with "fancy people" and "them professors." They had never traveled anywhere by train.

She had invited Victor too, but he had responded with a breezy postcard: "Congratulations, college graduate! Would love to see you at Hancock, but we're working on a coast-to-coast flight. We're aiming for the sky, both of us, Emma. Fondly, Vic." It was not a surprise, but it stung a little. Where was Victor now? Happily flying in the clouds in a noisy aeroplane? In some woman's bed?

Hannah and Piet Oosterfeld surprised Emma by accepting her invitation. They closed their grocery store for three days and came by train to Hancock. Emma greeted them at the station, more warmly than she would have greeted her parents. In a way, they had become her parents, glowing with pride, gamely walking all over the campus as Emma excitedly showed them every building and insisted on a tour of the biology lab and introducing them to Dr. Weatherbee, who was gracious and slightly regal.

On the day of graduation ceremonies they sat in the audience smiling when she marched in black robe and cap with the small band of graduates to the stage. On her white blouse beneath the robe, Emma wore a pin bearing a coiled golden snake with a minuscule ruby eye mounted on a shield embossed with three capital Greek betas. She had been elected to the Beta Beta Beta national honorary society for biologists and surrendered to the sin of pride by wearing it. Most astonishing of all, the Oosterfled's graduation gift to Emma was the forgiveness of her college loans, nearly five hundred dollars! Emma had pleaded with them not to be so generous, then wept with gratitude, exacting a promise that they not tell her parents, who she knew would be humiliated if they learned of the gift.

Then followed Emma's two years as a biology and Latin teacher at a high school not far from Hancock. She had been admitted to Cornell University and even was awarded a tuition waiver, but she had to earn the cost of her transportation to Ithaca, room and board, books, and—as she was about to learn—graduate students were required to pay all of the research expenses incurred while working on their doctoral theses.

She persuaded the university to delay admission until she could afford to begin post-graduate studies. Emma heard that Mr. Witherspoon had retired from Stanton Mills High School because of health problems. She hoped for the opportunity to return to her hometown and to be near her family. The Oosterfelds invited her to live with them and work in their store as she had from 1912 to 1916, but the principal, Mr. Ramsey, who had the memory of an elephant for their disagreement about Emma's valedictory address, refused to even consider her application for the position.

When Emma announced her decision to accept a teaching position far from home, Mama fretted. "You are turning your back on your family, Emma. Couldn't you find a job closer to home?"

"Mama, I have to take a job where I can find one. Why is it so terrible for me to leave home and make my own way? Kristin did it."

"That's different. She got married. She has to go with her husband. Your place is with your family until you get married."

The small town where Emma taught was close enough to Hancock College that she could spend some of her weekends and most of her summers working in Dr. Weatherbee's tiny laboratory. She continued her studies of the perplexing genetics of paramecium. Why on earth did they need multiple nuclei, when other organisms managed their business of heredity with just one nucleus per cell?

She wasn't able to solve that problem, but she did demonstrate that the number of micronuclei was correlated with nutritional conditions, which in turn determined how frequently the cells divided. Since it was generally agreed that the determinants of inheritance—genes, whatever they were—were carried in nuclei, her observations suggested that more copies of genes were needed to drive rapid cell division. Her paper on this work was published in the summer of 1924.

But they were lonely years. Was this to be the price of her single-minded pursuit of science?

SINGLE FEMALE STUDENTS at Cornell were required to live in women's dormitories, although "single" and "female" were largely redundant terms because married women were not admitted, and those co-eds who married while in college were expected to drop out. As a graduate student Emma was allowed a single room, and she settled into an intense, but socially isolated routine. On the strength of her teaching experience and prior laboratory work she had been able to persuade the reluctant head of the Biology Department to award her an assistantship to teach freshman biology laboratory—mostly dissections. She intended to introduce work with microbes in the future if the objections of the faculty could be overcome.

The assistantship greatly relieved Emma's financial worries, but when her teaching duties were added to her heavy load of advanced biology courses, little free time remained to her. She was regarded as an oddity by the other women in her dorm, not only because she worked so hard and was so professionally ambitious, but because she was a few years older and she came from a rural Midwestern background.

Nearly all the women—girls, really—were undergraduates from northeastern cities and towns who were much more interested in Cornell's lively social scene and finding a husband than in their studies. A few planned to become teachers, but Emma's determination to become a college professor and research scientist struck them as unrealistic and absurd.

"I wouldn't want to spend my life cutting up frogs and staring into a microscope," one co-ed scoffed.

"You'll scare off all the boys and end up an old maid," another giggled. "You're already twenty-four."

Emma shrugged it off. The last thing she needed just now was a *husband*, who would surely expect her to cook, keep house, and do his laundry, not to mention begin having babies. Good God, no.

What she did long for, if she allowed her mind to dwell on it, was a boyfriend, a man who would understand and support her goals in life the way Henrik had before the Great War destroyed his spirit, a man who would offer affectionate companionship and gratification of the physical desires Victor had awakened. Perhaps one such might be found among her fellow graduate students, but the prospects so far had not been promising. The men either failed to take her seriously or seemed put off by her obvious intelligence and outspoken questions. What they respected among themselves they saw as odd and slightly repellent in a woman.

An exception to the undergraduate women who struck Emma as superficial was Rosa Levin, a young woman to whom she was drawn because of her seriousness, passion, and obvious intelligence. They were an unlikely pair of friends because they had so little in common.

Rosa was the daughter of Jewish immigrants from Russia and had lived all her life in Brooklyn—which Emma had to be told was part of New York City—before coming to Cornell. She had never been on a farm and admitted that she found upstate New York to be dull and empty. Emma was tall, fair and blonde; Rosa was small and dark with hair like reddish black sheep's wool. Her speech was strangely accented and nasal with th's elided to d's and oddly distorted vowels. Furthermore, she had no interest in science.

Rosa was majoring in history and economics, but her true passion was political philosophy. She was an outspoken Marxist-Leninist and keen to persuade Emma to adopt her point of view. Emma had little interest in politics beyond her youthful pacifism, which had been intensified by her revulsion at the aftermath of the Great War. Their discussions were lively, but seldom ended in agreement. They also enjoyed exploring the great differences in their prior lives. Emma preferred those conversations to their political debates.

"You're a smart woman, Emma," Rosa said one evening. "I just don't see how you can devote all your mind and energy to your bugs and skeletons, and embryos and all that when there are great revolutionary changes sweeping over the world. The Bolshevik Revolution and the new Soviet Union are leading the way, can't you see that?"

"No, I can't. I'm against violence, and you keep saying that capitalist governments have to be overthrown by force—like in Russia."

"They do. You don't expect the capitalists to surrender power willingly do you?"

"Well, maybe in Russia where they had to get rid of the czar and the nobility, but not here in America. We have a democracy. We can vote for changes if we need them."

"Oh, you are so naïve about political power," Rosa retorted. "Look, how about things you care about? You say you're a pacifist. Don't you see how the armaments manufacturers, the industrialists, the steel magnates, they all profit from war? And they control the politicians. You have to break that."

"Hmmm."

Rosa's intensity glowed in her eyes. "And the farmers. You come from a farm family. I've read there's a big depression on American farms."

"There is. But that's because demand was so great during the War, and they produced too much, so prices went down."

"Hah! Don't you know that the big meatpackers and stockyards conspire to keep prices down? The farmers have nowhere else to sell their produce. And the banks and the railroads, they all combine against the little farmers. In the Soviet Union the farmers are forming big collective farms, farms where everyone owns the land and shares in the labor and the crops."

"Oh, Rosa, now you're being naïve. You don't know farmers like I do. They all want to own their own land and be their own boss. They'd never go for that. They're not former serfs like in Russia. Have you ever even been on a farm?"

"Well, no. Maybe it would be interesting to visit your family's farm some day."

Emma flushed with embarrassment. Her family hardly knew how to react to her these days. What would they think of this radical city girl? What would Rosa think when she saw how primitive the farm was, that she had to go to an outhouse? No electricity, no running water, no central heat, the stink of the barn everywhere?

"Oh, I don't think you'd find it very comfortable."

Rosa's boyfriend, Herschel Greenspan, occasionally joined them. Herschel shared Rosa's left-wing opinions, but he was less passionate, more light humored. And—this was awkward—he fascinated Emma. Short and stocky, with dark curly hair, large blue eyes and a full mouth, he carried himself with confidence and a virile energy that attracted her almost involuntarily.

Herschel and Rosa broke into an argument in Yiddish one evening, and while Emma couldn't understand what they were contending, she deduced from one or two glances toward her that Herschel's flirtations with her were the cause. She decided to distance herself somewhat from them after that, which was easy to do because, in addition to her teaching and coursework, she had decided to join Professor Hutchison's laboratory as a research student.

CHAPTER 8
1925

MORE IMPORTANT TO Emma than her friendship with Rosa Levin was the friendship she formed during her first year at Cornell with Barbara McClintock, although perhaps it couldn't be called a friendship—Barbara was too solitary and preoccupied for that. When Professor Hutchison learned of her interest in genetics, he suggested that Emma should talk to Barbara.

"She's very, very bright," he said, "but a bit eccentric, can be short with people. Don't be put off."

"Oh, Barbara McClintock," a grad student said when Emma asked about her. "She's the one that wears pants like a man."

Although she was two years younger than Emma, Barbara had already graduated from Cornell two years ago and was well into her Ph.D. research. Emma wondered whether she had been advised to seek out Barbara because of her scientific ability or because she was the only other female graduate student in genetics. She fought feelings of intimidation as she approached the corner of the lab where she found Barbara peering intently into a microscope, and she stood quietly waiting for her to look up. When she did so, Emma was confronted with a small young woman with intense brown eyes behind round dark-rimmed glasses. Her dark hair had been cut unfashionably short.

"Yes, may I help you?"

"Excuse me. Miss McClintock?"

"Yes."

"I'm sorry to interrupt your work. I'm Emma Hansen, a new grad student. I'm interested in genetics, and Professor Hutichson . . ."

" . . . told you to talk to me."

"Yes. If you don't mind."

"What sort of genetics are you interested in?"

"Well, I'm not sure yet. I did some work with paramecium at . . . my undergraduate school."

"Hmmm. Paramecium. Not much to work with there. Look, I can't tell you what to work on, but I can tell you what I'm excited about and what I think are some important questions."

"I've heard that you work on corn genetics . . . uh, maize."

"Yes, a lot has been done with the genetics of maize already. A lot to build on. What I'm trying to do is identify the chromosomes of maize by specific staining, so genetic markers can be mapped to linkage groups on specific chromosomes, the way Morgan is doing with the fruit fly Drosophila. Are you familiar with Morgan's work?"

"Um, yes, somewhat."

"Well, *read* his papers. Study them until you understand them completely."

"I will."

Barbara's eyes shone, and for the first time since Emma had approached her, she smiled. "What I'm doing is called cytogenetics. I've been working out modifications of Belling's method with carmine dye to stain the maize chromosomes. See, maize has ten chromosomes, and in metaphase they have distinctive sizes and shapes. I'm getting the staining good enough to tell reproducibly which is which. Once you can do that, you can begin to observe crossing over and map some of the genetic markers that are already known. The plant breeders out in the field don't yet understand why that's important, but they will. They will."

Emma was silent, awed by Barbara's intensity and unwilling to admit that she didn't understand why her work was important either.

"Maize is a good choice for study," Barbara continued. "Look here." She pulled a dried ear of corn from the shelf above her workbench. The ear carried neat rows of mature kernels, but unlike the field corn that Emma had seen at home, the kernels were not all yellow; they were a mosaic of colors: red, blue, yellow, and white.

"You see this single ear of corn is a whole collection of genetic crosses. When a pollen cell fertilizes each kernel embryo, the kernel expresses the phenotype of the resultant cross. Each kernel is a different cross. And the color of the kernel is far from the only phenotype one can observe. You have to look at the plants for most of those. And, of course, you have to do the crosses out in the field. I can show you next summer, if you like." She shrugged. "You've probably been told that I wear pants. But that's when I go out into the fields—practical, don't you agree?"

"Of course. I grew up on a farm, Miss McClintock."

"Barbara, please." She turned the ear of corn over and over. "See these kernels with streaks of different colors in them? Each kernel results from a single cross when a pollen grain contacts the silk and fertilizes the embryo. Why don't all of the cells in a given kernel express the same phenotype? There's something interesting going on there. I want to understand that."

"I'm still trying to decide whether I want to work with . . . maize. I really liked working with paramecium because they're so easy to grow and reproduce so fast. Practical, you know, if you have to work in some small college, as I will probably have to."

"Cornell is a wonderful place for maize genetics. Maybe you should start with that, then switch systems later."

"I'll think about it."

"Come back and talk to me when you decide. A bit of advice, though. Don't bother with a Master's. Just go straight for the Ph.D. They'll take you more seriously that way. But you'll have to take it in botany or biology, because women aren't accepted into the genetics program."

"I wanted to ask you about that. Has it . . . been . . . more difficult for you because you're a woman? Some faculty and students have been, well, hostile."

"Oh, you just have to overcome that. Cornell is pretty good that way. If you're smart and you do good work, there are people who will listen to you."

"Not a problem, then?"

"I wouldn't quite say that. Look, my mother didn't want me to go to college. She was afraid no one would want to marry me if I did. Fortunately, my father came home from the War and persuaded her. You just have to do what you love and work, work, work."

"You don't think about getting married, then?"

"No. Don't see the need for it. Marry your work. Now, if you'll excuse me, I need to look at the rest of these chromosome smears."

EMMA REFLECTED ON her conversation with Barbara McClintock. It had frightened her. Did she have Barbara's high intelligence and single-mindedness, her capacity to focus so acutely on her experimental work, her confidence that she was on a productive line of research? Could she earn the respect of her professors as Barbara had? She certainly had not acquired Barbara's intimidating mastery of genetics.

And "marry your work"? Was that the price of success for women in science? Was she willing to pay that price? It seemed that her mentor at Hancock College, Professor Weatherbee, had. But perhaps she had never been interested in marrying, as Barbara did not seem to be. Probably Emma was willing to forego marriage, but she longed for the intimate companionship of a man who understood and supported her scientific ambitions. The chances of finding such a man did not seem good.

PROFESSOR SUMNER BENT over the large beaker of cloudy fluid, which was suspended in a water bath, withdrew a thermometer, tilted it to read the temperature, then added a couple of ice cubes to the water bath.

"Got to keep it close to ten degrees," he muttered to no one in particular. "See if I get better separation of the urease than I do at zero or room temperature."

He turned to Emma. He was a sturdy, round-faced man, late thirties, with disheveled hair.

"Jim Sumner," he said, extending his right hand.

Emma shook the proffered hand and tried, unsuccessfully, not to gaze at the empty left sleeve pinned back to his shirt.

"Yes." He nodded. "Lost it in a hunting accident when I was seventeen. You don't see many one-armed biochemists, do you? My professor at Harvard, Otto Folin, told me to go to law school, said I could never do research with one arm, but I showed him. It takes determination, this business I'm in, Miss . . . I'm sorry, what was your name?"

"Hansen, Emma Hansen. I'm a biology graduate student. I'm afraid that I don't know much biochemistry, Professor Sumner, but my advisor, Professor Hutchinson, suggested that I talk to you about filling the gap."

Sumner waved Emma to a lab stool and sat opposite her on another stool. "I hope you don't mind talking here in the lab. I've got to keep checking the temperature of this water bath. See, I'm trying to find the optimal conditions for extracting urease from jack bean meal with thirty percent ethanol. Most of the proteins are insoluble, but my enzyme stays in solution and I can harvest it by centrifuging out the precipitate."

"I'm sorry, Professor, but I don't know what urease is."

"It's an enzyme, Miss Hansen. Cleaves urea into ammonia and carbon dioxide. Do you know what an enzyme is?"

"Yes, sir, it catalyzes chemical reactions in cells."

"Yes, but do you know what it *is*? Chemically, I mean?"

"No, sir."

"Well, neither does anyone else. I think they are proteins, but this famous professor over in Germany, Richard Willstätter, says they're small organic molecules, just riding along on protein colloids. The only way to tell is to isolate a *pure* enzyme and analyze it, right? That's what I'm trying to do. Been at it for seven years now. My colleagues think I'm crazy."

Emma laughed. "Well, I hope you prove them wrong, sir. I admire your determination. But I only came to get your advice about the best way to learn a little biochemistry. I'm a student of biology with an interest in genetics."

"Hmmm. Not sure about a little biochemistry. That's like being a little pregnant. How much chemistry have you had?"

"One year of general chemistry. I must say I couldn't see much connection to biology. It was all about the Periodic Table. Solubility of metal ion sulfides, rare gases, what not."

"That's inorganic chemistry. Have you studied organic chemistry?"

"No, sir."

"Well, you need to. Then you can take my medical biochemistry course. You'll have to work hard because one course is not really sufficient. But, I think you're wise to make the effort. Tell me, Miss Hansen, what do you think is the fundamental question of biology?"

"How does it work?" Emma blurted without thinking, then wondered if it was too childlike.

"Exactly. How does it work? But before you can even get to that, you have to answer an even more fundamental question: *what is it made of?* What are the chemical structures of the molecules that make up cells and confer function on them? Until you know that, how can you understand how *structure determines function?* That's the axiom of biochemistry."

Emma shivered. A sickening wave of uncertainty passed through her. None of her training approached biology in this strictly chemical and reductionist way. She had learned to look at plants and animals carefully and identify the details of their anatomy, and with the aid of good microscopes and stains, she could make out some of the internal structures, but she knew next to nothing about the chemical makeup of cells. She had learned to observe the behavior of living creatures under carefully controlled conditions, modify those conditions and determine what changes resulted.

"I'm afraid I'm not well prepared for that kind of research, Professor Sumner. I've done all of my work through observation of living creatures. Can't one learn a great deal about biological function that way? Genetics seems a powerful tool for that, don't you think?"

"Well, yes, it's a different approach. More descriptive, but useful, of course. But someday it will all come down to biochemistry." He stood up and examined the thermometer he pulled from the water bath. "Excuse me for a moment. The temperature has dropped to nine degrees. I need to add a little hot water and stir the bath a little." He laughed. "If you think this is a primitive, you should have seen my first lab. I didn't even have an ice chest." After a few moments of intense attention to his procedure, he sat back down on the lab stool. "Tell me, since you're a student of genetics, do you know what a gene is?"

"Of course. It's the fundamental unit of inheritance." An edge of irritation had crept into Emma's voice. That was elementary.

"No, no. I mean, what is a gene, *chemically?* What is it made of?

"No, sir, I don't know that."

"Neither do I."

"But there's good evidence that genes are carried on chromosomes, which you can see under a microscope."

"And chromosomes are made of what?"

"I'm sorry. I don't know." Emma's irritation was now mixed with embarrassment.

"Mostly proteins and desoxyribonucleic acid. So genes are probably made of one of those two kinds of molecules. Possibly both. I'm betting on proteins. They seem to me to be the only molecules with the structural complexity needed for such sophisticated functions as genes have." Sumner grinned and ran his only hand through his hair. "There's a challenge for you, Miss Hansen. Isolate a pure gene. A real long shot."

"Oh, my. I have no idea how to do that."

"Well, you'd have to devise an assay. A way to measure how much gene activity you have. Not sure how you'd do that outside of a living cell." Then he smiled kindly. "First, you'll have to learn some biochemistry. And do something much more cut and dried for your Ph.D. Tackle the big problem after you're settled somewhere."

"Thank you, Professor Sumner. You've given me a lot to think about."

"Sure, sure." He turned back to his water bath and stirred the milky solution in the beaker. "What do you think? Should I try acetone instead of ethanol? It's miscible with water."

EMMA SLIPPED QUIETLY from the laboratory, her confidence shaken. The world of science was so vast. She had only mastered a small corner of it. Was it even the best corner for her to explore? The mysteries of the living cell—tiny as it was—were so many, so large, so complex, and so difficult that understanding them seemed an almost impossible goal. The many scientists studying these mysteries were like a group of primitive savages who have come across of box of fine Swiss watches and who strive to understand how and why they work. How does it work? That was the question.

The savages contend among themselves for the best way to understand the strange objects. Some insist that their significance lies in the regular ticking sounds they emit. Others puzzle over the symbols on the dial or the slow movements of the hands. Still others smash the watches with rocks and exclaim over the tiny gears and springs that spill out. Will they ever be able to integrate their observations into a coherent understanding of how a watch works? Emma saw herself as one of the savages staring at her own mysterious watch, turning it over and over in her hands. How does it work, and how can I find out?

CHAPTER 9
1926-1927

A SHADOW FELL across Emma's lab bench. She replaced the glass cover on the Petri dish she had been studying and glanced up.

"So, Emma, still fiddling with your red bread mold?"

She shrugged with annoyance. "Of course. Don't you have anything better to do, Lenny?"

"Aw, be nice. Just a friendly visit. After all, you're the prettiest grad student in the building. Of course, the others are all men. Heh, heh."

Emma remained silent. She knew she wouldn't be able to concentrate on her cultures until Lenny went away. Leonard Lansing Hallowell III was the eldest son of a well-off farming family from Ohio. He had been sent to Cornell to pursue a graduate degree in plant genetics by his father, who was determined to pursue scientific agriculture, a passion that Lenny did not share. He lounged around the lab and engaged the other students in conversation about their research and genetics, picking up ideas that he often offered as his own in classes and seminars. His excuse for his research inactivity was that he had to wait until next year's corn crosses were performed in the field and the offspring were available for analysis. His family paid all his expenses. He lived comfortably in his own apartment, entertained guests with bootleg gin, and was in no hurry to complete his degree and return to the farm.

Lenny had no interest in Emma's research—she was the only student in the building not working on maize genetics, so there was little he could pick from her brain—but he was flirtatious and often asked her out. She always declined. Lenny was attractive and companionable, but Emma resented his lack of seriousness and his easy sense of entitlement that flowed from little more than growing up in wealth and comfort.

Besides, there was the thing with Herschel Greenspan.

"So, convince me, Miss Lady Professor Hansen, why it's important to work with this useless moldy stuff instead of a commercially important crop like corn." Lenny seated himself comfortably on a lab stool, settling in to kill a half hour or more.

"Please don't call me that." Emma growled. Word had gotten around of Emma's future ambitions, which most students considered completely unrealistic.

"OK, sorry. But tell me about this, this, fungus you've been working on for more than a year. It's not of any use to anyone, is it?"

Emma was reluctant to discuss the reasons for her unconventional choice of research topics with this superficial young man, but she felt that they were good ones. She had come to realize that, as a woman, she would never be able to obtain a faculty position at the research university. Her best hope for a faculty position, if she could obtain one at all, was to teach at a small college, perhaps a college for women. But she was determined to continue research in biology, presumably in genetics, when she was established in her independent career. She couldn't imagine a career in science without the possibility of the joy of discovery.

"You will never be able to amass the resources needed to compete with university scholars in the established fields of genetic research, such as with maize or the fruit fly Drosophila," Dr. Weatherbee had written her, when Emma wrote of her concerns for her future. "You should strive to develop your own research objects, a new system not pursued by other investigators. Moreover, it would have to be a kind of research that can be done with meager resources and little assistance."

No fields of corn with carefully removed tassels and bagged ears, no multiple cages swarming with fruit flies for Emma's independent career. But what? Until now she had been able to pursue research projects out of pure curiosity, for the fun of solving problems and discovery. Now she had to limit her choices to practical considerations. What novel, but feasible research should she attempt?

Emma struggled with this question until, a few months into her Ph.D. program, she heard a lecture by a U.S. Department of Agriculture scientist, Bernard O. Dodge, who had studied a strain of fungus, which he called *Neurospora crassa*. The fungus was known to reproduce asexually, growing as chains of fuzzy white filaments, but Dodge had discovered a sexual mode of reproduction. When strains of two different mating types were mixed, the cells differentiated and formed little packages, called perithecia, that contained tiny tubes filled with eight spores each in neat rows.

Dodge had stumbled by accident on the finding that these little spores could be induced to germinate by heating, and the progeny of each spore could be grown into fungal colonies, which were genetically identical cells, all descended from one spore. Even more exciting, it appeared that genetic characters from two different parents were segregated in the spores into four of one type and four of the other, a pattern consistent with Mendel's law. Perhaps this simple fungus could be used to study genetics in the same way that others had done using much more complex species.

Because of her experience with paramecium at Hancock College, Emma was strongly drawn to this possibility. The fungus reproduced rapidly, and it could be studied without great cost. She would need only inexpensive growth medium, Petri dishes, and a dissecting microscope. Best of all, Dodge had told her when she talked to him after his lecture that he did not intend to continue genetic studies with Neurospora because the USDA had reassigned him to other projects. He offered to send her his strains and copies of his procedures. Emma had eagerly accepted his offer and set to work on her Ph.D. research. The members of her research group thought she was making a big mistake, but Professor Hutchison agreed to let her, as he told Emma, "sink or swim."

"This fungus isn't of any agricultural importance, is it?" Lenny asked again, when Emma didn't respond.

"Well, people don't grow it to eat," Emma replied. "They don't eat fruit flies either, but they've been a valuable research tool. Besides, this fungus is a serious contaminant in bakeries and sugar cane processing plants, if you have to have a practical argument for studying it. Now go away. I'm trying to work."

"OK, OK. But I really just came by to invite you to a party at my apartment on Friday night. Nine o'clock. Please come. We'll have a merry time."

"Thank you, but I can't. I have a date."

Lenny's eyebrows rose. "A date? Who with?"

"None of your business."

Emma had not told Lenny the truth, not strictly speaking. She did have a date, but it was on Saturday night, not Friday night. Herschel was never with her on Friday nights, nor during the day on Saturdays. It had to do with observing the Sabbath.

Six months ago Rosa suddenly announced that she was dropping out of Cornell and going to Germany to support the Revolution over there. Rosa and Herschel argued vehemently about it in Emma's presence.

"You're nuts," he shouted. "You're just going to be beaten up by the police or the fascist bully boys. What can you—one American girl—do over there?"

"The moment is ripe for the Revolution." she retorted. "The workers can't find jobs and those with jobs are on strike; the inflation has wiped out the middle class; the Weimar government is wobbling. The Party has sent out a call. I speak German. I have to go."

"The timing is wrong. Maybe in twenty or twenty-one when the economy was so bad, you might have had a chance, but now the Socialists are weak and disorganized. Besides you speak Yiddish, not German. They hate Jews over there."

"I speak high German too. And the Communist Party rejects all religion. They're not anti-Semitic."

"Hah! The Party is run by Russia. The Russians drove my family out thirty years ago. You're going to get bloodied. For nothing."

"Armchair radical. Do you think the Junkers and the industrialists will give up power without a struggle?"

SO ROSA LEFT for Germany, and Herschel remained behind. Emma could not imagine having such passion for a political cause. Only biology meant so much to her. With Rosa gone, Herschel never came by the women's dorm, so Emma didn't see him until they met by chance on the campus two months later. Herschel fell into step beside her.

"I'm so glad to see you, Emma. I have missed you."

"It's nice to see you too, Herschel. I've been so busy that I hardly see any of our friends these days."

"Me neither. But . . . it's you I have missed. Uh, perhaps, now that Rosa is away, uh, maybe there is an opportunity for you and me?"

"I have no idea what you're talking about, Herschel."

"Oh, I think you do."

They stopped walking, and Emma looked directly at Herschel.

His dark brown eyes shone with mischievous invitation; his prominent lower lip moved from a pout to a grin. "I'm terribly attracted to you, and I get the feeling that you, maybe . . ."

"Damn it, Herschel, I, uh, I like you, but it wouldn't be right. Rosa's your girl. I couldn't see you behind her back."

"Oh, we have a, uh, an understanding. C'mon. Just for fun. Let me take you out for coffee, maybe go to a movie. You work all the time. A little relaxation would be good for you. Please."

"Well, maybe just for fun. I don't want a serious beau, you know. I don't have time for that."

"Oh, that's OK with me. I'm sure not looking to get married. Besides, my family would never stand for me marrying a *schicksa*."

"A what?"

"A gentile woman."

"Oh."

"So, may I come by your place on Saturday night? After sundown?"

So Emma and Herschel began seeing one another in her rare free evenings. Herschel's big-city sophistication and cynicism, his fluency in foreign languages, his strange religion, which he practiced and mocked in equal proportions, aroused Emma's curiosity. Perhaps inevitably, given the strong physical attraction between them—and despite the need for secrecy—they became intimate within a month.

Herschel had no interest in her scientific activities, but he quizzed her relentlessly as though she were a member of a foreign tribe—which, perhaps to him, she was.

"So, so tell me this. What would people back in—where is it you come from?" he asked one evening when they were together in his apartment.

"Stanton Mills, Illinois."

"Stanton Mills. I love it. Right out of Sinclair Lewis. Anyway, what would the folks back in Stanton Mills think of you spending time with a Jew?"

"I dunno. I guess they'd think it was pretty strange."

"They must have an opinion of Jews, don't they?"

"Oh, I suppose so. We think of them as merchants, maybe a bit slippery, you know. We say 'I jewed him down' when we're talking about bargaining. There was a cattle dealer by the name of Goldberg who came around; people said he was a Jew. I think some of the stores in Rockford are owned by Jews. I don't think there were any in a little farm town like Stanton Mills. I didn't know any Jews at Hancock either. I guess there wouldn't be any at a Lutheran college. Is it so important to you, the Jewish thing? I thought you Reds were atheists. Do you believe in the Jewish religion?"

"Not as the literal truth, no, but it's an important part of who I am. The people I belong to. When I observe the Sabbath or the High Holy Days, the traditions and rituals, I . . . I guess, it's always been a part of my life, my family and friends, my background, my history. Do you know what a *seder* is?"

"No."

"It's a gathering where we celebrate Passover. You know about Passover?"

"Um, well, sort of. I remember the story from Exodus. The Angel of Death passed over the Jewish homes."

"That's it. Well, we gather for a meal of special foods: matzoh, wine, and so on. There're readings and prayers in Hebrew. It starts when the youngest child asks 'why is this night different from all other nights?'" Herschel shrugged. "I dunno. It just feels very close and special. Don't you have some things like that? I mean, as a Christian, or being Swedish?"

"Not really. We'd go to church at Christmas and on Easter, and I like the music, hymns, and all of that, but I don't do anything these days. I don't miss it. And I don't think of myself as being Swedish. My father's parents came from Sweden, but my mother's family is mostly English with some German mixed in. We're just Americans, I guess."

"You really don't know about the persecution of the Jews, do you?"

"No."

"Well, I could go on and on about pogroms, Jews tormented in Russia and Poland, Jews not allowed to own land or to enter certain professions, being forced to live in ghettos, condemned by the Catholic Church as Christ killers."

"Not in America."

"Oh, there's plenty in America. Did you know that all the good medical schools and law schools have quotas on how many Jews they will let in?"

"Sort of like women, huh?"

Herschel laughed. "Touché."

EMMA'S EXPERIMENTS WITH Neurospora proceeded slowly. She had difficulty finding conditions for cultivating the fungus so that the cells progressed reproducibly through mating and its sexual cycle of development. Isolating and germinating the fungal spores required her to learn tedious techniques. No one at Cornell had any experience with fungal culture or genetics, so Professor Hutchison suggested that Emma travel to Washington to spend two weeks working with Bernard Dodge in his laboratory at the Department of Agriculture to learn his techniques directly.

Fortunately, Dodge welcomed Emma, and, when he discovered that she had grown up on a poor Midwestern farm, walked through the snow to a country school, and struggled to obtain an education, just as he had, a warm bond grew between them. Working hands-on with Neurospora cultures under Dodge's experienced guidance and encouragement gave her the tools and experimental competence she needed for successfully carrying out her thesis research.

Emma learned that if she were ever to be so fortunate as to train novice scientists herself someday, she would serve them best by acting as a mentor, teaching them directly in the laboratory how to execute experiments. The "sink or swim" philosophy of graduate education that she saw often at Cornell was inefficient at best and inhumane at worst.

The train journey that brought Emma to Washington required a change of trains at Grand Central Station in New York City. She was so intimidated by the huge city that she never left the vast, ornate spaces of the station to see the sights. When she confessed as much to Dodge, he insisted that she spend a half day touring Washington with him in his car before he took her to Union Station for the return journey. They puttered along wide avenues through far more automobile traffic than Emma had ever seen while she gawked at the city's famous sights and monumental buildings.

"Let's go wake up President Harding from his nap," Dodge joked, as they passed the White House.

When they drove up to the grandiose D.C. station and Emma stepped to the curb to join the crowds, she turned and grasped Dodge's hand.

"You have been so kind and have taught me so much. I can never repay you."

"Oh, yes, you can. Do wonderful things with my little fungus. Make discoveries. That will be my reward. Good luck, Emma."

IN THE COMING months Emma had another scientist to thank for supporting her thesis research: the usually reclusive Barbara McClintock. After hearing Emma describe her experiments in a research group seminar, Barbara approached her quietly at her desk.

"Emma, I think you could add a lot to your characterization of Neurospora genetics if you did a preliminary cytogenetic characterization. It would be valuable to determine the number of its chromosomes and follow their behavior through the sexual cycle. You would have to develop techniques for preparing the cells and staining the chromosomes as I did with maize. I could teach you how to get started, but a lot of trial and error experimentation will be necessary."

It was a generous offer. Emma had been questioned severely during her seminar. There were very few well-characterized genetic markers in Neurospora. How did she expect to do genetics with no genes to analyze? Combining cytogenetic work with her preliminary genetics would give her thesis added significance and novelty. Without saying so, Barbara had provided a way around the shortcomings in Emma's research plans. If the chromosome staining experiments were successful, the path to her Ph.D. would lie clear. After two months of tedious work at the microscope with Barbara's stains and advice, Emma had achieved sufficient success to proceed on her own.

Her indebtedness to Bernard Dodge and Barbara McClintock taught Emma a valuable lesson about the collective nature of scientific discovery. She might work alone day after day, but she was not truly alone.

If Emma was gratified by the support she had received from a few fellow scientists, she was troubled by her growing isolation from her family back in Stanton Mills. Some of the fault was her own. She had not been home in three years, and she wrote letters only infrequently.

Her classes, teaching responsibilities, and long hours of research consumed her mental energy, and when she did sit down to write to her mother—no one else in the family ever wrote to her—she struggled with what to write. Her older sister Kirsten, her mother's favorite, had followed the expected path for a farm girl: early marriage to a farm youth, children, and establishing a home close to the Hansen farm. In contrast, Emma had always had "peculiar" interests, had gone far away to study God knew what and was still unmarried at twenty-seven.

When Emma had written about her biology classes and her struggles to establish experimental genetics of *Neurospora crassa*, there was no response. What was left in her life to write about? She certainly could not write about her romantic life. Her family would have been scandalized if they knew of her relationship with Herschel. Her family had approved of her friendship with Victor—what little they knew of it—but Emma had not heard from him in over a year. When he transferred to the Transcontinental Mail Service in 1925, he didn't provide a new mailing address.

The letters Emma received from her mother did not overtly describe her unhappiness, but veiled references to it permeated them. "Life on the farm just goes on and on," she wrote. "It don't seem like anything changes. Just cooking and washing and ironing, milking the cows, working in the garden, canning, the same as it was when you were home. Not much to write about, I'm afraid." Her mother wrote of sultry heat in summer and bitter cold and snow in winter. Emma knew that her mother and her sister-in-law Susan often quarreled, but the letters did not mention it. Her mother was overworked and depressed, but Emma did not know how to comfort her.

Hannah Oosterfeld regularly sent news of events in Stanton Mills along with polite comments on Emma's attempts to describe her studies and research, but her most recent letter contained a troubling paragraph: "I am a bit worried about your mother, dear Emma. She seemed rather thin and weak when I saw her in the store last week. It had been some time since I last saw her, as Bjorn and Susan have been getting the groceries for your family lately, so I could see how much she had changed. When I asked after her health, she said she was fine, just rather tired lately, but I do wonder and worry. Has she written anything to you about it?"

In fact, Emma had not received a letter from her mother in three months. When Emma wrote to ask if she was unwell, there was no reply.

Then came a letter from her brother:

> *May 26, 1927*
> *Dear Emma,*
>
> *I hope you are doing okay at that college. Seems like you have been gone forever.*
>
> *Mama hasn't written because she didn't want you to worry, but she asked me to write to tell you that she has got to have an operation. Her insides haven't never been right since she had such a hard time having Aaron, and seems like they have got a lot worse lately. She has been losing a lot of blood. We took her to a doctor in Rockford and he said she has to have an operation to take out her baby bed and fix things up inside. We're taking her to the hospital next Monday and she will have to stay for a week or so. The doctor said there's nothing to worry about, but we figured you'd want to know.*
>
> *Bjorn*

Emma taught her biology classes and worked in the laboratory as usual throughout the week that followed. Bjorn had said that there was nothing to worry about, but she grew ever more anxious as day followed day with no news from home. The Hansen farm had no telephone, so there was no fast way to find out how Mama's surgery had gone or how she was recovering. Her anxiety rising, Emma obtained permission from Professor Hutchison to use his office phone to place a long distance call to the Oosterfeld grocery store to see if they had any information. They did not, but promised to contact the Hansen farm and call back.

The next day Professor Hutchison summoned Emma to his office to receive a telephone call from Stanton Mills. The first voice she heard was Pieter Oosterfeld.

"Oh, Emma, I'm so sorry. Here, here, it's your brother, Bjorn."

"Bjorn, I've been so worried. How's Mama? Is she all right?"

"Naw, Emma, I've got real bad news. Mama died day before yesterday."

"No. What. How could that happen? I thought the doctor said . . . Oh, my God. Oh, my God. Why didn't you call me?"

"Well, we didn't know . . . we didn't have no phone number . . . we was going to send you a telegram. Then Mr. Oosterfeld came out and said we could call you on his phone."

"But, but, what happened?"

"She was bleedin' real bad. They couldn't get it stopped. Just seemed like it was so quick."

Emma was slack-jawed. A greenish fog enveloped her. She couldn't think; she began to cry. How was this possible? Her mother dead? Just like that? She had been so far away. Even now she was struggling to understand. Unwelcome emotions overwhelmed her: confusion, grief, guilt.

She had long known that Mama was unhappy and suffered from female troubles, but she had pushed that knowledge away and concentrated on her own urgent struggle to become a scientist. She had never been very close to her mother. She had never told her or written to her to tell her that she was grateful for all she had done for her or to convey her understanding and sympathy with her unhappiness. Such frank expressions of intimate feeling were never exchanged in the Hansen family. Now it was too late to make amends.

"Bjorn, oh, I can't believe this. I feel so bad."

"Uh, Emma, the funeral's the day after tomorrow." Static fuzzed Bjorn's voice. Has she heard correctly?

"What? What? Day after tomorrow?"

"Uh, ja."

"Why so soon? I can't possibly get there by then. It takes two days by train. There aren't that many connections from Ithaca to Stanton Mills. Bjorn, I can't get there."

"Well, we figured you wouldn't come anyways."

"What? Why did you think that?"

"Emma, you ain't been home in over three years. Besides, the undertaker was kind of in a hurry. He had another funeral."

"Well, I feel terrible about this."

"I'm sorry, Emma. It's too late to do anything now." More static on the line. Emma struggled to comprehend all she had just heard. Her belly burned; she feared she would vomit.

"Emma?" Bjorn's voice was distant and fuzzy.

"Well, if I can't come to the funeral, I'll wire you some money for flowers. Put them by the casket for me, OK?"

"Ja, OK."

EMMA TEARFULLY EXPLAINED the call to Professor Hutchinson, thanked him for use of his phone, and fled to her lab, where she wrestled with her emotions. Perhaps attending her mother's funeral would have helped her to express her grief and soften her guilt. Perhaps the sight of her mother's waxen body in her coffin would have helped her to accept the finality of her death. Perhaps she and her family could have comforted one another. Perhaps.

Attending the funeral would have been a sentimental, symbolic act of little practical value, but such gestures were important to her family and in Stanton Mills. Her absence would be noted, seen as a sign of coldness, of indifference. Emma was ashamed to be thought of in such terms, but she was also relieved not to have to undertake the long, tiresome journey. She had used every bit of her savings to pay for the trip to Washington to work with Bernard Dodge and would have had to borrow funds for the trip. From whom? Emma had never felt so alone. How could they have assumed that she wouldn't come home for the funeral?

A week after her mother's funeral she received a letter from her sister Kirsten:

> *Dear Emma,*
>
> *Well, we buried Mama the day before yesterday. It was a nice sunny day, but awfully sad. Lots of folks were there. Papa just don't say much. He says he'll keep going like before, but I think Bjorn and Susan are taking over the farm.*

*I hope Mama can rest in peace. It like to broke my heart that
of her five children, only two was there. Aaron dead years ago,
and no one knows what became of Henrik. And you didn't bother
to come home. I guess your bugs or whatever it is you are doing
out there are more important to you than your family. I hope you
haven't gotten to thinking you're better than the rest of us because
you have been to college and wanting to be a lady professor and
all.*

    Kirsten

The letter infuriated Emma. It was so unjust. Had not the family
scheduled the funeral so as to make it impossible for her to be there?
Had Bjorn described his phone conversation to Kirsten? Probably not.
He was so taciturn. Like their father. Kirsten was transforming her
grief into resentment of Emma. Did she really think that Emma felt
no grief too? How could she respond? Was it even worth attempting?
She was desolate: her favorite brother Henrik first destroyed by war,
then disappeared, the death of her mother made even more bitter by her
regret that they had not loved one another more, now her sister slapping
her face like this—from a safe distance with such an unfair, hostile letter.

Sitting at her lab bench with tears flowing down her face, Emma read
the letter for a final time, then thrust a corner into the blue flame of the
little Bunsen burner that she used for sterilizing her inoculation needles.
A yellow flame flared up and quickly consumed the sheet. Delicate black
flakes drifted across the stone lab bench like dead leaves.

CHAPTER 10
1928

DEAN ELIAS WOODROW sat back in his upholstered chair and peered over his glasses at Emma, who sat nervously perched on the edge of a hard chair facing him. Her new blue suit—the only suit she owned, recently purchased for this interview—was too warm; or was it tension that made sweat form between her breasts and moisten her back? The Dean's decision had the power to transform her life.

Since completing her Ph.D. in June Emma had mailed out dozens of applications for teaching positions in small colleges around the country. Many had not been answered, even after she sent letters requesting a response. Some were curtly declined with no reasons given. She had received no offers or even invitations to interview. Her teaching and research assistantships ended. None of the maize geneticists at Cornell were interested in engaging her for postgraduate work because her research had been with "some fungus." She was facing unemployment, new Ph.D. or no. Would she be forced to return to teaching in high school, as she had done four years ago? Was all that she had fought for to come to nothing, no professorship, no chance to continue research?

Emma forced herself to sit calmly and willed a pleasant expression onto her face. She sensed that the Dean was savoring the power that his long silence projected. Woodrow, she had learned from her study of Harrington College's catalog, held a Ph.D. in history from Harvard, which gave him great stature among the faculty, a significant fraction of whom had not earned doctorates. He had been elected Dean of the College while still in his forties, and for the past fifteen years had ruled with magisterial hauteur.

Emma had traveled at her own expense the day before from Ithaca to Harrington, an Ohio town of about fifty thousand people located about halfway between Columbus and Cincinnati, to be interviewed for the position of Assistant Professor of Biology. The invitation had come very late in the summer, which suggested that the college was scrambling to fill the position before classes started next month. Dared she hope that this was the chance she had searched for—the only serious consideration she had received after an agonizing summer?

"Well, Miss Hansen, I have examined your credentials carefully," Dean Woodrow said, finally.

"Yes, thank you, sir. But, excuse me, it's Dr. Hansen."

"Um, yes, of course. Your letters are quite supportive and a Ph.D. from Cornell is, well, in your favor. Most of our faculty are, uh, not from such, uh, distinguished institutions, and one of my goals at Harrington is to elevate the, uh, regard in which our faculty are held by others. However, I have some concerns. It appears that your doctorate is in botany, whereas we are seeking a biologist, a generalist."

"Oh, that's a peculiarity of Cornell's genetics program, sir. They have a rule—a silly one, if you want my opinion—that women may not receive degrees in genetics, so I was compelled to take a degree in botany."

"Um, yes, but genetics is also rather too specialized, Miss Hansen. Harrington is an undergraduate institution, as you surely know. Our candidate must be able to teach a wide range of topics in biology: general biology, zoology, anatomy, bacteriology, embryology, as well as botany and genetics."

"You have examined my transcript, Dean Woodrow. You can see that I am broadly trained in all those areas of biology. Also, I have several years of teaching experience in high school and as a teaching assistant at Cornell. My interest in genetics is strong, of course, and I would like to continue doing research in genetics here at Harrington. But I certainly expect to teach biology, broadly defined, and I look forward to it."

Woodrow's eyebrows rose. "Research? You understand that this is not a university, but a teaching institution. Undergraduates only. You would have a substantial teaching load, little time for research."

"I understand. However, I would like to maintain a small program of research. In part, I want to provide an opportunity for bright and motivated advanced students to do research projects under my supervision. I believe that there is no more effective way to teach the true nature of science. Mere presentation of facts and generalizations is inadequate without providing an understanding of how scientific knowledge is arrived at. That is by observation and experimentation, of course."

"Um, yes. Provided that you are appointed to our faculty. We do value scholarship here at Harrington. Our best faculty have published scholarly work. But you must understand that your research activities would be on your own time and at your own expense. Unless you can raise funds from external sources."

"Yes, I understand that. I am prepared to make the effort."

"Let me be candid with you, Miss Hansen. We thought this position had been filled, but our candidate withdrew recently without advance notice. Um, most unprofessional."

"I see."

"So, we are compelled to fill the vacancy very quickly to, uh, meet our teaching needs. I will be very frank. I would have preferred to hire a man. Men are naturally superior leaders and command respect in the classroom. Whereas a woman . . ."

Her cheeks growing hot, Emma dared to interrupt. "Sir, I only ask to be judged by the quality of my performance, not by my sex. If I am offered the position, I assure you that the college will not be disappointed."

"Um, well, I hope not." The Dean studied the papers on his desk— or pretended to, it seemed to Emma—before he finally spoke. "Shall we proceed? I am prepared to offer you a position as Instructor in Biology, renewable after review annually. The salary would be twenty-six hundred dollars per annum."

"Dean Woodrow, please understand. I am keen to join the faculty of Harrington College, but the position was advertised as for an Assistant Professorship at a salary of three thousand dollars. Surely, with my credentials . . ."

"Ah, yes, well, that was for a male appointee, who would have to support a family. And who would, ah, you will recognize, be in, uh, greater demand."

Emma hesitated. *God knows, I want this chance, but if I allow this man to run over me now, what can I expect in the future?* "Very well, I will accept the lower salary for the first year, but I require appointment as an Assistant Professor. With the opportunity to earn tenure. That costs the college nothing. You can still do your annual review. I believe I can earn tenure. It is my intention to make the college very, very glad to have me on the faculty."

Woodrow leaned back in his chair. Emma knew that the college had to have an instructor ready to teach its biology classes in three weeks. It was obvious that she was tougher than he expected or liked, but she was well prepared. She wondered if he had received any applications from men who were as well qualified. Still, he stretched out the wait.

"Very well," he said. "Don't make me regret taking a chance on you, young lady."

EMMA WALKED QUICKLY down the hall, the wooden floor creaking under her feet, and descended the stone steps leaving MacAllister Hall. Her white blouse clung to her damp body. Because there was no one walking on the campus at the moment, she removed her suit jacket.

For the first time since leaving the Dean's office, she breathed deeply and took in the world around her. She permitted herself a tiny thrill of joy. At last. This stately academic grove would be her home for the coming years. In late summer the campus was deeply shaded by mature elm trees and, in the absence of the eight hundred or so students who would soon return, it was quiet, green, cool. MacAllister Hall, behind her, stood at the south end of a grassy quad. It was a handsome four-story stone structure with high narrow windows and a mansard roof, built in the Second Empire style that was popular in the 1870s. Other brick and stone buildings in various styles surrounded the quad and two other adjacent lawn-like areas.

Emma felt tension slowly easing from her body. The campus comforted her as Hancock College had years earlier. Harrington College was about twice the size of Hancock and enjoyed a strong reputation among small liberal arts colleges. Founded shortly after the Civil War by Presbyterians, the college was now secular and well endowed. It began admitting women around 1900, and they were now about a quarter of the student body. Yes, Emma could feel at home here.

Still, the frosty negotiation with Dean Woodrow and his obvious reluctance to hire her rankled. It polluted her pleasure. Why was each achievement so hard-won? Even when she had finally received her Ph.D., it had felt anticlimactic. Her emotions were more akin to those of an exhausted runner than the exhilaration of victory that she had imagined.

Perhaps it was because the faculty had seemed more grudging than congratulatory. During the long and tedious oral defense of her thesis, "A Preliminary Genetic and Cytogenetic Characterization of the Heterothallic Ascomycete *Neurospora crassa*," the examining professors had seemed disengaged. She knew that most of them considered the object of her researches to be of minor scientific and no practical importance, but in the end they agreed that her work was sound and original and that she had a thorough understanding of genetics.

She was asked to step outside of the room while the committee deliberated her fate. One of the professors had an unfortunately loud voice because of his poor hearing, and Emma was stung to hear him say,

"Well, she's not as brilliant as McClintock, but, frankly, more capable that one expects of a woman. I don't see any future in her research, but since she will end up teaching in a lady's academy somewhere, I don't believe she will embarrass Cornell."

Besides, Emma had been disappointed that she had no one to share her achievement with. Rosa Levin had returned from Germany, much embittered by Stalin's crushing of his rival Leon Trotsky, whose ideas she had favored. She returned to Herschel's arms, and Emma and Herschel pretended that they had only been friends. He slipped quietly out of her life.

She had heard nothing from Victor in over two years. Emma sent invitations to the graduation ceremonies to her family and to the Oosterfelds. She wrote notes telling them that she understood that it was impractical for them to come to Ithaca, and, indeed, they wrote back politely declining. But Emma was damned if she would forego the pleasure of donning a black robe with three velvet hashmarks on the sleeves and having the long doctoral hood placed over her shoulders in the formal ceremonies held in June 1928. Barbara McClintock attended the ceremony and congratulated Emma warmly. Bernard Dodge was not able to be present, but sent a telegram that ended with the words, "You will make Cornell and me proud."

EMMA TOOK THE train back to Ithaca to take her leave of her friends and colleagues and pack her belongings for her return to Harrington. She bundled her books and papers into boxes. Her clothing all fit into a single suitcase. It was a sad little collection, very worn. She would need some better clothing for teaching. The Dean had advanced her two hundred dollars from her salary, so Emma bought two more simple suits, tan and pale blue, to go with the dark blue suit she had worn for her interview, and two white blouses. New shoes would have to come later.

At the lab Emma packed her cultures and research materials for shipment to Harrington. Since she had been forced to buy all of her own supplies and equipment, she was entitled to take them with her. She said goodbye to Professor Hutchison, who congratulated her.

"You are very fortunate, Emma," he said. "Harrington is a good small college."

Then she sought out Barbara McClintock, who was in her lab as usual, and shared her good news.

"I want to thank you, Barbara. Your assistance with my cytogenetic work was really a very important part of my thesis."

"Good luck, Emma. I wish you well. I don't suppose you will be able to continue your research with Neurospora there. Too bad. You were off to a good start."

"Oh, I'm going to try. I know I won't have much time or support, but I'm determined to try."

"Well, I've been holding out for a professorship at a research university. Some place that will allow me to keep working on maize genetics, but so far, no one will take me."

"Oh, that's too bad. You are so capable. Much more than I am. Do you think it's because . . . ?"

"Because of my anatomical 'deficiencies'? Yes, I do. They just won't hire a woman."

Emma returned to Harrington the next day. There was so much to do and little time to get it done. She rented a room by the week in a campus rooming house for single women. A search for a suitable apartment would have to wait. Dean Woodrow had suggested that she live in Franklin Hall, the women's dormitory, but when Emma learned that she would be required to serve as a house mother to the co-eds— "resident faculty supervisor" was the formal term—she declined.

"I lived in a women's dorm for four years," she told the Dean. "I need a quieter, more private place to work. Besides, I expect to be in my office and laboratory in the evenings and weekends."

The next order of business was to meet with her colleagues and get settled in the Biology Department and to learn more about her teaching assignments for the fall semester. Emma had, rashly she now realized, accepted her appointment without meeting them or seeing where she would work.

The Science Building faced the central quad on the west side. It was a stolid, three-story brick building with a vaguely English Gothic stone façade built in 1890, and Emma would soon learn that its laboratory facilities were antiquated. She entered the office of the department chairman, Professor Morris Foster, at nine in the morning on her first full day on campus. Foster's office was a spacious second floor corner room with tall windows looking out over the quad. He rose to meet her, but did not offer his hand.

"Ah, Miss Hansen, welcome. We are glad to have you here." His deep and resonant voice carried a New England accent.

With a full head of white hair he appeared to be about sixty. Dressed in a three-piece suit and with aromatic white smoke curling from his pipe, he looked most professorial. Emma fought feelings of intimidation.

"This is our colleague, Mr. Rothermel," he continued.

A small, bald, nervous-seeming man rose from his chair and nodded without speaking.

"In the normal course of events we would have become acquainted before you were hired, of course, but, as you know, the Dean was rather in a hurry," Foster rumbled. "I . . . we . . . reviewed your credentials, of course. Ph.D. from Cornell, most impressive."

It occurred to Emma that the introduction of Rothermel as "Mister" indicated that he had not earned a doctorate and that he might feel threatened by her.

"I am eager to get started, Professor Foster," Emma replied. "Could we discuss my teaching duties first, because I don't have much time to get prepared."

"Indeed. Let's see now. We will expect you to take over General Biology I this fall and General Biology II in the spring. Three lectures a week. Not much to it. Just grind through the textbook, two chapters a week. About twenty-five students. Most are taking the course to meet their general education requirements in science, not biology majors. You'll need to give frequent quizzes and exams to force them to keep up with the reading. Quite a bit of grading, I'm afraid. Here's a copy of the text we use."

"I see." Emma hoped to do much more than grind through a textbook. "Is there a laboratory section?"

"Yes, once a week. Mostly dissections."

Emma leafed through the textbook. It had been published in 1916, the year she graduated from high school. "I was a teaching assistant in courses like this at Cornell. Is there any problem if I make changes? Adopt a new textbook? Introduce new lab exercises?"

Foster shot a glanced at Rothermel, who shrugged, but did not speak. "Well, there's no time for changes this fall, but after that, it's up to you. I'd like to review your proposed changes, of course. Um, there's a bit more, Miss Hansen. I see that you specialized in genetics, so naturally, we'd like you to take over the genetics course. Frankly, neither of us like teaching it. We don't really know much genetics, rather arcane subject, seems to me."

"Oh, there's a lot new that's happening. I'd be excited to teach genetics. Is that in the spring?"

"Uh, no, this fall. And, um, one more thing—bacteriology. You seem to have worked with microbes, so we'd like to assign that course to you also this fall. There's no laboratory for that."

"Oh, there should be. But I'll have all I can handle as it is for now." It was a staggering load for a new faculty member, but Emma chose not to protest. She'd have to do the best she could by following the content previously used in the courses this fall, then revise them in the future. "And what will you gentlemen be teaching?"

Foster drew deeply on his pipe and exhaled a white cloud. "I take care of the courses in botany. My doctorate was in botany. One naturally prefers to teach in one's specialty." More smoke.

"I do embryology and comparative anatomy," Rothermel said. "Used to do gross human anatomy, you know, dissection of cadavers, but we discontinued that. Most of the students who took the course were going on to medical school, where they made them do it all over again."

"Oh." It was clear to Emma that her colleagues had reserved small, specialized courses for themselves, and that their teaching loads were much lighter than hers. "May I see the teaching laboratory? My office? And, another thing: I'd like a small laboratory space for my own research."

Rothermel and Foster exchanged glances and frowned.

"Well, I should hardly think that you will have time for research . . ." He pronounced the word "research" as though it were an unclean activity.

"Not at first, I realize that, but later. I'll have weekends and more time in the summer."

"Hmmmm. I take it that you are not married."

"No."

"Of course, you are still quite young. Perhaps . . ."

"May I see the laboratory now?"

The main teaching laboratory for biology was a large, poorly lit room equipped with three rows of wooden benches topped with soapstone. Wooden stools lined the aisles between the benches. Cabinets with glass doors held a few microscopes, dissecting equipment, and several jars of specimens—worms, starfish, frogs, and large grasshoppers—floating in preservative fluid, awaiting dissection. A large stone sink stood at the end of each bench. Emma stalked the room as though she were considering buying it. The lighting was poor. She would have to press for improvements.

"Is this where I would teach bacteriology lab?"

"Yes."

"Well, do you suppose we could arrange for more electrical outlets for microscope lamps and gascocks equipped with natural gas for Bunsen burners to be installed? An incubator? And an autoclave? A big one. I'll have to have one for my research anyway. Could we put in a request to the Dean to have these improvements made as soon as possible?"

Foster and Rothermel rolled their eyes at one another, but Emma ignored it. "Now where do you propose to put me? My office, my lab?"

"Well," Rothermel offered, "we discussed that. You can have my old office. When Professor Whisnant retired, I moved to his second floor office. And I've been thinking about this business of your lab. We hadn't planned on that, but you could have the old gross anatomy room. Since we don't use it any more. It's just down the hall from your office."

"That would be good. May I see them?"

The office was small, but suitable. It was equipped with a desk and chairs, two bookcases with glass doors, shelves and a wooden filing cabinet. A hot water radiator stood under the single window, an ornate accordion-like apparatus coated with silvery paint. Emma would discover that it hissed and groaned during the winter months and was difficult to adjust. Her office was often too cold or stiflingly hot.

The human anatomy room that was to become Emma's laboratory reeked of formaldehyde embalming fluid. A large zinc topped table stood in the center of the well-illuminated room; a large porcelain sink and shelves and cabinets lined one wall. There were only two half-height windows; the floor was concrete, not wood as in all of the other rooms, with a drain set into it.

"I think this can be made to do," Emma said after a careful inspection. "But some modifications are required. Can this large cabinet be removed and replaced with a lab bench with shelves over it?" She pointed to the cabinet in which cadavers had been stored. "And I'll have to have electrical outlets installed from my microscope lamp, and for two incubators. Oh, and a couple of gas outlets for Bunsen burners on the benches. I'll make a list and ask the Dean to make it part of the work done when the teaching lab is updated."

Both of her new colleagues were now shaking their heads and frowning.

"Ah, don't you think you are . . . perhaps, um, a bit overly ambitious? These are expensive renovations," Foster said.

"I don't want to seem presumptuous, but we should ask for what we need. I realize that it may take a year or so to get the work done. If you will support me in this, I can promise modern, well-taught courses in biology. And that would reflect well on all of us, don't you think?"

"Um, yes, of course. I'll support your requests to the Dean. Um, perhaps if we all three take the petition to him, he will, uh, be more receptive." There was an awkward pause. "Well, we'll let you get to it. You have quite a lot to do."

Emma needed three trips to bring her boxes of books, papers, and research materials from the rooming house to her office. She would have liked to ask her new colleagues to help her carry them, but a bite of stubborn pride forbade her from asking. She was about the take a box of research supplies to the room that would become her lab, when she realized that Foster and Rothermel were inside. Perhaps they were preparing a list of the renovations she had requested.

"She seems rather pushy, don't you think? Somewhat full of herself. I'd bet nothing will come of this 'research' pipe dream. What is she working on, anyway?" Rothermel's nasal voice.

"The genetics of some obscure fungus, I think it was. Let's see how she handles her classes," Foster rumbled. "That'll take the wind out of her sails, I'd wager. You have to admit that she'll take a big burden off of us. And if she pushes old Woodrow into modernizing the labs, well, I'm all for that."

WHEN CLASSES BEGAN in September, Emma started taking her main meal of the day at noon in the main dining hall in the faculty dining room adjacent to two, much larger, noisier rooms where the students ate. The first time she entered, heads—all male—turned.

An older man approached her with a kind smile. "Excuse me, young lady. You must be new here. This is the faculty dining room. The students take their meals in the next room."

"But, but . . ." she stammered. "I am on the faculty."

Fortunately, Professor Foster, who was seated at a nearby table, stood up and announced in a loud voice. "I'd like to introduce our new assistant professor of biology, Dr. Emma Hansen, recently of Cornell University."

Emma smiled in gratitude. He might be a bit stuffy, but not unkind.

"Oh, I beg your pardon," the professor who had intercepted her said. "My goodness, you are so . . . um, youthful."

Emma's lunchtime conversations with her colleagues were cordial, but a little stiff. After a few polite questions, the men generally returned to their own conversations. Two days later she noticed two women seated at a table by themselves and she approached them.

"May I join you, ladies? I'm Emma Hansen. New in the Biology Department."

"Oh, yes, we've heard all about the new lady professor. I'm Rosalee Bendix and this is my colleague Miss Erica Jameson. Please join us." Both women appeared to be in their fifties and were dressed in a rather old-fashioned manner with long skirts and full-sleeved blouses, hair piled on their heads, rather than cut short and bobbed as Emma's was.

"Thank you. My goodness, are we the only women on the Harrington faculty?"

"I'm afraid so, dear."

"Have you found that to be . . . ah . . . difficult?"

"Oh, no, I wouldn't say so. Would you, Miss Bendix?"

"No. You see, we're both in the Domestic Science Department. The men have always been content to leave that to us ladies. They don't know anything about cooking, sewing, homemaking, or child care, and all of our students are co-eds."

"How are you getting on, Dr. Hansen?" Miss Jameson asked.

"Oh, please, call me Emma. Well, I'm nearly swamped, I admit. I only arrived four weeks ago, and I'm teaching three courses for the first time. Courses that have been rather . . . let go, if I may speak frankly. I have begun asking for improvements, but I suspect that my colleagues think I am too pushy."

"Well, I'd encourage you to be patient. Try not to antagonize them. You are a bit of a pioneer, you know," Miss Jameson replied. "Where are you living, dear?"

"Rooming house for the moment. Mrs. Stockdale's. I haven't had time to look for an apartment of my own. One I could afford."

"I take it you aren't married then?"

"No."

"Perhaps we can help you. The building where we live has some small apartments. One-room efficiencies with a little kitchen and bathroom. Close enough to walk to campus."

"Oh, that would be a great help. Thank you."

"Shall we arrange to meet this weekend? I'll talk to the landlord."

They settled into small talk over their meals. Delicate questioning revealed that neither Miss Jameson nor Miss Bendix held doctorate degrees or had any interest in biology or research. When Emma brought up new research on the discovery of vitamins, which she thought would connect to their teaching about foods and nutrition, her two new friends did not express much interest, so she retreated to questions about the college and campus life.

At the end of the lunch, Miss Jameson softly clearly her throat. "Um, Miss Hansen, if I may make a suggestion? I could show you a way to do your hair that would be . . . um . . . would make you appear a bit more . . . mature. My goodness, you look like one of the co-eds. Perhaps the students would . . . take you more seriously . . . ? If you don't mind my suggesting it?"

Emma stifled a little flash of irritation. It was kindly intended, and she would need all the friends she could find. "Yes, yes, of course, if it doesn't require too much fussing in the mornings."

CHAPTER 11
1930

AS EMMA SURVEYED the assembled students in the lecture hall, she experienced a surge of nervous excitement, a feeling like she had experienced when she waited to begin the oral defense of her Ph.D. thesis before a panel of professors at Cornell. Even though this was the start of her third year of teaching at Harrington College, she still felt this way at the beginning of a new semester, the first time she faced a new class. She had learned to accept the edgy feeling, learned that it actually made her more articulate, more quick-thinking, more intellectually alive—not a nervous teacher, but a better one.

Emma stood at a lectern in front of a large blackboard and demonstration table. The students sat expectantly in four raised tiers on benches with wooden writing desks curving in front of them. Fifty-two students this fall, the most ever. Enrollments had increased each term as word spread across the campus: there was a new lady professor of biology who was really good.

Emma had learned much about teaching in the past two years. Her first year had been stiff and clumsy in spite of her experience teaching high school and at Cornell. At the beginning she had felt as though she were a fraud to stand as a professor in front of a college class. But by now she had gained confidence. She had learned not to open the class with a review of the course requirements and objectives, but to start by sharing her excitement about biology, to invite her students to join her on a journey of discovery.

"This term we are going to explore the living world together," Emma began. "And we are going find wonderful things, sometimes scarcely believable things, about how living organisms solve their problems of finding food, reproduction, and avoiding predators; how they adapt to their environment; how they have evolved throughout great periods of time. As we take this adventure, I want you to constantly ask questions. What is it made of? How is it put together? What is the function of each organ, tissue, and cell? How do the organisms function in groups? Because that is a question that always makes sense in biology—what is its function? In the nonliving world, you wouldn't ask 'what is the function of a cloud, of a rock?', but in biology you must ask it. And then a deeper question: *how* does it work? Sometimes we don't know. Not yet, but we must always ask. And, finally, you should demand to know: *why do we think so?* What is the evidence that leads the scientific community to conclude what it does and for your textbook to state as though it were certain fact. What is the evidence? What observations and experiments led to the conclusion? Could it be wrong?"

Emma stood back from the lectern for a moment. The nervousness she had felt moments ago was replaced by quiet joy. This, yes, this was what she had dreamed of doing for so long.

"And if you develop these habits of critical thought, you will not only obtain a deep appreciation for biology, you will understand the nature of science itself, and you will have learned skills that you can apply fruitfully to most of life's problems."

The students' eyes followed her, wide with attention. She had them. It was almost like the spell cast by the traveling evangelist preachers who set up their tents in small towns. Well, perhaps she was an evangelist, an evangelist for science.

She beamed at the students. "Shall we begin?"

WITH THE HELP of Bernard Dodge, Emma had been able to secure a five-hundred-dollar grant from the U.S. Department of Agriculture, which she had used carefully to purchase equipment and supplies to begin her studies with Neurospora genetics. She was not yet in a position to invite advanced undergraduates to work with her in the little laboratory. The few students who had accepted her invitation to do independent studies did work in more traditional areas of field biology, such as collecting and analyzing specimens, searching for ecological relationships, and she helped them with such projects as Dr. Weatherbee had helped her.

A recurring criticism of Emma's work at Cornell had been that there were so few readily identified genetic variants of Neurospora to use in her studies. The famous T. H. Morgan had a large collection of fruit fly strains that had hereditable variants in body morphology or eye color that allowed his coworkers to conduct crosses and genetic mapping. Emma had to concede that she was limited by her lack of an equivalent collection. Then she read a paper in which Morgan reported using x-rays to obtain new strains, mutant strains, with a much higher frequency than was possible by simply hunting through a huge number of individuals hoping to find such variants arising by chance. Somehow, by an unknown mechanism, x-rays increased the frequency of mutation.

Emma decided to try this method with her pet fungus. But where would she get a source of x-rays? No one in the physics department had an x-ray tube; there was not one on the campus. So Emma approached the local hospital. They used x-rays for diagnostic purposes all the time. Would they permit her to expose her little cultures to x-rays? The physicians were skeptical and amused, but when she convinced them that her fungus presented no danger of disease to patients, they gave consent.

The first exposures to x-rays killed all the cells; Emma concluded that lower doses were needed. Lower doses seemed to have no effect. The critical question was: how would Emma know if mutations were occurring? Unlike fruit flies, the fungal colonies had no readily observable anatomy in which changes could be detected. What was she looking for?

On a Saturday afternoon in May of 1929 Emma sat on a lab stool in her basement lab poring over a collection of Petri dishes on which colonies of fungal cells that had been exposed to x-rays had been grown and stimulated by heating to differentiate into colored ascospores. Some colonies failed to sporulate and just grew as thread-like mats. Those probably arose from mutations, which was encouraging, but they weren't useful to Emma because spore formation was essential for subsequent genetic analysis. Then she noticed on one of the dishes that a single colony of cells differed in color from the others. It formed white spores. Normal Neurospora cells produce a bright red-orange pigment during ascospore formation.

Excitedly, Emma replaced the cap on the Petri dish and ran out from her lab. She had to show this to someone. But on a Saturday afternoon the Science Hall was quiet as an abandoned graveyard. On the second floor she found a janitor pushing a broom down the hall.

"Look!" she exclaimed. "What do you see?"

Puzzled, the man peered into the glass dish that Emma uncovered and presented to him. "Well, a lot of orange spots, I guess."

"Yes, yes, and what else?"

"There's a white one, just one that I can see."

"Yes. I think it's a mutant. It can't make the color that the others do. Like an albino. That's what I'll call them: *albino* mutants."

"Yes, ma'am."

"But I'll have to subculture it. Make sure all its progeny are white too."

"Yes, ma'am."

In the coming weeks Emma found that subcultures derived from the original white colony always gave rise to more white colonies: the *albino* characteristic was inherited; it must have resulted from a genetic mutation. Delighted, Emma screened dozens of irradiated cultures for more *albino* mutants and eventually found a few more. Better still, over the following months she eventually found colonies that had other alterations in their color: some were pale yellow; some were bright yellow. Emma carefully collected and stored those that consistently inherited the mutant characteristic (called "phenotype" in genetic jargon). It was just a beginning, but she now had some tools to work with. She could now begin serious research on the genetics of Neurospora!

THESE WERE HAPPY years for Emma, the happiest in a long time, but there were shadows across her sunny fields. She longed for male companionship, not only the open, cheerful sensuality she had enjoyed with Herschel, and especially with Victor—both of whom had disappeared from her life—but a deeper, more committed friendship with a man who understood and respected her passions for teaching and science and who brought his own passions to the relationship. An equal. The prospect of finding such a man at Harrington College or in the surrounding community seemed depressingly remote.

Emma had not communicated with her sister Kirstin since she had received her resentful letter after their mother died. She wrote, but not often, to her father, her brother Bjorn and his wife Susan, and they replied infrequently with spare descriptions of farm and family activities. Although they did not say so, Emma deduced that the Hansen farm was struggling with low milk and pork prices brought on by last year's stock market crash, a worsening of a decade of low farm prices that followed the Great War.

Emma had a more lively correspondence with Hannah Oosterfeld, who kept her entertained with news of Stanton Mills and occasional insights into Emma's family that she gleaned from their visits to the grocery store. Hannah and Piet expressed more interest in Emma's professional activities than her family did, and their letters glowed with praise and pride at her accomplishments, even if they had little understanding of the science involved.

What remained of Emma's connection to her family? It was with a mixture of anticipation, guilt, curiosity, and hope that Emma planned a trip to Stanton Mills in July of 1930, two years after she had moved to Harrington College. It would be a tiresome journey with a change of trains in Columbus and an overnight stay in Chicago because of infrequent connections to Stanton Mills. She arranged to be met at the station by Piet Oosterfeld so she could visit with him and Hannah before Bjorn drove the truck into town to pick her up. Like their neighbors, the Hansens still had no telephone service, so the arrangements were made by mail and confirmed by telephone to the Oosterfeld's store.

Emma trembled with nervous excitement as she stepped with her small suitcase from the passenger car onto the little Stanton Mills station platform. She was the only person to get off the train, but freight and bags of mail were quickly hustled off the next car. Piet walked toward her, much more gray and bent than she remembered him.

"Ah, Emma, our own lady professor! How good to see you again after so long," he called out. A warm handshake, but no hug in public. "Come, Hannah is so eager to see you. Won't you have some coffee with us while we wait for Bjorn."

The sights and smells of the grocery store were so familiar, so rich in memories, that Emma had to blink back tears as she entered and embraced Hannah, now a tiny old lady—when had that happened? The store was little changed from the days when Emma had lived upstairs and worked there, but the shelves and counters were somewhat depleted of stock, and surfaces were dusty. That would never have been allowed in the old days.

It was Monday—washday—so there were no customers in the store. Piet hung a "Closed" sign on the front door, and they climbed the stairs to the upper level apartment for coffee. It was so unchanged that Emma felt a rush of sentimental nostalgia, as though she were suddenly transported back to her days as a high school girl, first liberated from the farm.

"Emma, you look so well," Hannah said. "Let me just look at you. So pretty. Surely some man will want to marry you soon. Do you have a beau?"

"Oh, no. I haven't had much time for that, I'm afraid."

"No, I suppose not. You've been so busy. Accomplished so much. Doctor Hansen, no, Professor Hansen. Just think of it. But you mustn't neglect your personal life. Tell us, dear, are you happy?"

"Oh, yes. I love teaching in college. And I'm getting my research going well now too."

"That's wonderful, dear."

"But how about you two? How are you getting along? Has this depression made things difficult for you?"

Piet cleared his throat and replied carefully. "Well, yes, I'm afraid it is starting to. Most of our customers are farm folks. We've always carried them on credit, as you remember, but with farm prices so low, well, some of them can't pay their bills. And, of course, they spend less than they used to. I hear rumors that some are facing bankruptcy because the banks may foreclose on their mortgages. These are hard times."

"Oh, my, I'm sorry."

"Hannah and I aren't getting any younger. We'd like to sell the store and retire, but who wants to buy it with a depression going on? Seems as though we just have to hang on until things get better. Surely this can't go on for too long. "

"Listen, you were very generous with me when I was trying to get through college. You lent me money and then wouldn't let me pay you back. How about I pay you back now? I don't make a lot at the college, but I live simply. I could send, oh, I don't know, maybe twenty dollars a month. Would that help out?"

"Oh, Emma, you're very kind, but we could never ask you to do that."

"You *didn't ask* me to do it. I want to do it. Now that I can. So, please, let's just agree. No discussion. No one else needs to know. Now, tell me what you have heard from Papa and Bjorn and Susan. They hardly ever write. And, tell me, what can I bring them? Some things from the store?"

"SUSAN STAYED OUT on the farm with the kids," Bjorn offered by way of greeting the sister he had not seen in six years. "Here, gimme your bag. And what's this?"

He nodded toward a box of groceries that Emma had purchased at the Oosterfeld's store: sugar, flour, salt, canned goods, all items that Hannah assured her that the family purchased regularly. Emma hoped that the gift would not embarrass them.

Bjorn took Emma's hand to help her into the truck—the same Ford truck of her troubled rides with Henrik. Bjorn's hands were thick and callused, his face lined and deeply tanned, his hair now as much gray as blond, three days growth of blondish-gray bristles. He wore faded and patched bib overalls with a faint odor of the cow barn: manure, hay, sour milk. He would be nearly forty now, Emma realized. Some of her East Coast friends would regard him as a rustic hick, she knew, but she saw him as a familiar stranger, a taciturn, hard-working man whom she had once known, but no longer did.

They spoke little on the twelve-mile trip over dusty, rough roads. The surrounding fields were green, the corn thigh-high, sweet odor of freshly mowed clover hay, oats and barley turning yellow-gold. Emma's thoughts turned to hunting birds' eggs with Henrik in fields like these. Henrik. Long ago vanished.

Susan served dinner late in the evening after Papa and Bjorn came in from milking the cows. The sun glowed orange-red in the western sky. Emma helped light the kerosene lamps to illuminate the kitchen. It had been years since she had done this simple task.

After the men washed up, the family sat down at the kitchen table, Papa presiding at the head of the table, as he always had, Bjorn and Susan at one side, and their sons on the other. Emma was ushered to the opposite end of the table in Mama's old place. Papa's hair was white now and he moved stiffly. Even though he was only sixty years old, his face was an old man's face, weathered and lean with craggy bones and pale blue eyes, an aging Viking like his ancestors, turned to leather not by the sea, but by the land. The little boys, now aged six and four, rosy towheads in bib overalls like their father, peeked shyly at their aunt, but didn't speak. When the meal of ham and green beans, fresh sweet corn on the cob and boiled potatoes was served by Susan, Emma noticed that no one said grace. That practice must have disappeared when Mama died.

Papa and Bjorn talked with one another as though Emma had dinner with them every evening.

"I'm worried about old Blossom," Bjorn said. "Her right hind quarter is real bad, hot and hard as hell. She like to kicked me into the gutter when I tried to strip the pus out. Don't seem like the bag balm is doin' any good."

"If she loses the quarter, we might have to sell her. Too bad. She was a good milker," Papa replied. He looked across to Emma. "Don't suppose they taught you anything about mastitis at that college, did they?"

"No, not about mastitis specifically. I suspect it's a bacterial infection of the udder. Someday maybe there will be a drug against it. Paul Ehrlich has discovered one, but I don't think it's used for mastitis."

She considered adding that Ehrlich's drug, Salvarsan, was used to treat syphilis, but decided against it. She had begun requiring her biology students to read Paul de Kruif's *Microbe Hunters*, which contained the story of Ehrlich's studies, along with many other fascinating chapters. It generated so much enthusiasm that she planned to add deKruif's *Hunger Fighters* to the reading list in the fall.

"Well, 'someday' don't do much good," Papa muttered.

"No. The pace of discovery is slow, and practical benefits from it are even slower." Emma didn't dare tell her family that her own research was driven purely by curiosity and with no practical applications in mind. "There was a lot of work at Cornell on corn, though, that is leading to some much improved varieties of field corn. Hybrid corn, they call it."

"Oh, ja, I've heard talk about that. But you have to buy the seed instead of using your own."

"What we need to buy is a tractor," Bjorn interjected. "One of them Farmalls. We could work the fields and cultivate the corn a lot faster than with horses."

"And where do we get the money?" Papa retorted. "Eight hundred and twenty-five dollars. Plus more for the cultivator. Hell, you could buy ten acres of good land for that. We're still payin' off the mortgage on the barn. And milk down to seventy-five cents a hundredweight."

Emma sensed that this was an argument that had been repeated many times before. Eight hundred dollars was nearly a third of her annual salary; she could not afford to offer to help her family as she had promised the Oosterfelds, so she remained silent.

The next day Emma helped Susan can sweet corn. It was familiar work from her years on the farm. The little boys helped bring in and husk the fresh ears, although they were much slower than Susan and Emma, whose hands flew. Emma did not know her brother's wife well and was unsure of her attitudes, but she hoped to gain some insight into the family's life from her.

"How have you all been since Mama died? Has Papa been depressed?"

"Oh, he don't say much. Just work, work, work, him and Bjorn. They are a pretty good team, but they argue about the farm. Bjorn wants to modernize, and Papa don't. Your mama and me, we was a good team too, after we got used to each other, and I can't hardly keep up with it all now that she's gone. I put my foot down about milkin' cows, though. I don't work in the barn. The house and garden and two kids is enough."

"Oh, I agree with you. A farmer's wife works as hard as her husband." Susan glanced gratefully at Emma, then turned back to husking corn.

"What news do you have from Kirsten? I never hear from her. She was upset with me because I didn't come back for Mama's funeral, I guess, but, Susan, it just wasn't possible. I couldn't even have gotten here in time."

"She took it hard when your mama died. So sudden and all. We haven't seen much of her ourselves since then. We get together two, three times a year. Christmas. She became a Catholic, you know, after she married Kurt Reinhardt. They've got five kids. One ever coupla years. Oldest is thirteen, fourteen, I forget. Her and Kurt took over the Reinhardt farm after his father died. But Kurt's mother and his two youngest sisters are still at home. It's a handful."

"Well, the truth of it is, she was Mama's favorite. Not me." Emma hoped the bitterness she felt did not show in her voice. All she had accomplished mattered little to Mama.

"You ever think about gettin' married? You're what, thirty now? Or are the men all scared off because you're a lady professor and all?"

"Oh, I'd marry if I met the right man. Just haven't yet, I guess." Here we go again: first, Hannah Oosterfeld, now Susan. Why are they so worried about my marrying?

"Well, don't marry a farmer." Susan exchanged glances with Emma.

Emma nodded. This was as close to a confession of her unhappiness as Susan was likely to make. Emma hoped that her face conveyed understanding.

"The Hansens are pretty hard-driving," she said softly. "Maybe that's what got me through Hancock and Cornell. But, Bjorn's a good man, and you have two beautiful little boys. They were so sweet and polite when I gave them the hard candy."

"Well, take care you don't spoil 'em now. We don't buy 'em candy."

"No danger. I'm not here often enough for that." Was the family so hard up? When Susan did not reply, Emma probed gently. "The Oosterfelds said that things were getting pretty tight at the store because of the depression, and last night Papa was grumbling about the price of milk . . ."

"Oh, we'll never go hungry because we can grow our own food. Cash is awful short, though. Got to pay the taxes and interest on the mortgage so's they won't try to take the farm."

"I wish I could afford to help."

"Oh, Bjorn would never stand for that. Don't even mention it."

They continued cutting corn from the cobs in silence.

"What ever happened to that Midlothian boy you was going out with? Did he get away?"

"Oh, Victor." Emma felt a flush of remembered affection and pleasure tinged with disappointment. "He was never serious about marrying me. Or anyone else, I don't think. I don't know. A fellow scientist, a woman, once told me, 'Marry your work.' Maybe that's what I've done."

Susan laughed. "Well, work don't warm your bed at night."

Ha, Emma thought but did not say, I don't have to marry to have a bed companion. Although it had been a long time without one.

"True," she replied, "but there is something to be said for being the master of your own fate."

After three days on the farm, Emma was ready to return to Harrington, and she sensed that her family was ready for her to leave. As she rode on the train, she reflected: how little life had changed back in Stanton Mills and on the Hansen farm, while her own life had been utterly transformed.

No one had asked about her work. She longed to tell them how excited she was about teaching biology in college, the wonderful news that she had discovered how to generate mutants in Neurospora with x-rays, the new discoveries she read about in scientific journals. But it was a completely unfamiliar world for them and she didn't want to appear boastful, so she talked about what they wanted to talk about. We are from the same root stock, she mused, but I am not like them, perhaps never was. Maybe I, too, am a mutant.

CHAPTER 12
1931 - 1932

"PROFESSOR KÖHLER, I need a chemist." Emma entered the office of Harrington College's senior chemistry professor with energy and directness.

"Ach, Fraulein Professor Dr. Hansen. Good day to you. How are you?" Prof. Köhler replied.

He could never get accustomed to the informality of Americans, which he felt bordered on rudeness. Köhler was a native of Germany and had received his doctoral training in the famed school of chemistry founded by Justus von Liebig at Munich. During the economic and political chaos following Germany's defeat in the Great War, he emigrated to the United States and had been named professor of chemistry at Harrington in 1920. He retained his formal manners, insisted on the umlaut over the o in his name, and spoke heavily accented English. His courses in chemistry were well known for their thoroughness and rigor—and for being dry.

"I am well, thank you. And you, sir?" Emma realized that, in her excitement, she had been too abrupt and stood waiting until Köhler waved her to a chair.

"*Bitte*, sit yourself down. Now tell me, Fraulein Doctor, why does a biologist need a chemist?"

"Well, I have isolated a series of mutants in the fungus *Neurospora crassa* that have defects in pigment formation, and the way they fall into genetic complementation groups suggests to me that they are somehow involved in the chemical synthesis of the pigment. I can explain it more fully, if you wish."

"Ach, I'm afraid I have no understanding of this *Vererbungslehre*, what you call genetics."

"That's not important, sir. The point is this: if I knew what the chemical structures of the various pigments produced by the mutants were, I might be able to deduce what the genes do." Emma leaned forward in her chair.

Her conversation with James Sumner some years earlier rang in her ears: "*How does it work?*" she had posed as the fundamental question of biology. "*What is it made of?*" he had insisted had to be answered first. She now saw the wisdom of that.

"I don't know enough chemistry to do that."

"Hmmm. Any idea of the chemical nature of the pigments?"

"No, sir, but they are colored: yellow, orange, red orange."

"Not inorganic, you think?"

"No, I doubt that."

"Vell, then, why don't you talk to the new fellow, Joseph Bellafiori. He's a new Instructor in chemistry. Studied organic chemistry with Professor Adams at Illinois. Just got here. He might could help you."

"Thank you. I haven't met him. Thank you for the suggestion."

"*Ja, bitte schön.* Gudt luck."

She found Joseph Bellafiori the next day in the small laboratory where a few male students worked at stone-topped wooden benches on a project in the organic chemistry lab course. He was talking softly, but intently to a pair of students, who held a glass flask of bright yellow fluid for his inspection.

He looked up at her, his eyes widened and he broke into a grin. She had not expected him to be so young—almost boyish. Bellafiori was a smallish man, not much taller than Emma, and athletically built. His head was covered with dark loosely curled hair; his eyes were the color of horse chestnuts; and his complexion was surprisingly rosy.

Emma wrinkled her nose. "Hmm. Smells like boot polish."

"You're right," he replied, still grinning. "It's nitrobenzene. They use it in shoe polish. Or used to. I'm teaching the boys about aromatic nitration reactions." He paused. "What can I do for you?"

"I'm Emma Hansen. From the Biology Department. I . . ."

"Oh, so you're the brilliant lady professor in biology I've been hearing about. Wow, smart *and* pretty too."

Emma felt warmth in her cheek. Flirtatious fellow.

He extended his hand. "I'm Joe Bellafiori. Nice to meet you, Dr. Hansen. Why have you come to see me?"

"I'm looking for an organic chemist to collaborate with me on the genetics and structure of pigment formation in the fungus *Neurospora crassa*, and Prof. Köhler suggested . . ."

"So the Kraut sent you to me, eh?"

"Well, yes. Don't you like him? He seemed to think that you were well qualified."

"Oh, he's all right. Very Old School. Drives a hard bargain too. I thought with a Ph.D. from the great Roger Adams at Illinois, I might be able to get a good research position, but there's a Depression going on. No jobs. Köhler got me as an Instructor, yearly appointment for two thousand a year. I took it, but I'm going to be looking for a better job."

"I understand. I'm in my third year and still making what I earned when I was hired."

"That's terrible. I've heard you are a wonderful teacher and even managing to do research." Bellefiori turned his head and walked over to a student at the lab bench. "Mr. Woodley. Put out that Bunsen burner right now. Mr. Simpkins is heating benzene on the steam cone. The vapors are flammable as hell. You've got to pay attention to what your lab mates are doing." He stepped back to Emma. "Sorry for the interruption. Can't burn the lab down. Now tell me, Dr. Hansen . . ."

"Emma, please."

"OK, good. I'm Joe. Tell me about this research you want to do. Why do you need an organic chemist?"

Emma repeated her description of her collection of mutant strains that produced pigments of different colors and her idea that learning the chemical structures of the pigments would give clues as to the functions of the genes that had been altered in the mutants she had isolated. Bellafiori listened intently.

"The mapping studies I have done so far are pretty crude, but I don't think the mutations are alleles."

"Alleles? What's that?"

"Oh, sorry. I mean I think that separate genes are involved, not different mutations in just one gene."

"Oh. Well, if we work on this together, you're going to have to teach me some genetics. I don't even know what a gene is, haven't had any biology since high school. Now, the colors of the pigments suggest to me that that could be carotenoids. Do you know if they are soluble in organic solvents?"

"Now it's my turn." Emma laughed. "What's a carotenoid? And I have no idea what they are soluble in. You'll have to teach me a lot of chemistry if we do this."

"OK, sure. This sounds like it could be fun. I'd love to do some research. If we solve the structures, we could publish it together. That would be good for both of us. But I don't see how it's gonna tell you what genes do. Doesn't anyone know that?"

"No. Not really. Genes determine characteristics of living creatures. All kinds of characteristics, but no one really knows *how* they do it."

With what she soon learned was characteristic directness and enthusiasm, Joe gently grasped her by both shoulders and said, "Let's sit down and talk about it in detail. I'd love to work with you."

Emma and Joe spent the entire Saturday morning in her lab, talking about her research and discussing how to proceed. She showed him her collection of mutant strains and the colors of the pigments they produced. She tried to explain how she characterized the mutants by genetic tests, how the fact that crosses between two mutants sometimes led to progeny that produced pigment just like the parent strain indicated that they were mutations in two separate genes, how the frequency of crosses helped to map the mutations.

Joe admitted that he didn't fully follow her arguments, but he promised to sit in on her genetics course next semester. Emma in turn agreed to sit in on the second semester organic chemistry course.

"So, can you grow enough of this fungus so I can try to extract the pigments from it?" Joe asked. "I need enough to do structural studies and I have to figure out which solvents to use."

"I haven't tried to grow cultures in large flasks, but I think I can do it."

"Once I get 'em extracted, I'll probably get a mixture. I'll have to figure out how to purify individual pigments. That'll be a challenge. Lots of trial and error." He flashed the grin that was already growing familiar. "But I had a lot of experience with natural products chemistry at Illinois. This is gonna be fun."

"We do have to worry about how to pay for supplies and equipment," Emma replied. "I have spent all but about a hundred dollars of my USDA grant. I have to buy materials to grow the cells, and you will need solvents and, well, you know better than I what you will need."

Joe shrugged. "I might be able to bootleg the solvents from the lab course. And I'll beg the Kraut for a couple hundred dollars. That will get us started. Now, let's go get a cup of coffee over at the Dining Hall, OK?"

Emma was not fond of coffee, but she agreed without hesitating.

EMMA AND JOE met frequently in the months that followed. Both had to meet the many responsibilities of the classes they taught and squeezed out time for their project in the evenings and on weekends. Emma learned how to grow large-scale fungus cultures and to harvest the brightly colored fungal mats by filtration.

She did this in her lab and took the material to Joe, who had staked out a fume hood in the organic chemistry teaching lab for his experiments in extracting the pigments. Sharp odors of the solvents, sometimes sweetish, sometimes oily and suggestive of gasoline, clung to his clothing. Emma enjoyed watching him work because he was so intensely engaged. If something went wrong, he cursed in Italian and stamped around the lab. When an experiment succeeded, he shouted with pleasure, took Emma by both hands and swung her around the lab.

"Joe," she laughed after one such merry dance on a Saturday evening, "you are the most passionate person I've ever known. So full of feeling."

"Ah, it's because I'm Italian, you surely know that. I grew up in Little Italy in Chicago. Bellafiori. Means beautiful flowers." He ruffled his dark curls and wiggled his hands besides his ears. "Some flower, huh? Should be *bruttofiori*, ugly flowers."

"Oh, stop. You're a very good looking boy, and you know it."

"Boy?" he retorted, projecting his lower lip in pretended offence. "I'll have you know I'm twenty-six, hardly a boy."

"Well, that's a good bit younger than I am."

"And, of course, a gentleman never asks . . ."

"But you are no gentleman. I don't mind telling you. I'm almost thirty-two."

Joe shrugged. "Trivial difference. Besides, you're so pretty, you look like one of the co-eds."

Emma laughed. "You're a liar, but a charming liar."

He wrapped an arm around her shoulder and hugged her. He was very tactile, relaxed in expression of his affection, so unlike the family she had grown up with. "I will never lie to you, Emma."

JOE'S HUNCH THAT the pigments were structurally related to carotene proved invaluable, because he was able to draw on the prior experience of the German chemists who had isolated and characterized beta-carotene, the yellow pigment of carrots. He extracted colored materials from the parent fungus and different preparations from three of Emma's mutant strains.

Purifying the pigments proved more challenging. The usual procedure was to attempt to crystallize them. Crystallization from a solution occurs when a dissolved substance slowly becomes insoluble and assembles into highly ordered, regular arrays of identical molecules—crystals—so the very act of crystallization selects identical molecules to form the crystals and excludes impurities. But Joe's many attempts did not succeed.

"I think we're getting mixtures in our extracts," he told Emma. "I've got to find a way to resolve the mixtures."

They decided to attempt to isolate the bright red-orange pigment from the parent strain first because it seemed to be the most abundant. While Joe struggled with his brightly colored solutions and crystallization dishes, Emma screened hundreds of colonies after exposure to x-rays for more mutant strains, seeking those that produced more of the other pigments, and she continued the tedious mapping of her mutations.

Emma looked forward to working with Joe, and it was clear that he felt the same, teasing her with terms such as "my science pal," "lady professor," and "older, but wiser one." While they worked, they exchanged life stories. Although Joe had grown up in a large Italian family in the tenements of Chicago and Emma on a small dairy farm, they shared the experience of overcoming the relative poverty and indifference of their families to pursue careers in science.

"My dad runs a trucking business," Joe told her. "He wanted me to drop out of high school at sixteen and work with him, but this teacher got me all excited about chemistry, and I knew that's what I wanted. It was so beautiful and orderly. It explained so much about how the world is put together, and there were so many useful applications. So much more to discover. My teacher told me to go to Illinois, that they were really good in chem, so I did. Had to work my way through. The first couple of years I got a job on the ag farms. Mucking out barns, hauling hay and corn, stuff like that. I'm surprised they hired me, 'cause I didn't know anything about farming like most of the ag students did. But I guess you don't have to know much to shovel shit, huh? Oh, sorry, madam professor, for the naughty language."

"I grew up with brothers. I've heard worse. And I'm very familiar with what comes out of cows. Besides milk, I mean." Emma laughed. Then she frowned.

"What, Emma?"

"It still makes me sad to think of one of my brothers. Henrik. He was my favorite. He came back from the war shell-shocked. So changed, so unhappy. Started drinking a lot. Then he just disappeared."

"Really? No idea what happened?"

"No. Some people guessed that he hopped the rails, became a hobo, but we don't know. We don't even know if he's still alive." Tears welled in her eyes, and she turned away so Joe wouldn't see.

But he did see, and he gently wrapped his arms around her. "I'm sorry. You really loved him didn't you?"

"Yes, I did." She croaked and laid her head on Joe's shoulder.

"That's sweet. I guess I'm not that fond of my brothers and sisters. I'm the oldest of seven, and it was always crazy around home. Barely enough to eat. I never got to sleep without someone else in my bed until I went to college."

"I'm amazed that you made it through."

"It was a struggle. But you know all about that. Having to drop out and teach and borrow money like you did. After my junior year and in grad school I got jobs with the chemistry department, so it was easier. And I got a little bit from joining the Army."

"The Army?"

"Yeah, well, all male students had to join the cadet corps for two years, but I stayed in for four years and got a commission. They paid a little bit for drills and summer camp. I still have to go to drill once a month and summer camp. I'll show you my uniform sometime. Second Lieutenant Bellafiori." He drew himself up proudly and marched around the lab in mock military fashion.

"Oh, I don't want to see it. It will make me think of poor Henrik."

"OK. I understand. No soldier Joe." He returned to the table. "Do you think your folks are proud of you, all you have accomplished, a Ph.D., a lady professor and all?"

"You know, it's disappointing, but I don't think so. It's all so foreign to them. It doesn't mean anything. I feel rather isolated when I visit them."

"Me too. Same thing. They think I'm completely odd for loving something so much, something that's so hard to describe. They're having a really hard time since the Depression has got so bad, and I don't think they understand why I can't send money. They don't understand why I'm so happy. 'All those years in college and no more money than that?' "

"Are you happy?"

"Oh, yeah. And really happy now that I've found you. I love this project we've got going . . . and . . . and . . . I love being around you."

"I like it a lot too. But . . ."

"But, what?"

"Well, we're . . . partners in research. Collaborators. I'm not sure we should . . . let . . . other feelings . . . complicate things."

"Emma," Joe said, gently kissing her cheek. "I'm not sure we will be able to avoid that."

CHAPTER 13
1932

"YOU KNOW, I'M gonna have to give up on differential crystallization and try something new. Our mixtures are too complicated, too many chemically similar components, I'm guessing," Joe mused, as he sat with Emma in her office on a chilly Saturday evening in April. "There was this Russian guy, Tswett, who separated plant pigments by pouring solutions of them through a hollow glass cylinder filled with calcium carbonate and then washing through with various solvents. He called it chromatography—color writing—because the different pigments separated into colored bands that he could see on the white background in the tube. Maybe we could do that with our pigment mixtures."

The initial trials were sufficiently promising that Joe and Emma began a series of experiments using small glass tubes filled with materials other than calcium carbonate and washing the tubes, which he called columns, with various solvents and solvent mixtures. By the end of the summer of 1932, nearly a year after they had begun their collaboration, they had found conditions for separation of the pigments. The red-orange pigment from the parent strain, which they named Pigment A, separated well from three other colored bands under their best conditions.

Most exciting was the observation that the three colored pigments produced by Emma's mutant strains—one yellow-orange, and two pale yellow, which they designated Pigments B, C, and D—corresponded to the extra bands visible on Joe's columns. Joe proved that by deliberately mixing extracts from the various mutants in different proportions and showing that the most intensely colored band corresponded to the extract added in largest amount.

"Look at that!" he exclaimed to Emma, pointing to a tall glass cylinder packed with white powdered cellulose on which all four colored bands could be seen slowly marching down the tube as he added solvent mixtures. "Isn't that beautiful? We can collect the different colored solutions as they wash off of the column, and I'm going back to trying to crystallize them."

"It *is* beautiful, Joe. You have been so patient. This is brilliant. Has anyone else figured out how to use this method to purify things?"

"I don't know for sure, but I don't think so. I'll have to go to Columbus and search the Ohio State library. Harrington's chemistry library isn't complete enough. But I think everybody just forgot about old Tswett. I think we ought to write this up and publish it." Joe grinned with pride.

Only Emma really appreciated what he had discovered, and her enthusiasm was as genuine as his own. He swept her into his arms and hugged her, as he liked to do.

He was doing that a lot lately, and Emma enjoyed it. She was falling in love with this young man, in spite of her reservations, her concerns that scientific collaborators ought not to let their personal emotions intrude on their research. If they became lovers, wouldn't it change the balance? Wouldn't he become more like a husband, more dominant? Would he still take her as seriously? Would she be expected to mute her criticisms and questioning of his work?

She had not told him of her growing affection, though, and she was finding it more and more difficult to hide it. To the attraction she had felt from the start was added respect for his intelligence and diligence, his cheerful enthusiasm, and his easy acceptance of her, a woman, as an equal. For his part, Joe seemed content to continue as a friendly—very friendly—collaborator. Perhaps he thought that Emma's reserve, her coolness to his occasional hints of romantic interest, meant that his feelings were not reciprocated. Because they both had heavy teaching loads and much of their joint research was conducted in separate locations, Emma had been able to keep her subsurface feelings from Joe.

ON AN AFTERNOON IN late September, Joe burst into Emma's office, where she was grading the first quizzes of the semester in her general biology class.

"Emma, you have got to come see this!" he exclaimed. "Come now."

He pulled her up from the desk with both hands and led her to the door and across the Science Building to the chemistry lab.

"Look!" he cried, pointing to a glass evaporating dish.

There nestled in deep red-orange liquor was a cluster of maroon needle-like crystals jumbled together like a pile of tiny straws. "Isn't that the most beautiful thing you ever saw? That's Pigment A. Crystals, Emma, crystals."

"Oh, that's what you've been trying to do for so long."

"Yeah, and that's not all." Joe waved his arm in the direction of an odd glass apparatus shaped like a lower case letter b filled with fluid. A long thermometer and a capillary tube projected into the fluid through a stopper in the opening at the top of the device. There was a Bunsen burner under the apparatus, but with no flame burning. "I've run a melting point already in the Thiele tube. The crystals melt sharply at 178 degrees."

"Is that important?"

"Oh, yeah. A pure compound melts at just one temperature and the temperature does not continue rising while you're heating it until it's all melted. It's called heat of fusion. Just like I teach the kids in the lab. If it's not pure, the melting is smeared over a temperature range. Oh, man, this is so exciting. We've got it, Emma. I can do chemistry on it now. We're gonna get the structure of Pigment A!"

Joe danced around the lab then stopped in front of Emma, who stared at him wide-eyed. She had never seen him so happy. He grabbed her and kissed her full on the mouth. She hesitated for a second, then kissed him back with enthusiasm and relief.

Afterwards they looked into each other's eyes for a long time. No words were spoken, but none were needed; a bridge had been crossed.

"OK, madam professor science pal," Joe exclaimed. "I've been wanting to do this. You are invited to my apartment—my wretched little, messy apartment—for a celebratory dinner on Saturday night. I'll cook Italian for you: chicken cacciatore and polenta."

"Really? I didn't know you could cook."

"Oh, sure. Any chemist can cook. Recipes are much less precise than chemical procedures."

"I'd love to come, Joe."

JOE'S APARTMENT WAS the rear half of the second floor of an old house near the Harrington College campus that had been crudely converted into rental apartments. It was accessible by wooden stairs attached to the back of the house.

Emma climbed the stairs and tapped on the door. Joe pulled the door open. He wore a black rubber lab apron over a short-sleeved white shirt and trousers. He was barefoot, slightly flushed, and his hair was more tousled than usual. Wonderful aromas greeted her.

"Come in, come in. Sorry I didn't have time to clear up my mess. I figured I'd better concentrate on cooking. Have a look around, but please overlook the disorder."

The apartment had just two rooms: a large room with a small kitchen area installed at one end long after the house had been built, and a bedroom whose door opened off of the main room. Joe shared a bathroom down the hall with occupants of the front apartment. The big room was furnished with an upholstered sofa and chair of considerable age, a large wooden desk, bookshelves, and a table with four chairs. Papers and books were strewn over the desk, sofa, and floor, but the table had been cleared and set for two. Peeping into the bedroom, Emma noted that the double bed was unmade and clothing draped over a closet door and hung out of half-open dresser drawers. Cheerful chaos.

Joe dipped a spoon into a bubbling pot and carefully tasted a sample. "This is ready. Please, I don't mean to rush you, but shall we eat?"

"THIS IS SIMPLY DELICIOUS, Joe," Emma exclaimed. She smiled across the table to where he sat illuminated by the light of a candle he had set between them. His dishes were an odd collection of mismatched pieces. He had served the salad in a large porcelain evaporating dish obviously borrowed from the lab.

"Glad you like it. It's my mother's recipe. Sorry I don't have any wine to go with it. If Roosevelt gets elected, they'll finally repeal Prohibition, don't you think? Then I'll invite you again and serve it with wine."

"Oh, don't make me wait that long." Emma laughed. "Of course, now I must invite you for dinner. I'm afraid my dishes won't be so flavorful. I only know how to cook what we used to make on the farm. Country food. About the only spices we used were sugar and salt. Maybe vinegar, things like pickles and sauerkraut."

"I'd be delighted with whatever you made, I'm sure."

After dinner Emma helped Joe clear the table and wash dishes. They occasionally bumped shoulders while working. When a lock of Emma's hair fell over her forehead while she was washing dishes, Joe gently brushed it back with his fingers. Their eyes met; Joe blushed and looked away. Perhaps because he was unsure of Emma's response. Joe began enthusiastically talking about the next stage in his research plans.

"Now I get to do some real chemistry," he said. "Determine the structure of Pigment A."

"How will you do that? You've shown me the structure of beta-carotene. It looks awfully complicated to me. All those methyl groups and double bonds and funny little cyclohexene rings at the ends. And didn't you say it was unstable in air and light?"

"Yeah. You've got to keep it in the dark, and it oxidizes easily. Well, here's how I'm going to go about it. I need a really good elemental analysis, you know, exact percentage of carbon, hydrogen, and oxygen. There's a really good microanalysis lab at Illinois. I think I can get them to do it for us. There better not be any nitrogen in it."

"Why not?"

"Carotenoids don't contain nitrogen, so the chemistry will be easier if it's a carotenoid, instead of something I don't recognize. But first, I've got to go through the literature and make sure no one has described this exact molecule before. I don't think so, but we've got to be sure."

"And if it's something new?"

"If I had to do the structure from scratch, it would be a real challenge, but I think it won't be that hard. I'll try to convert it into a carotenoid that is already known using procedures where we know exactly what chemical changes we have made. That way, we can reason back to what we started from."

When the kitchen was cleaned up, they swept aside the books and settled on the sofa, Joe at one end and Emma at the other. Joe leaned back happily and put his bare feet up onto the sofa between them. Emma was fascinated. He had beautiful feet: small for a man, pale and smooth with high graceful arches, and slightly spatulate toes. She took his left foot into her hands and gently massaged it. She caressed first one foot, then the other. Uncharacteristically, Joe stopped talking.

"That feels nice," he whispered after a while.

"You have pretty feet. Did you know that? Like the rest of you."

Joe quickly rose from the sofa and fell to his knees in front of her. "Oh, Emma, Emma, I'm crazy about you. I know you don't think we should get romantically involved, but damn it, we are. At least I am. Please, oh, please." His face was flushed; his eyes shone.

"Joe, you're babbling." Emma laughed. "Just hush up. I will. Yes, yes, yes."

CHAPTER 14
1932-1934

"HOW'S YOUR GERMAN?"

Startled, Emma looked up from her cultures. She had not heard Joe come in to her lab.

"Oh, Joe, you startled me. You should knock first."

"Sorry, love."

Since they had become lovers, Joe had been unable to conceal his happiness and growing familiarity with Emma. He came frequently to her office and lab. Rumors had begun to circulate. They had to be more discreet. If their affair became known to the Dean, they ran the risk of being fired for moral turpitude: conjugal relations between unmarried persons were strictly prohibited. But Emma was as happy as Joe and no more willing to hide her feelings than he was. She took his hand and pulled him to a lab stool beside her.

"My German is OK. I can read it. Used it for one of my two languages for the Ph.D., but I don't speak it well. My Latin is better. Why?"

"I need to go up to Columbus again, to the chemistry library at Ohio State and dig out everything I can about carotenoid chemistry. Most of it is gonna be in German. I'll have to start with Beilstein."

"Beilstein?"

"*Beilsteins Handbuch der organischen Chemie.* It's a huge compendium of everything that has ever been published about every organic compound in the world. Very German: *sehr gründlich.*"

"Really? Every one? There must be, what, hundreds of thousands."

"Yup. They fell behind for a while because of the war, but I think they will have everything up through 1929. The listings give you citations to the original papers, and I'll need to look all of those up. Most of them will probably be in German too. I'll be taking a lot of notes." He flashed his usual big grin. "Maybe I should take the Kraut, Professor Köhler, along. But I'd rather take you. How about it, Emma? Come to Columbus with me?" His eyes twinkled. "It won't be all work and no play."

Emma cancelled her Friday class and took a Thursday evening train to Columbus with Joe. They registered—a bit nervously—at the hotel as Dr. and Mrs. Bellafiori. To deceive the clerk Emma had turned a ring on her left hand so that the stone faced down and it looked like a wedding band.

During the days they worked intensely in the Ohio State library. Emma found the indexing system used by Beilstein baffling, but Joe was familiar with it, so he identified research papers for Emma to translate and take notes from. Emma did not fully understand the chemistry, but she knew what Joe was looking for and filled pages with notes on characterization and chemical reactions of compounds they suspected of being related in structure to their four fungal pigments.

As they left the hotel on Sunday morning, they passed an older man in the hall whom they did not know, but Emma recognized as a Harrington College professor of classical languages. He nodded curtly and continued down the hall without speaking.

"Do you think he knew who we were?" Joe said softly after the man was out of sight.

"I don't know," Emma replied. "I hope not. Or if he did, he has the decency to keep his mouth shut."

THE FOLLOWING MONTHS were so full that Emma and Joe were almost oblivious to the growing economic disaster that had engulfed their country. True, as a consequence of falling enrollments and declining tuition income, Harrington College had forced them, along with the rest of the faculty, to take a ten percent reduction in their already meager salaries, but they lived so simply that there were no serious consequences. Emma was compelled to write to the Oosterfelds and apologize that she would no longer be able to send small sums each month, as she had done for the past two years. The rare letters she had from Susan admitted that the Hansen family farm was struggling, but never asked for help.

"We're scraping by," Susan wrote, "but on a farm you always have something to eat."

They were very busy teaching their classes, but they were distracted by a series of exciting successes in their research. Emma had submitted a paper to the journal *Mycologia* on the isolation of mutant strains of Neurospora using x-rays that included a preliminary description of her collection of mutated strains that exhibited defects in pigment formation, and it had been accepted with only minor revisions required by the journal's editor.

Joe had sent a paper describing his method of differential elution from columns of powdered cellulose for isolation of Neurospora pigments to a new journal called *Analytical Chemistry*, and that paper was also in press. Most exciting, he had cleverly deduced the structure of Pigment A from microanalysis and chemical conversion to a known carotenoid and was preparing a manuscript to submit to the *Journal of the American Chemical Society*. He had succeeded in isolating crystals of Pigments B and D, although Pigment C was still resisting his efforts at crystallizing it.

In October 1932 the Depression tightened its grip on them when the State Bank of Harrington failed. Rumors that the bank had lost a great deal of money on foreclosed mortgages and defaulted loans sparked a run on the bank as frightened depositors sought to withdraw their money. Neither Emma nor Joe had much money in the bank, but both had relied on checking accounts there to pay bills.

A far greater problem was that Harrington College used the bank for most of its financial activity, and its funds were now either frozen, or worse, lost. The college could not issue monthly salary checks to the faculty or other employees, so they printed paper scrip, which amounted to promises to pay the printed amounts some time in the future. Would local landlords and merchants honor the college's scrip? No one knew. Most initially refused, but were later forced to do so or receive no payment at all.

In March of 1933 the newly elected President Franklin Roosevelt pushed the Emergency Banking Act through Congress, but it was well into the year before the Harrington State Bank was certified to re-open. By that time Emma and Joe had exhausted the meager fund that had supported their research expenses. Emma could no longer buy medium for growing the fungal cells that provided pigment for Joe to purify, and Joe could not purchase the chemicals he needed or pay for microanalysis of his samples.

He paced the lab in frustration. "We can't just stop, Emma. Things were going so well."

"Maybe we can borrow a little from our salaries?" she suggested. "I'll apply to the USDA again and maybe the Rockefeller Foundation. We can show how much progress we have made. If I don't get the money, we'll move a lot more slowly, but we're going to keep at it."

The following months were difficult ones. Joe's research nearly halted, and Emma was only able to do a few additional genetic mapping studies. There were many months when they did not know whether they could pay their rent or buy groceries.

A bit of encouragement arrived with the notice that the *Journal of the*

American Chemical Society had published Bellafiori and Hansen's paper, "Structure of Neurosporaxanthin, a Novel Carotenoid Pigment from *Neurospora crassa*." Joe and Emma had the pleasures of their love affair to comfort them, but they had to be careful to avoid discovery of their times of intimacy by nosy neighbors, gossiping colleagues, and students.

LATE IN THE summer of 1933 they celebrated a reunion when Joe returned from his obligatory six-week Army summer training camp. It had been a long six weeks. Harrington College had cancelled all summer classes because enrollments were so small, and Emma had been able to do little more than revise her plans and notes for the classes she would teach in the fall and fuss over the genetic mapping data she had collected when she still had funds for research. She missed Joe terribly. He had become the most important figure in her life. She walked the abandoned campus every day, imagining conversations she would have with him.

"I'm just going to lie here with you until dark, so I can slip home without being seen," she whispered as they lay in Joe's scrambled bed.

"You know, if we got married, we wouldn't have to sneak around like guilty adulterers," Joe replied. "We could save some money too, with just one apartment."

Emma sat up in mock indignation. "Joe Bellafiori. Is that a proposal of marriage? If so, it must be about the most unromantic one ever."

Joe laughed, climbed naked out of the bed, pulled Emma, also naked, to a standing position.

"I'm sorry," he said, and knelt before her. "Emma Hansen. Love of my life, my partner in science and love, precious Emma, will you marry me? Will you make me the happiest man on the planet? Please marry me."

"That's better." She laughed. "Yes, Joe Bellafiori, yes, I will marry you. If I hadn't known if before you went away to Army camp, I discovered it then. My life is empty, terribly incomplete, without you."

Joe rose to his feet and enfolded her in his arms. "I'm so happy. Don't know why I took so long to ask. When shall we do it?"

"That's a problem, Joe. We're so hard up. Our future is insecure. I think we have to wait. This fall I will go up for tenure. Once I'm promoted—assuming that I am . . ."

"Oh, you will be. They'd be idiots not to promote you!"

"Have you not noticed an abundance of idiots in this college? Dean Woodrow has never liked me. Anyway, I think I have a strong case. Once

I have a tenured position, maybe even a decent raise, we will be more secure. And you, you must go to old Köhler and demand to be made an Assistant Professor on the tenure track. With all your teaching and two research papers already . . . My God, none of the other chemistry professors have ever published *anything* since they got here. Biology professors either, for that matter."

"OK, I'll do it. You're right. It's one of the things I love about you— your toughness, the fire in your belly." He bent to kiss it. "Your lovely, lovely belly."

LATE THE FOLLOWING spring Emma received a telephone call from Dean Woodrow's office, a summons to meet with the Dean. She knew that he was likely to deliver the College's decision on her promotion to Associate Professor of Biology with tenure. Now, in 1934, she had been on the faculty for six years, and the usual academic rules required a decision to be made, so that she would have a terminal seventh year to find another job if promotion was denied.

It had been a tense wait. Emma knew that her senior colleagues in Biology, Foster and Rothermel, were supportive. How could they not be, when she taught twice as much as they did and had published original research, which they had not? But the review process had been secretive and the Dean had been silent for months, so she paced nervously outside his office until he came to the door and invited her in.

"Ah, Miss Hansen, come in, come in," he rumbled. "Sit down, please." Still refusing to call her Doctor Hansen, but this was not the moment to correct him. He offered a weak smile. "I have good news. The President and the Board of Trustees have approved the recommendation of the College that you should be promoted to tenure with the rank of Associate Professor."

"Oh, that is good news. Thank you. I look forward to serving the College in the future."

Dean Woodrow cleared his throat. "Um, yes. I, uh, must confess that I underestimated you at the time of your hiring."

A silence hung in the air. Was that all he had to say?

"If I may ask, Dean Woodrow, uh, I have been told that it is customary to make some, uh, adjustment in one's salary at the time of promotion. I have had no increases since 1928. In fact, my salary was reduced by ten percent three years ago."

"Surely you are aware that the College is in a very difficult financial situation because of the prolonged depression that afflicts our nation?"

"Of course."

"So, you will understand that no increase in your salary is possible at this time."

Emma fumed, but decided to save this battle for another day. She began to rise from her chair

Dean Woodrow raised a hand. "Uh, a moment more, Miss Hansen. There is another matter, a, ahem, rather delicate matter, that I wish to discuss with you."

"Yes?"

"One has heard, um, rumors, of, um, shall I say, a . . . personal relationship between you and Dr. Bellafiori, a, uh, relationship that is said to exceed the bounds of propriety."

"Yes?" Emma replied coldly. The bastard.

"I hardly need to remind you that the College cannot countenance any, ah, behavior of, ah, um, less than the highest moral character on the part of its faculty. Our professors are expected to serve as models of behavior to our students. Any, ah, intimate relations between you and Dr. Bellafiori would violate our standards of conduct and, ah, constitute grounds for dismissal. Ahem. That would be most unfortunate, I'm sure you would agree."

Emma detected a gleam of satisfaction in Dean Woodrow's eyes, even as he put on a most serious face.

"Well, I hope I can put your, uh, concerns to rest. Dr. Bellafiori and I are engaged to be married." She paused until her anger calmed and she could speak without a constriction in her throat. "I presume that marriage will make us respectable."

Dean Woodrow smirked. "Yes, yes, of course." He cleared his throat. "But it does give rise to another problem."

"What problem?"

"If you marry, one of you will have to resign."

"Whatever for?"

"Harrington College—like virtually every other college and university in America, I might add—has an anti-nepotism rule. Only one member of a family may hold a position with the college. It avoids the problem of a faculty member, or other employee, from exerting undue influence to hire a spouse or other family member. Quite properly so, I feel. So, if you and Dr. Bellafiori were to marry, one of you will have to resign. Under normal circumstances, that would be the wife, of course, but as you have just been promoted to tenure and Dr. Bellafiori was just made an Assistant Professor without tenure, perhaps, ah, you might arrive at a different decision."

Emma jumped to her feet. "That's absurd. Joe—Dr. Bellafiori—was already on the faculty when I first met him. I had nothing to do with his hiring. Surely an exception can be made because our situation doesn't fit the sense of the rule."

"Oh, no, no, no. Rules are rules. One cannot go about making exceptions. Otherwise, soon we have no rule at all," Dean Woodrow lectured, as though talking to a dull student. "Besides, would you not attempt to apply pressure at the time of Bellafiori's tenure decision? Oh, no, that would not do. You and Dr. Bellafiori must decide. If you marry, one of you must resign. And, I must repeat my warning that any cohabitation outside of marriage will not be tolerated by Harrington College."

CHAPTER 15
1934

SWEATING IN THE same blue suit she had worn for her interview with Dean Woodrow six years earlier, Emma sat before the large oak table, willing herself to remain calm. Her mouth was dry, her mind racing. She and Joe had decided to petition the Harrington College Board of Trustees for an exception to the college's anti-nepotism rule. The Board had been meeting in MacAllister Hall since ten and now convened in the afternoon to hear their appeal. Joe and Emma had waited all forenoon, twisted in growing agitation, uncomfortable in their best clothing, far too nervous to eat any lunch.

The five members of the Board of Trustees, the President of the College and Dean Woodrow sat around three sides of the table, their faces impassive. Dean Woodrow had nodded curtly to her and Joe as they entered the room, but the others showed no reaction. All of those who now stood in judgment of her and Joe's petition were men. Gray-haired or bald, one bearded, serious men of substance, each dressed in nearly identical grey three-piece suits with gold watch chains drooping over their ample vests.

All but one. An older lady, dressed in an elegant, but old-fashioned, long mauve dress with a high collar that was closed with an ivory cameo brooch, her gray hair set in perfect rows of waves, wearing wire-framed glasses and a serious expression, sat among the male Board members. Elizabeth Harrington, a granddaughter of Clinton Harrington, the founder of Harrington College, was a majority shareholder in Harrington Steel and Manufacturing and the only female member of the Board. No doubt she had been appointed because of her family connections and continued financial support of the College.

Emma knew nothing of Miss Harrington's opinions of feminism. Would she have become conservative and traditionalist, as the holders of inherited wealth often do? Would she resent this aggressive lady professor who wanted special consideration so that she could marry, when Miss Harrington was a spinster? Emma knew only that Miss Harrington had lived a rather secluded life. She was rumored to play a strong role in managing the family fortune, but Emma had not been able to learn much about her. Miss Harrington was her best hope. Emma sought her eyes and was answered with a stern, undecipherable expression. Yes, speak to Miss Harrington.

"As you see from the typed petition before you," the President intoned, "Professor Hansen and Professor Bellafiori request the Board to grant an exception of the anti-nepotism policies of Harrington College so that they may marry without one of them having to resign. You will recall that at our last meeting, the Board voted unanimously to promote Professor Hansen to the rank of Associate Professor with tenure. Professor Bellafiori, on the other hand, was promoted from the rank of Instructor to Assistant Professor without tenure one year ago. Dean Woodrow has recommended that the petition be denied. Professors Hansen and Bellafiori have asked to address the Board in person. Professor Hansen?"

Before speaking, Emma looked briefly at each of the faces before her. She hoped her own face conveyed both respect and calm, intense determination, but not her fear. If their petition failed, she and Joe faced bleak choices: one of them would have to leave Harrington College and seek employment elsewhere—a grim prospect during the ongoing Depression—and they would be forced to live apart. Or they could both leave, presumably have to abandon their academic careers and try to build a new life together somewhere else. Did the Board understand the cruelty, the waste of this?

"Thank you, President Thomas. Lady and gentlemen of the Board of Trustees, Professor Bellafiori and I thank you for granting us the opportunity to plead our case before you. Let me begin by saying that we fully appreciate the reasons for the College to adopt an anti-nepotism rule. Pressures from faculty members to hire spouses or favoritism shown to the spouses of employees would be wrong and potentially harmful to the college. I'm sure we all agree that hiring and promotion should be based on merit alone. Marital status or sex should have nothing to do with it." Emma glanced at Miss Harrington. Was there a glint of agreement in her eyes? She couldn't tell. Did the others even agree that marital status or sex had no role to play? Ohio and many other states required that female elementary school teachers be single and to resign when they married, but did such Victorian rules make sense at a co-educational college?

"Not long ago you reviewed my performance during the six years I have served on the faculty of Harrington College, and you voted to promote me to Associate Professor with tenure. I was overjoyed with your decision, because I have come to love this college and I wish to devote my career to it. You have given me the opportunity to share my knowledge and excitement about biology with your students and to initiate a productive research program that I believe brings professional respect to the college and new avenues for introducing our undergraduates to biological research. I wish with all my heart to continue to do these things and to do them even better."

Did the Trustees really value original research as she and Joe did? Even some of their colleagues seemed to resent it more than respect them for pursuing it.

Here Emma took a gamble. She turned to Dean Woodrow. "Dean Woodrow, didn't you agree that my performance has been outstanding and merited promotion?"

"I did," he said, "but—"

"You are concerned about the consequences of breaking the anti-nepotism rule, correct?" Emma interrupted.

"Yes. If the Board does so, I expect many further requests for exceptions to this important policy. This is not a question of your qualifications. Or Professor Bellafiori's. It is a matter of principle."

"Good," Emma continued. "I'm glad that you agree that our fitness to serve on the Harrington faculty is not in question. Now let me tell the Board why I do not think they need fear the consequences of granting an exception. Professor Bellafiori had already been hired in the Chemistry Department when we first met. I had nothing to do with his hiring; I had been appointed some three years before he was. No favoritism or special considerations of any kind were involved."

Emma again locked eyes with Miss Harrington. Here goes. "Who can account for the workings of the heart? Even I, who aspires to be a rational scientist, cannot. Professor Bellafiori and I began working together purely as scientific collaborators. I had been studying the genetics of pigment formation in a fungus, mostly as a way of developing a convenient experimental system for obtaining a better understanding of the science of heredity. Professor Bellafiori is a talented and well-trained chemist who agreed to work on solving the chemical structures of the fungal pigments accumulated in my mutant strains. He has made excellent progress in his work. It has been a productive collaboration." Emma turned both palms upward in appeal. "We didn't plan on it. We didn't expect it. It was inconvenient and now it threatens our professional careers, the research we have built together. We fell in love. We want to marry. We want to live in the same city. And we both want to continue serving Harrington College. I believe we both have a great deal to offer. No nepotism was involved in our hiring." Emma turned to Dean Woodrow. "When Professor Bellafiori is considered for promotion and tenure, I expect the decision to be made on the basis of merit alone, the quality of his teaching and his research. I will not interfere and I will accept the judgment of the College. We are asking the Board to grant an exception to the anti-nepotism rule in this special case, not to abandon the rule as it is intended to be applied. Thank you."

Emma sat down. Was it enough? Had they been listening and seriously considering her case, or had they already made up their minds? Even if Miss Harrington supported her, would she be able to persuade the others?

"Professor Bellafiori, do you wish to address the Board?"

Joe stood, tense and serious in his dark suit, white shirt, and tie, the only good suit he owned. His cheeks glowed with unusually high color. I am risking my entire, hard-won career for this handsome young man, Emma thought.

He nodded and seemed to relax. "I won't repeat the arguments, the compelling arguments, that Emma . . . Professor Hansen . . . my fiancé," he turned to her and smiled, "has made. If you decide in our favor, we'll make the College proud. I know it. If you decide against us, I will resign. There is no way on earth that the College should lose such a fine teacher and scientist as Professor Hansen because of this policy. You have already decided to grant her tenure. I will leave. Find another job. I don't know if she will stay or follow me. We don't know." He gazed around the room, his eyes hot with fury, looking so intently at each trustee that they looked away—all except Miss Harrington. He raised a finger. "But, by God, we will marry. Please don't force us to live apart."

Joe sat down. Emma bit her lip, fought tears. She didn't dare look at him. His intention to abandon his career in favor of hers if the Board turned them down moved her deeply. He had not told her of that decision.

"Um, very well," President Thomas said, after a long silence. "If that concludes your . . . uh . . . remarks to the Board, would you please retire to my office down the hall while the Board deliberates?"

Alone in the President's office, Joe and Emma embraced and settled in for an agonizing wait.

"Joe, would you really resign if they turn us down?"

"Yes, I've thought about it a lot. You've got a tenured position doing what you love, and you'd have a hell of a time getting another. You know that. I can find another job."

"Maybe at Ohio State? Then we could continue our project. I'd hate living apart though."

"I called the Head of Chemistry there. They're not hiring. The whole University. Maybe I could get a job doing chemical analyses at one of the rubber companies in Akron."

"Oh, God, that would be such a waste of your talents." Emma took Joe's hand and pressed it warmly. "Thank you," she whispered. "No one has ever loved me as much as you do."

Two hours passed while they fidgeted nervously, rarely speaking. What more was there to say? They'd been over and over it. From time to time Joe jumped up from his chair and strode out of the office, down the hall and back. What was taking so long? Were they arguing? Had they gone on to other business?

Finally, they heard voices, sounds of the meeting breaking up. President Thomas came into his secretary's office, his face expressionless, and waved Emma and Joe into his private office and closed the door.

"Well. It was quite a discussion. We even got into the Epistles of St. Paul on the proper role of women in society." He shook his head. "But you prevailed. The Board has granted an exception, just in your case, with the explicit statement that it does not set a precedent."

"Oh, what a relief. Thank you," Joe exclaimed.

Emma was unable to speak.

"I feel it was the right decision," President Thomas said. "But I should warn you, in confidence of course, that Dean Woodrow does not. I would do my best not to antagonize him further, if I were you."

"No, sir, certainly not," Joe replied.

"Perhaps I shouldn't tell you this, but you have an . . . uh . . . effective ally on the Board. Miss Harrington." For the first time President Thomas smiled. "She was . . . ah . . . most persuasive."

Emma finally found words. "Thank you, sir. And thank the Board for us. Thank Miss Harrington. Privately, of course."

The President took each of them by the hand. "You're welcome. Now then, when's the wedding?"

CHAPTER 16
1935-1936

"JOE, I'M GOING to have a baby. I've just been to the doctor and he confirmed it," Emma blurted as soon as she had caught her breath from climbing the stairs and pulled off her winter coat.

She had moved into Joe's second-floor apartment after their marriage in the summer of 1934. It was very crowded, but she had imposed orderliness over Joe's chaos. They planned to accumulate funds to purchase a small house near the Harrington campus, but that looked to be a year or two in the future. Joe stood in the kitchen stirring a fragrant sauce for spaghetti. He dropped the spoon and spun around to embrace Emma.

"Oh, that's wonderful. I'm going to be a daddy. Oh, sweetheart."

Emma's face crumpled and tears rolled down her cheeks. "Oh, no, it's not. Don't you see? How in the name of God can we manage if I have a baby?"

"Aw, you don't want this baby?"

"It doesn't matter if I want it or not. I'm stuck with it." Then seeing the hurt and confusion in Joe's face, Emma softened. "Oh, I know you're happy about it, and I'm proud to bear your child, but don't you see? It's too soon. The burden all falls on me. Teaching all my classes while I'm pregnant. And then, what happens after, after he . . . she . . . is born? How can I take care of a child and do everything I'm doing now? I won't give it all up. All I've fought for. I won't give it up to stay home with a baby. Teaching, our research? I won't."

"Sweetheart, you're overwrought. We'll figure it out so you don't have to give up your work. Let's take it a step at a time. When is the baby due?"

"October, the doctor said."

"So, can you get through the spring semester OK? I mean, doing what you're doing already? The teaching, anyway?"

"I guess so. I've been feeling sick in the mornings, but the doctor said that would get better. It won't show much until summer."

"I thought you were acting funny lately. Oh, my love, why didn't you tell me?"

"I don't know. I guess I was trying to pretend it wasn't happening. Then I had to be sure." Emma calmed herself, laid her head on Joe's shoulder. The tears began again. "It's next year I'm worried about. And the years after that. I'll be obviously pregnant in the fall and then when the baby comes . . . I can't teach then. I'll need to take care of the baby. And, Joe, we have to get a bigger place."

"Can't you get a year off next year?"

"You're joking. Can you imagine me asking the Dean for that? I can just hear the pompous 'I told you so; this is what comes of hiring female faculty' lecture. The Dean was furious with us when we went over his head and appealed to the President and got the Board of Trustees to grant an exception to the nepotism rule, you know that. If I do manage to get the year off, I won't get any salary. How can we get by on just your salary?"

Joe held a sobbing Emma and repeated over and over, "We'll get through this. We'll get through this."

It was the first serious crisis of their young married life, although the very act of getting married had proved more troublesome than either of them expected. They planned to marry after the end of the spring semester in 1934 when they were free of teaching duties and before Joe had to leave for his six weeks of military training.

Emma decided that they would not return to Stanton Mills for the ceremony. Her connections to her family there were tenuous, she had no involvement with a local church, and arranging even a simple wedding would impose awkward obligations on her family. Joe suggested marrying in his home parish in Chicago, but learned by correspondence that the priest would not marry them unless Emma adopted the Catholic faith, which she refused to do. In the end, they abandoned the idea of a religious ceremony or including family members and were married by a cheerful old justice of the peace in Harrington with two friends from the college faculty as witnesses. Because they were so concerned about accumulating funds to buy a house, they did not take a wedding trip.

"We've had our honeymoon already," Emma joked.

"And we're gonna keep having it," Joe replied.

News of their marriage did not surprise anyone who knew them at Harrington College, and they settled into domestic life. There were questions and complaints behind their backs about how they had escaped the nepotism rule and some clucking about Emma's declaration that she would continue to be known as Emma Hansen, not as Emma Bellafiori. Their fall teaching schedule was intense, and they made little progress on their research projects.

And now this. Before marriage, Joe and Emma had been careful to use the newly available latex condoms, but after the wedding that they had occasionally been careless. They had agreed that they wanted children "someday," and they were vaguely aware that, at thirty-four, Emma's years of fertility were limited, but they had not decided on a time to start a family—except "not yet."

"It's a good thing you have nine months to get used to the idea," Emma said after she had regained calmness.

Her students were not aware of her pregnancy during the remainder of the spring term, but she and Joe made preparations. They pooled their savings, took out a frightening mortgage, bought a small house five blocks from the campus and moved in at the start of summer. It was much smaller and shabbier than the house they had dreamed of, and it was very sparsely furnished.

Emma and Joe persuaded the other two professors of biology to join her in petitioning the Dean to reduce her teaching obligations to a half-time load (and salary) by dropping two course offerings for a year and accepting modest increases in the teaching her two colleagues took on. The Dean adamantly refused the request.

"Mrs. Bellafiori, a lady ought to have the decency to go into confinement when she is, ah, in the family way. We cannot have the scandalous parading of a . . . uh . . . gravid . . . woman in front of classes of impressionable students. It's simply not done. You must take a leave without pay for the coming year. Indeed, if you intend to care properly for a child, you should resign, just as I said you should last year. This was all foreseeable when the Board of Trustees foolishly overruled the nepotism policy."

"Well, I think it is a shortsighted and puritanical policy," Emma retorted. "Pregnancy and childbirth are perfectly natural, normal events, not some shameful disgrace to be hidden from view. For a professor of biology to lead a class through the science of human reproduction while experiencing it herself is a unique educational opportunity."

"Outrageous. Next thing you'll be inviting your class to witness the birth itself. Have you no sense of propriety, Mrs. Bellafiori? No, no, and no."

FOR SOME TIME Emma was troubled by her conflicted feelings. She did not share Joe's joy in the prospect of having a child. Did she lack normal maternal instincts? She was aware of whispers around the college that she was an unnatural woman. Was this true? Why could she not feel greater happiness in the coming blessed event? Did other women share her feelings when they learned of their pregnancies? There was no one whom she could ask. Even Joe didn't fully understand.

Over the course of the spring and summer, however, Emma came to see her pregnancy less as an unexpected inconvenience and more as a fascinating biological phenomenon, a phenomenon going on in her own body. She studied textbooks of physiology and embryology to gain a deeper understanding of the remarkable, but invisible events occurring under her slowly swelling belly.

"Here, this is what our baby—Fetus Bellafiori—looks like about now," she said to Joe as she pointed to a colored drawing in the embryology text. "Such a big head and tiny little hands."

When she first felt the tiny fluttering of quickening, she was thrilled, and the first feelings of tenderness toward the little creature growing inside her uterus awoke. By the end of summer Emma was visibly expecting. Her abdomen enlarged and her belly button inverted. The baby's movements became more frequent and vigorous. She called Joe over to feel them, which delighted him. If the movements occurred while they were in bed together, she bared her great round tummy so they could see little disturbances moving her skin.

"Fetus is active tonight." Emma giggled. "Sometimes he stands on my bladder and I suddenly have to go pee."

When the students returned to campus in September of 1935, Emma was very obviously in the family way. She was not permitted to teach, but she refused to go into hiding. She continued to spend a few hours each weekday in her office. She posted a sign on her office door:

> Professor Hansen is on leave during the 1935-36 academic year and will not teach her usual classes. She is expecting a child to be born this fall. However, she will be pleased to meet students privately and answer questions, including questions about pregnancy and childbirth. Each week's office hours will be posted below.

Word spread quickly that the lady biology professor was informally teaching about pregnancy and childbirth, and her office was soon crowded with coeds, many of whom were not biology students. Very cautiously at first, they asked about what it felt like to be pregnant and what they somewhat fearfully expected during delivery. The girls also found that Emma answered questions about sexual intercourse and contraception frankly and in detail. She was astonished at how little most of them knew about these topics and how grateful they were for her candid and unembarrassed explanations. There was a need, Emma saw, for an organized course on human sexuality, marriage, and pregnancy, and she would likely be the only person on campus who would have the credentials—and courage—to teach it.

As the time of her delivery drew nearer, Emma began to think seriously about how she was going to get this big thing out of her. She knew that her body was adapted to childbirth, but the details were obscure. Her mother had told her next to nothing.

She had witnessed the birth of kittens and piglets on the farm; those slippery little creatures appeared to slide out of their mothers in a single pulse, but the birth of a calf took longer and more exertion. Her father and brothers had ordered her out of the barn once when they had to assist a cow with a difficult calving, but she had hidden behind a stall and watched while the calf was extracted from the bawling cow with an arrangement of ropes and pulleys. It was a disturbing memory. She had vague and frightening recollections of her mother's breach delivery of her baby brother Aaron twenty-three years ago and recalled that her mother had breast-fed the baby, but she needed to know much more than that.

She turned to textbooks in the library, and at her insistence, her doctor reluctantly loaned her a medical school textbook of obstetrics. Because the book devoted so much attention to the problems that can occur during pregnancy and delivery, it made for troublesome reading, as Emma's doctor had warned her. She was able to extract detailed information on the normal course of labor and delivery, and she decided to prepare detailed notes and anatomical sketches. Someday, she was determined, this should be taught in a Harrington College course.

EMMA GAVE BIRTH to a baby boy on November 2, 1935 whom she and Joe named Enrico Hansen Bellafiori. The name was chosen in memory of Emma's beloved lost brother Henrik and to honor his father's Italian heritage. Although the baby presented in the ideal left anterior occipital position, it was a long and painful birth.

Emma decided to refuse anesthesia with ether, because she had learned that it often required delivery of the baby with forceps and the newborn sometimes had difficulty starting breathing. At the doctor's insistence because Emma was a first-time mother at age thirty-five, she entered the Harrington County hospital as soon as she and Joe were certain that labor was under way.

Joe stayed with Emma through the long hours before she moved to the delivery room. He struggled to maintain calm as labor intensified and Emma rode out increasingly frequent mountainous waves of exertion and pain.

"I see now why they call it labor," he would say for years afterward.

He was excluded from the delivery room and paced frantically until a nurse came to tell him that he was the father of a little boy. From her experience of the birth of calves on the farm, Emma knew to expect dramatic groans, blood and a slimy, vein-rich purplish placenta, and she was just as glad that her excitable, city-bred husband was not present to witness the gory expulsion of his son.

During her pregnancy, Emma had privately worried that she lacked motherly feelings toward her unborn child. Her plans had been disrupted by this stranger who had invaded her body. Will I come to love this child? she wondered unhappily. Her fears dissolved after Enrico was born. Emma was flushed with tender love toward the little warm, pink fellow as he suckled gently at her swollen breasts with soft sighs and grunts, his tiny hands curled into fists. The unique, indescribable smell of his skin and breath was sufficient to provoke tears and the involuntary leaking of breast milk. He was so sweet, so helpless, so peaceful when sleeping. Emma fell quickly and deeply in love with her baby. I needn't have worried, she reflected. The mothering instinct is built-in, a necessary part of mammalian biology.

After Thanksgiving, Emma did not return to her office, but asked Joe to post a notice that she would be glad to see students in their home. Occasionally a coed or a pair of them visited Emma while she was nursing the baby, which she quickly learned to do discreetly while she answered the student's questions. Dean Woodrow sent her a letter complaining about the practice, which she ignored.

"What I do in my own home," she told Joe, "is none of the Dean's business."

Emma made a note to include lactation and breastfeeding of infants to the course on human reproductive biology that she intended to initiate.

Emma and Joe would later remember the first year of Enrico's life as a mixture: the exhausted blur of night feedings, walking a restless, colicky baby, changing diapers and endless laundry—a haze that alternated with delight in Enrico's first smiles and giggles, his learning to crawl and toddle, his babbling and obvious curiosity about the world. Unlike most husbands, Joe shared in the tasks and did most of the cooking, and he took delight in his infant son.

Even after Enrico was weaned at the end of the summer of 1936, Emma and Joe were too occupied with their teaching responsibilities and childcare to work on their research projects. Emma returned to her normal teaching duties in the fall of 1936. She installed a crib in her office and hired Mrs. Schroeder, an older widow, to come with Emma to the campus to care for Enrico while Emma taught her classes. Coeds, even some male students, came with growing frequency to Emma's office to see her child. Again, Dean Woodrow sent a letter complaining about activities that he characterized as unseemly, undignified, and disruptive, and again Emma ignored him.

Emma and Joe were troubled by their lack of progress on their joint research. There was simply no time for it, and they had no funds for the work in any case.

"We can't just let it die," Emma said.

"I know, I know. If I could just work out the structures of the other three pigments . . ." he replied.

They agreed to submit a proposal to the Rockefeller Foundation for a thousand dollars to support their research.

"Joe, they'll never give us that much money," Emma exclaimed.

"Well, let's ask for everything we need anyway. If they give us less, we'll make do with less."

CHAPTER 17
1938

THE INSIGHT INTO the deeper consequences of their research did not come to Emma and Joe in an instant, a dazzling moment of clarity, of understanding replacing bafflement, as was the common layman's notion of scientific discovery. Rather, it developed slowly, first as a hypothesis that Emma developed to make sense of her collection of mutants that were unable to form the normal orange-red pigment of the sporulating fungus, the pigment that they named Pigment A. Later, when Joe solved the chemical structures of Pigments B, C, and D, which were accumulated by various mutant strains, the pieces fit together to form a coherent whole—a whole of far-reaching implications.

Emma classified her mutant strains into two groups: *albino* mutants, which were white; and *pig* (for pigment) mutants that produced colored pigments, but not the red-orange Pigment A of the parent fungus. The majority of the mutant strains were *albinos*. By mapping and genetic crosses, Emma determined that there were at least six separate *albino* genes, but she had no idea how each gene differed from the others.

The *pig* mutants were more interesting, however. Emma had isolated twenty-three of them and established that they mapped to four separate genetic locations, which correlated with which of the three colored pigments they accumulated.

When she and Joe carefully analyzed the pigments using his new method of separation on glass tubes filled with powdered cellulose, they found that one set of mutants excreted only Pigment D; Emma named these *pigD*. Another set, dubbed *pigB*, produced mostly Pigment B, but also small amounts of Pigment D. The final group of mutants formed predominately Pigment C and small quantities of both Pigment D and B; these were named *pigC* mutants. The *pigC* mutants mapped to two distinct locations, so Emma classified them as *pigC1* and *pigC2*.

"I think we are looking at genes involved in different steps of a linear pathway for making Pigment A," Emma told Joe as they studied her data. "It's like one of Henry Ford's assembly lines. The car chassis comes down the line and there's one worker to put on each wheel. If the first worker is injured and can't work—that's basically what happens to my mutants—the workers upstream don't realize it, and cars with no wheels pile up. If the first worker is OK, but the second one is unable to work, both cars with no wheels and cars with one wheel accumulate, mostly the latter. If the third worker is knocked out, you get cars with two wheels and some with one wheel and some with no wheels. And so on."

She drew a scheme on the blackboard, talking excitedly as she wrote.

albino		pigD		pigB		pigC1, pigC2	
Unknown	→	Pigment D	→	Pigment B	→	Pigment C	→	Pigment A
colorless		yellow		yellow		orange		red

"It works this way: the *albino* genes are needed to make Pigment D. If any one of them is defective, as in my mutant strains, they can't make Pigment D or any other colored pigments. There must be several steps because I have found six genes, but whatever they make, it's not colored. The *pig* genes are needed for the last three steps. Pigment D comes first, then Pigment B, then Pigment C and finally Pigment A."

"Why is Pigment D first?"

"Because it's the only pigment that accumulates when *pigD* is defective. The others accumulate more than one pigment."

"Yeah, that makes sense. Like the assembly line with the first worker knocked out. The *albino* genes make the car chassis," Joe exclaimed. "And *pigB* has to come after *pigD* because it accumulates both B and D. D must be converted into B somehow by the *pigD* gene."

"Exactly," Emma replied. "And by the same logic *pigC* comes after *pigD* and *pigB*, because it accumulates all three intermediate pigments, but no Pigment A. And Pigment B is converted to Pigment C by the *pigB* genes because you don't get any of it in the *pigB* mutants."

"Yes, yes, and *pigC* converts C into A. But how come there are two kinds of *pigC* mutants?"

"I don't know. Maybe there's a step we haven't discovered. Or maybe two genes have to work together."

"Emma, this is a beautiful hypothesis. Now I have got to determine the exact structures of the rest of the pigments, because it ought to make chemical sense. If one pigment is converted into another, they should be pretty similar in chemical structure, shouldn't they? Like the cars that are the same except for the number of wheels."

"Yes, exactly. And the idea is that each gene is like an assembly line worker: it carries out one step in the assembly of the final pigment. The thing we haven't figured out yet is *how*. How do genes work?"

"That would be really exciting if we could understand that, wouldn't it?" Joe exclaimed.

He grasped Emma by the hands and danced her around the floor in a burst of boyish enthusiasm that was familiar from the early days of their collaboration, but she had not seen in a long time. Their research had been overshadowed for the past three years by the demands of raising a young child, their relentless teaching duties, and an acute lack of funds for research materials. Finally, a grant from the Rockefeller Foundation for five hundred dollars had allowed work to begin again. Most of the funds were being used by Joe for his attempts to determine the chemical structures of Pigments B, C, and D

His parents' commotion brought little Enrico running on his short legs into the room. "Mommy, Daddy dancing," he piped, reaching up with his arms. "'Rico dance too."

"Enrico, *il mio bambino!*" Joe cried as he swept the child up, swung him around and handed him to Emma. "Did you know that your mother is the smartest woman in the world?"

The little boy squealed with laughter. He was, like his father, very expressive, quick to laugh, quick to cry. Though he slept in a crib in his own room, he had learned to climb out and often joined his parents in their bed when he woke in the morning or if disturbed by dreams at night.

Joe's love for him was exuberant, Emma's quieter, steadier—and, as the willfulness of a two-year-old emerged, firmer. He had his father's dark curly hair, brown eyes, and sun-tanned complexion, so Emma sometimes called him Little Joe.

Mrs. Schroeder still spent many hours during the weekdays with him. Emma had given up feeling guilty about this; her child's happiness and loving security was sufficient evidence for her to be content. She and Joe occasionally remarked that they could no longer remember what life had been like before Enrico. There was no love, they had discovered, more unconditional than parental love for a child.

IN THE SPRING of 1938 Emma was selected as the faculty member to give the annual Harrington College Lecture. The lecturer was chosen by popular vote of the students. Emma did not know this, but she had been elected College Lecturer twice before, but Dean Woodrow had suppressed the vote and named the runner-up, in both instances a male member of the humanities faculty. However, Dean Woodrow reached mandatory retirement age in 1937, and his successor, Dean Nibblock, honored the students' selection without question.

As Emma considered the topic for her lecture, she decided not to lecture on the exciting ideas that she and Joe were developing. The work was incomplete; vital evidence had yet to be obtained. Furthermore, the genetics and chemistry would be difficult to present clearly to a large general audience of students and faculty, most of whom had little or no knowledge of science. So, she chose a topic that had arisen from time to time and that, as recent events were showing, deserved attention. She titled her lecture "Why I Do Not Teach Eugenics."

Emma's title provoked some puzzlement, but her lecture was well attended by students because she had a reputation as a lively and stimulating teacher, and the faculty always attended the annual College Lecture. She began by describing briefly the central idea of the eugenics movement: the use of genetic selection for the improvement of the human race.

"I am a biologist with a strong interest in genetics," she said. "I am persuaded of the power of genetics to predict and understand the inheritance of many traits in all species. There can be no doubt that the principles of genetics apply to humans, as well as to other animals and plants. Everyday experience shows us that. We observe how children resemble their parents."

She presented evidence that some human diseases are inherited, using the example of hemophilia. Then she described some of the ideas developed by Charles Davenport and his followers, but she avoided the long, censorious description of the Jukes family that Professor Gillespie had read with such relish to her genetics class at Hancock College back in 1922.

"From these descriptions of families with long histories of socially undesirable behavior, the eugenicists have jumped to the conclusions that such behavior is inherited, and that such individuals should be prevented from reproducing, even by such drastic means as forced sterilization. But they have failed to demonstrate the genetic basis for such behavior. They neglect the effect of environment. What would happen, for example, if a child born to a family of paupers, alcoholics, or other social deviants were to be transferred to the care of a normal family and given loving care, good nutrition, and a sound education? The so-called heritable social deviance of the child might never be expressed at all. Furthermore, we know that the expression of genes is conditional.

Consider the simple case of the arctic hare. Many genetic experiments have proven that hair color in rabbits and hares is inherited. Yet the arctic hare has brown color in the summer and white in the winter.

"I reject eugenics, not because it is science whose conclusions I dislike—although I do—but because it is faulty science whose conclusions are not logically supported and are being woefully misapplied. The most appalling illustration of this is now being seen in Germany under National Socialist rule. Citing the careless and sweeping generalizations of so-called *Rassenkunde* or racial science, the Nazis are removing a broad swath of undesireables from society into confinement and conducting forced sterilizations, without a shred of evidence for the genetic transmission of the various illnesses and disabilities in question. Even more extreme is their designation of entire racial groups, particularly Jews and gypsies, for exclusion from the self-identified *Herrenvolk* or master race. These people are being deprived of their fundamental rights of citizenship; their property is being expropriated; they are being denied their means of livelihood and being forced into exile."

Emma realized as she prepared these lines how much her affection for Rosa Levin and Herschel Greenspan had opened her eyes to these atrocities, which received remarkably little attention in the US. It was easy to be indifferent to cruelty suffered by those whom we did not know.

"This is an appalling misuse of science—no, not science, faulty science—for political ends. We may in coming years gain a deep and valuable understanding of how human behavior is governed by inherited characteristics, but we cannot do experiments with human beings. Humans are not to be bred like cattle or dogs, even if we understood the genetics adequately to do so—and we most assuredly do not."

Emma's lecture was greeted with tepid applause. The audience had expected something more cheerful, more like her enthusiastic lectures in general biology classes. Certainly, nothing political was wanted. Secure behind her oceans, still struggling to recover from the Great Depression, America wanted to ignore the ugliness of Hitler's Germany and its growing aggressiveness toward its neighbors. And many were not particularly sympathetic toward Jews, at home or abroad.

Even Joe's reaction was muted. He admired Emma's spunk and forcefulness and agreed with her conclusions, but they had rarely discussed the evolving situation in Europe. Many of Joe's Italian relatives admired Mussolini, although Joe thought he was a strutting clown.

A couple of days after the lecture, he said to Emma, "Well, I may have a hell of a time getting promoted to tenure. Old Köhler was really upset by your lecture. Said you were attacking the German people."

"That's nonsense. I was attacking the misuse of genetics by the Nazis."

"That's what I told him, but I don't think he objects that much to the Nazi government."

"Ugh. Well, even so, your promotion shouldn't be affected by your wife's opinions."

"No, but you know it is dependent on Köhler's recommendation."

"Joe, you are an excellent teacher and carry a heavy load of classes. You've published research, and we'll have more by then. You come up in forty, right?"

"Yeah, two years from now."

"Maybe Köhler will have retired by then. It's like me and Dean Woodrow. You just have to wait for the dinosaurs to die off."

CHAPTER 18
1938 - 1939

EMMA'S PREDICTION THAT the colored pigments accumulated by her mutant strains were intermediates on a step-wise pathway leading to the final product, Pigment A, was an insight that greatly speeded Joe's elucidation of their chemical structures.

Once he had figured out Pigment D, he quickly found that it was chemically closely related to Pigments B and C. Pigment B gave him the most trouble until he realized that it was an aldehyde that was readily oxidized during handling, a problem he solved by converting it into a stable phenylhydrazone derivative. Now, as he sat down at the kitchen table with the structures of all four pigments drawn on a sheet of paper, he saw how logically Emma's postulated pathway was arranged. His sunny spirits mirrored the warm weather and fresh green of the June Saturday morning. Enrico sat on the floor near him, humming to himself as he constructed a tall, narrow tower of wooden blocks. Emma came into the kitchen and draped her arm fondly over Joe's shoulder.

"You've been so happy ever since you worked out the structure of Pigment B."

"Yes, because it all clicks together. Look at this. Your fungus cells are little chemists, Emma. Each intermediate pigment is converted into the next one by a chemical reaction that we might use in the lab. The first one, Pigment D, is an alpha, beta unsaturated primary alcohol. You predicted that it is converted into Pigment B, and all that takes is a simple one-step oxidation to an aldehyde—not so easy in the lab, but chemically simple. And the next step is another simple oxidation of the aldehyde to a carboxylic acid to make Pigment C."

"Oh, that fits perfectly with some things I've been reading in a biochemistry review," she replied. "People have reported enzymes catalyzing those kinds of oxidation reactions in yeast and muscle."

"Remind me," Joe asked. "What's an enzyme?"

"It's a substance that catalyzes a very specific chemical reaction inside of cells. They make the reactions go much, much faster than they would otherwise. It's pretty clear now that they are proteins. My old Cornell professor, James Sumner, has proven that. So why couldn't the same kinds of oxidizing enzymes catalyze these oxidation steps: D to B and B to C?"

"Makes sense to me."

"Don't you see?" Emma said in a mixture of thoughtfulness and excitement. "I've been toying with this idea for a while now. Each gene is somehow responsible for one step in the pathway. And we think each step is a chemical reaction catalyzed by an enzyme. Ergo: *the function of genes is to* make *enzymes.* Not only in our fungus, but maybe in all living cells. Either the genes themselves *are* enzymes or they somehow *instruct the cell how to make enzymes.*"

"Like little workers on an assembly line. Each one doing his little chemical job. Only they also teach their descendants how to do the same thing. Because genes are inherited, right? My God, Emma, you're saying that's *how genes work*—they make enzymes. That's a big discovery, isn't it?"

"If it's right, it sure is. One thing bothers me, though. What about the last step, C to A? That's a funny looking reaction. The tail of the molecule curls around and forms that strange methylcyclohexene ring at the end of the chain."

"Yeah, that's not such simple chemistry. It explains why Pigment A has a dark orange color, though, because it adds two more conjugated double bonds to a whole string of them."

"I've never heard of an enzyme that catalyzes any reaction like that."

"Me neither, but I don't know anything about enzymes. Maybe no one ever looked for it. Besides, it's a step that requires two genes, remember? *pigC1* and *pigC2*. Maybe there are two steps and we never found the intermediate."

"Well, I think we're on to something, something important. Why don't you submit your structures to the *Journal of the American Chemical Society?* We have to wait until that's published first, because our genes to enzymes hypothesis depends on the structures. Then I'm going to try to write this up for the *American Journal of Genetics.* That's a really good journal. If it's published there, people will take it seriously. After all, we're not from one of the big universities."

They were interrupted by the clatter of wooden blocks onto the kitchen floor and a wail of distress from Enrico.

"It doesn't stable!" he cried. "It doesn't stable!"

Emma knelt beside her son. "No, 'Rico, a tower isn't very stable when you make it so tall. But look. Let's build another one. If we start with the biggest blocks on the bottom and put the littlest ones on top, it will be more stable."

"Mommy's right, 'Rico," Joe added, joining them on the floor. "And if you are careful to put each block squarely on top of the one below it, they won't be so likely to tip over."

Smiling, but with tears still wet on his cheeks, Enrico returned to building his towers.

Emma and Joe sat back.

Emma caressed Joe's hand. "Just like building a scientific hypothesis, huh? Block by block."

"Yeah." Joe laughed. "And, like 'Rico says, it better stable."

EMMA HAD NEVER worked harder on the writing of a manuscript. She marshaled tables and a figure to present her genetic data and maps clearly and convincingly. Joe helped her create a figure that showed the chemical structures of the pigments and emphasized the simple steps in their conversion to the final Neurospora pigment.

Emma concluded that the pigment was formed in a linear pathway in which each step was catalyzed by an enzyme. She cited examples of enzymes that catalyzed similar oxidation reactions, but had to concede that the final ring closing reaction was without a known precedent. She emphasized that each step corresponded to a specific gene and that mutations in those genes caused the step associated with it to be interrupted.

She then reached the generalization that she knew had consequences far beyond the details of this study: "We propose that each of the *pig* genes specifies an enzyme that catalyzes a chemical step in pigment formation. It seems likely that the *albino* genes function in a similar fashion, but proof of that conjecture must await the isolation of the earlier intermediates in pigment formation, determination of their chemical structures, and correlation of defects in their formation with specific *albino* genes."

Then, as Joe would later put it, she reached for the moon. "We wish to suggest that our findings on the role of *pig* genes in determining pigmentation phenotypes in *N. crassa* may well be generalized to the mechanism of genetic expression in many, if not all, species. That is, we propose that, in general, genes exert their effects by, in as yet unknown ways, determining or causing the formation of specific enzymes, which in turn by virtue of their catalytic capabilities lead to the expression of phenotypes. Mutations, then, represent heritable alterations in the structures of genes that alter or obliterate the enzymes that execute the expression of those genes. Furthermore, since enzymes are now known from the work of Sumner, Northrup, Kunitz, and their colleagues to be comprised of proteins, we venture to suggest that some genes may specify proteins other than enzymes, proteins that confer structure or other properties on the cells that contain them."

Emma admitted that it was not known by what detailed mechanism genes might "specify" proteins, but commented "since genes must be capable of undergoing precise duplication during cell division, perhaps their method of dictating or causing protein formation is related to the process of gene duplication."

She was privately inclined toward the idea that genes were actually self-duplicating proteins, but decided that such an idea was too speculative to include in a paper that already reached well beyond its data.

Joe's enthusiasm grew each time he read Emma's latest revision of their paper. "This is really exciting. Imagine, a lady professor at little Harrington College explaining to the whole world how genes work." He pushed his chair back and pulled Emma onto his lap. "Did you ever expect to come up with anything this big?"

"No. I always wondered how genes work, but I thought that problem was too hard for me to solve. All I was trying to do was develop a fungus system that was simple and cheap enough to do genetics with here at Harrington. The pigment mutants were just a handy phenotype. We just kind of stumbled into it. I say *we*. It's not just me, Joe. This paper is going to be by Hansen and Bellafiori. I couldn't have put this together without your chemistry."

"Yeah, but you were smart enough to see that you needed a chemist."

"I needed *this* chemist. I didn't even realize how much I needed you until I found you."

THEN CAME A period of waiting. The editor of the *Journal of the American Chemical Society* paper on the determination of the structure of the pigments required some revisions before it was accepted and could be cited as in the press, so three months elapsed before Emma finally submitted the paper by Hansen and Bellafiori entitled "Genetic Determination of Biochemical Steps in Carotenoid Pigment Formation in *Neurospora crassa*" to the *American Journal of Genetics*. More waiting: two months passed without a word from the journal, then three. Emma and Joe busied themselves with their usual obligations, but their anxiety grew as the period of silence lengthened. Should Emma contact the editor to ask about the review?

Finally in February 1939 a thick brown envelop arrived in Emma's campus mailbox. The large envelope meant that the mailing included a copy of the manuscript along with the editor's decision letter. That was to be expected; editors almost always required revisions and returned the manuscript for that purpose. Emma nervously tore open the envelope, pulled out the letter, and hastily read it. Then read it again.

The concluding line slapped her face. "I therefore regret to inform you that your submitted manuscript is not acceptable for publication and is being returned to you herewith."

CHAPTER 19
1939

"LISTEN TO THIS!" Joe shouted to Emma, waving the letter around as he stalked their kitchen. "'The referee finds that the central conclusion of the manuscript, namely, that the genes of pigment formation act by specifying enzymes that catalyze reactions of pigment biosynthesis, is not logically compelling, because the authors have failed to demonstrate that the reactions they postulate are in fact catalyzed by enzymes. The mere isolation of putative intermediates in pigment formation that *might be* converted from one to the other by enzymes is not sufficient to establish that fact.' That's ridiculous. How else would those reactions occur? They'd be too slow and nonspecific without enzymes."

"Joe, I've read the letter a dozen times." Emma replied wearily.

"And all this hogwash. 'The authors have extrapolated a modest study of an incompletely characterized pathway for pigment formation in a minor fungal species into a grandiose general hypothesis for the mode of action of all genes in all species. Such sweeping generalizations reflect an ignorance of the complexities of genetic expression and cannot be supported without further evidence. Particularly troubling is the authors' failure to provide an explanation for precisely *how* genes could act to "specify" enzymes.' Emma, that's impossible. This guy has set the bar so high that no one could overcome it."

"Well, we won't give up. I still believe that we're really on to something. Let me think about it for a while."

After a few days Joe was still fuming, but Emma had shaken off enough of her anger and disappointment to begin thinking about how to respond to the rejection of their paper.

"I guess we'll have to do some enzymology," she told Joe. "The referee is right. We didn't prove that enzymes catalyze the steps we identified, but if we do that, I think we can re-submit the paper. I might have to tone down some of the discussion, but still get our basic new idea in."

"I don't know anything about enzymes," Joe grumbled. "How do we do that?"

"It would be a lot easier if we could work with a biochemist. Is there anyone in the chemistry department?"

"No. I told Köhler we should hire a biochemist, but he wouldn't hear of it. Said it is a specialty for medical schools and it was sloppy science anyway. Stubborn old duck."

"Well, we'll have to do it ourselves."

"What do we have to do?"

"We'll have to make cell-free extracts of the fungal cells and show that they catalyze the conversion of Pigment D into Pigment B, Pigment B into Pigment C and so on. The activities should be missing from extracts of the mutants. And they should be destroyed by treatments that are known to inactivate proteins, such as heat and enzymes that degrade proteins. That should be enough to convince any skeptic."

"That is a lot of work. And we don't have any experience with it."

"I know it. But what choice to do we have? When you come up with a really new scientific idea, I guess you have to expect a lot of doubt. You need a lot more proof than for a paper that doesn't challenge current ideas."

So they set to work. Progress was slow. Emma had to figure out how to make extracts of fungal cells that she harvested during the phase when they produced pigment actively. She had to remove all the remaining cells from the cell juice she prepared, because she knew that if she did not, a critic would say that the whole cells, not the cell extracts, were responsible for the reactions. She also knew from her reading that she would have to use gentle methods because enzymes are usually not stable in cell extracts. Joe had to devise ways of measuring the activity of the enzymes they were trying to study. That required separating one pigment from another. The column methods he had used to purify the pigments required far too much material be practical for measurements of enzyme activity. He needed a new, more sensitive separation method.

Before Enrico was born, Emma and Joe had done most of their research work in the evenings and on weekends, but now they wanted to spend those times with their son, because they were away from him most weekdays teaching classes, meeting students and grading quizzes and exams. Enrico was a very bright, lively, and cheerful little boy. Emma and Joe took so much pleasure in their time with him that they willingly pushed their frustrating research to the side. They read children's books—*Mother Goose*'s rhymes and *The Little Engine That Could* were favorites—to him over and over. Recently while chanting, "I thought I could. I thought I could," with him, Joe playfully asked Enrico to point to the words. He did so correctly, tracing with his finger and repeating, "I . . . thought . . . I . . . could."

"Emma," Joe called out. "Look, 'Rico can read these words."

Enrico glowed in his parents' excitement.

"Teach me more."

Thus began a game of writing words from his books on scraps of paper and asking Enrico to identify them, which he learned to do quickly.

Emma took him on nature walks pointing out birds and flowers. Enrico was delighted when a robin built a nest on a tree branch where it could be observed from his upstairs bedroom window. He and Emma checked daily on the progress of its construction, the mother's incubation of the eggs and the parents' tireless feeding of their babies.

"Are you trying to turn him into a biologist?" Joe teased.

"You can take him to the lab and teach him chemistry when he's older." she replied.

During the summer of 1939 Harrington College taught no classes, so Emma and Joe had more time to work on their attempts to study their enzymes. Emma found that she could grind fungal material with fine sand in a mortar and pestle and filter the extracted cell juice through diatomaceous earth to prepare solutions that were free of intact fungal cells on microscopic examination. Joe was stumped in his attempts to devise a sensitive assay for the enzyme activities they wanted to study until he stumbled across a report from two English biochemists who were using paper sheets to separate small quantities of materials in a way that was similar to how he had used columns of powdered cellulose.

Paper strips could be hung from a tough of solvent—the same solvents he had used before—and mixtures spotted on the paper near the top were separated into colored bands of different pigments as the solvent slowly soaked its way down the paper. The strips had to be hung in glass tanks to keep the solvent from evaporating. Joe improvised this setup by using large glass pickle jars he got from a local grocery store. They were ready to start testing for enzyme activity.

Joe's work was interrupted by his six weeks of military summer camp, however, and after his return in August, they agreed to take a short vacation, which they had never done before. They would travel by train to Chicago and Stanton Mills to visit their families, whom they guiltily agreed they had neglected. Since the death of her mother, Emma had exchanged letters only infrequently with her sister-in-law Susan; her father and brother never wrote.

"My father is getting old," she said. "We should go see him and my brother and his family. Maybe my sister Kirsten too, if she decides she's speaking to me. Enrico will love the farm. His cousins are quite lot older, but maybe they will get on."

"Fine. It's way past time that they met your husband and our boy. And, if you can stand the racket, we'll stay with my family in Chicago. Enrico's got a whole lot of aunts and uncles and cousins to meet. Mama is always complaining that she hasn't seen us since Christmas '36, when Enrico was only one. I'm embarrassed that we haven't been there in three years."

They visited the Bellafiori family in Chicago first, arriving by train in the mid-afternoon, and took the el and a streetcar to Joe's old neighborhood. Emma was glad he knew his way around the city. She was intimidated by the noise and traffic, the tall buildings and clattering elevated trains. Enrico, who had only known the quiet, shady streets of Harrington, Ohio, stared and clung to his parents.

Mama Bellafiori enthusiastically greeted them. "*I professori!* "*E Enrico, che bello.* She embraced Enrico before kissing Joe and Emma on both cheeks.

Emma would recall the following three days as a haze of cheerful noise and confusion, great meals of rich Italian food, some of which she recognized from Joe's cooking, and red wine. The house was so filled with Joe's brothers and sisters, aunts and uncles, cousins, nieces, and nephews that she struggled to learn their names and connect them with faces. Joe coached her when they were finally alone at night.

Much of the conversation was conducted in Italian. Emma had heard Joe use occasional Italian phrases and curses, but now she saw that he was completely fluent. Though lost to its meaning, Emma loved the sounds of a language so rich in vowels and rhythms. She recognized some words from her years of studying Latin and resolved to persuade Joe to teach her to speak Italian—whenever they might find time for that.

Eventually, though, she began to feel excluded by the flood of florid, unintelligible language. Couldn't the family try harder to include her? Enrico was so often inspected and admired, hugged and kissed that he was exhausted and fretful by night. Most of Joe's family had never met Emma before, and they treated her warmly, but with an air of respect that seemed to place a distance between them, addressing her as *Signora la professoressa*. She repeated, "Please call me Emma," and wanted to add, "Joe is a professor too," but did not. Surely they knew that already.

On Saturday they took their leave and headed for the train station for the two-hour trip to Stanton Mills.

"If we stay until Sunday, they'll make us go to Mass," Joe warned Emma. "And I know you don't want to do that. Nor do I."

"My ears are stilling ringing." Emma laughed. "I always thought you were lively and emotional, but now I see you are one of the quiet ones. Wait until you meet my family. They're practically frozen mutes compared to your lot."

IN STANTON MILLS they had arranged to meet the Oosterfelds before going to the Hansen farm. Piet and Hannah had sold the grocery business, but still owned the building and lived in the familiar upstairs apartment. They had grown old and fragile. They moved slowly and carefully; a quaver had crept into their voices.

"So this is the lucky man who married our dear Emma," Hannah said as she grasped Joe's hand. "And look at this beautiful little boy."

Enrico hung shyly by Emma's leg.

"I'm the lucky one," Emma told them. "Joe's a professor of chemistry at Harrington College, and he's my partner in everything we do."

"Emma has told me how much you have helped her over the years. She's living her dream now, thanks to you," Joe said as he offered his hand.

"Oh, we didn't do much," Piet said. "Emma did it. She's a very determined young lady."

"I've noticed." Joe laughed.

Their conversation was slow, polite. Twenty-seven years had passed since Emma first sat in this room with its fussy furniture and lace doilies. Her life had been completely transformed since then, while the life of this dear old couple, whom she had regarded as substitute parents, changed only with the passage of the seasons, the weakening of old age. The Oosterfelds understood that she and Joe were teachers, but when Emma tried to explain that they had discovered something important about how genes work, they simply smiled, and Hannah said, "That's wonderful, dear."

As they prepared to leave, Emma said, "Please don't bother to come down the stairs," and they did not argue. She wondered if she would see them again before they died, then suppressed the thought.

Bjorn picked them up in town in a nine-year-old Ford Model A sedan instead of the truck Emma recalled from years before. There were other changes too. Most of the twelve miles of rural road leading to the farm had been graded and covered with gravel, so the trip was dusty, but less rough than Emma remembered. Thanks to the Rural Electrification Act, the Hansen farmhouse now had electric lights and simple appliances, but there was still no indoor plumbing. Water was still carried from the well and heated on the kitchen range. Joe was amused by the wooden outhouse, but Enrico was frightened by the big holes in the seat and had to be coaxed to perch his little bum nervously on it.

"Just be glad it's not winter." Emma laughed.

Bjorn and Susan's sons, now fifteen and thirteen, had grown from shy little boys into tall, lean adolescents. The older boy's voice was now a deep rumble, and he looked so much like Henrik that Emma nearly broke into tears when she first saw him. Dear, beloved, lost Henrik. Nothing had been heard about him since his disappearance years ago, and the family rarely mentioned his name, as though he had been a disgrace.

But Emma's greatest shock was seeing her father. Why had they not told her? Papa was gaunt, his hair completely white and thin. His head jerked from time to time with small involuntary twitches, and his hands trembled constantly. His speech—what little there was of it—was slurred.

"I had no idea Papa was in such a bad way," Emma said to Susan when they were out of his hearing. "You didn't say anything in your letters."

"Would it have mattered? Nothing you could do anyway," she retorted. Then, seeing the hurt in Emma's face, she softened. "The doc says it's Parkinson's disease. It's gotten a lot worse in the past year, so I didn't tell you. I guess we're trying to pretend it isn't so bad. He tries to work as hard as he ever did. Won't listen to Bjorn, never did."

Most hurtful, the old man seemed indifferent to Emma, Joe, and his grandson Enrico, whom he had never seen before. Preoccupied with his failing body, he had turned cold.

And what of Kirsten, her older sister? "Did you tell Kirsten that we were visiting?" Emma asked Susan. "I'd like to see her and her family. Surely it's time to get over her resentment over my not returning for Mama's funeral. That was years ago."

"Sure. I called her and told her you and Joe and the little one were coming. She said, well, never mind what she said. I guess she's not over it. I'm sorry."

A painful knot twisted in Emma's stomach. What a stubborn, spiteful family this could be. Why couldn't they talk about their feelings? What could she do? Beg her sister for forgiveness? Well, damn it, she could be stubborn too.

Bjorn and Susan were now clearly in charge of the farm and were responsible for its modernization. Susan showed Emma her electric refrigerator and washing machine.

"Just like in town," she said. "I'm working on Bjorn to put in running water and a bathroom, soon's we get enough money. Maybe a furnace after that."

Bjorn, quiet as ever, led them on a tour of the barn and outbuildings, proudly pointing out the new tractor and machinery and the electric milking machine, which had allowed a doubling of the farm's dairy herd. It was all new to Joe, and he was fascinated. He bombarded Bjorn with questions and comments, earning the respect of his brother-in-law.

"That Joe sure is interested in farming for a city boy. Smart too, catches on real quick," Bjorn told Emma.

Perhaps to avoid the emotional complexities of her return to her family, Emma spent much of her time with Enrico, showing him the farm's animals. He squealed when a calf ran a long, wet sandpapery tongue over his hands and giggled when a cow arched her back, raised her tail, and released a great stream of yellow urine from her backside. Such everyday sights from Emma's girlhood were exotic adventures to her son.

She led him on walks into the fields and pastures, naming plants and birds they saw and searching out a redwing blackbird's nest in a grassy ravine. They even found a dung beetle patiently rolling a ball in the dusty cowpath. Emma could not resist explaining to Enrico why the beetle was doing that and how she had discovered a dung beetle thief.

Three days on the farm were enough. Joe and Enrico had a good time, but for Emma a mixture of estrangement and sadness dimmed the pleasure of the visit. They slept poorly because they and Enrico were forced to share a narrow bed with a lumpy straw mattress. Emma was keenly conscious that their presence added to Susan's burdens, and she no longer knew how to be very helpful. So, pleading the need to return and prepare for the coming fall classes at Harrington, they asked Bjorn to drive them to the train station in Stanton Mills.

On the train ride back, Emma was unusually quiet. The gentle rocking of the train car soon put Enrico to sleep.

"Joe, will you think less of me if I admit that I no longer feel as though I belong there? I'm so much happier at Harrington with you. I'm a little ashamed of feeling that way."

"That's OK, sweetheart. I feel the same way sometimes when I go back to Chicago. We're the family now: you and me and 'Rico.'"

IN THE FALL, Emma and Joe wrestled with the problem of demonstrating the conversion of Pigment D into Pigment B and of Pigment B into Pigment C by cell-free extracts, as predicted by their scheme. They had little success.

"The problem is that Pigment B is an unstable aldehyde," Joe complained. "We can't keep it around long enough to use it as starting material for the B to C reaction, and it doesn't accumulate cleanly in the D to B assays."

"But D is a stable alcohol, right, and B is a stable carboxylic acid. Why don't we try to run both reactions together?" Emma asked.

"You mean test for conversion of D all the way to B? Two successive oxidation steps?"

"Right. Both enzymes acting one after the other. If that works, then we can use extracts from the mutants. Extracts from *pigB* or from *pigD* mutants ought not to work because they're missing one of the required enzymes, but if you mix them . . ."

"The missing enzymes will be provided, and it will work just like the extracts from the parent strain," Joe interjected. "Emma, that's brilliant. Let's try it."

By the end of November they had shown experimentally that cell-free extracts from normal and mutant strains behaved exactly as they had predicted. The activities were destroyed by heating and by digestion with a preparation of protein-destroying enzymes from beef pancreas. Joe and Emma felt they had adequate evidence for the role of enzymes in the first two steps of their proposed three-step pathway, and they now turned to the vexing problem of finding evidence that an enzyme catalyzed the last step, the conversion to Pigment C into Pigment A. So far, they had not been able to demonstrate that reaction in the lab.

Their excitement was greatly tempered by their alarm at events occurring that fall in Europe. Germany invaded Poland; Britain, France, and their allies declared war on Germany; Russia took possession of eastern Poland, forced the Baltic countries into submission and went to war against Finland. The war between Japan and China advanced in intensity. The world was once again at war, only twenty-one years after the end of the Great War. Emma was distraught.

"We've got to stay out of it. The only result of war is death and destruction."

"Roosevelt says that America will stay neutral. Don't you think the French and the English will be able to beat the Germans?"

"Oh, God, Joe, I can see all that horrible trench warfare like the last war over again. I've told you what it did to Henrik. If we go to war, won't you have to go? You're an officer in the Army."

"I suppose so, but I'm thirty-three already and with a Ph.D. in chemistry, they'd probably send me to a proving ground for ordnance. Testing weapons or something like that. Not combat."

"Still, isn't that dangerous?"

"I'd imagine they're pretty careful. Certainly it'd be a lot safer than being shot at."

"Oh, don't even joke about it. I could not bear to lose you."

CHAPTER 20
1940

IT WAS AN exceptionally lovely spring on the Harrington College campus. A sustained period of warm weather in late April following earlier rains stimulated a glorious display of flowering trees, blooming bushes, and lush green lawns. Emma could not recall the campus so beautiful. Students strolled the quads, holding hands and hugging books, laughing and frolicking like innocent children in an Arcadian glade. The warmth made Emma happy to be a respected professor among them, happy to be married to Joe and mother of Enrico, happy simply to be alive.

In what little free time they could squeeze out, Joe and Emma continued their attempts to demonstrate the enzymatic character of the reactions of pigment formation in cell-free extracts made from Emma's fungal cultures. They discovered that the conversion of Pigment D to Pigment C could be much accelerated by the addition of a boiled extract of yeast; the active ingredient in these extracts had properties that indicated that it was the so-called "nicotinamide coenzyme" that had been described previously by a German biochemist, Otto Warburg, who had shown it to be involved in oxidation reactions. That fit perfectly with the fact that conversion of Pigment D to Pigment C required two oxidation steps. However, they were stuck with the last step of their pathway, the conversion of Pigment C to Pigment A. Nothing they tried permitted them to observe that reaction with cell juice in the test tube. They were missing something.

Because the Harrington College library only subscribed to a few scientific journals, Joe and Emma had to make occasional trips to Columbus to use the science library at Ohio State University, and Joe decided that another search of the biochemical literature for clues to their problem was needed. He and Emma had bought a used Chevy sedan that spring, so he drove off on a beautiful Saturday morning, leaving Emma to look after Enrico and grade papers.

He returned in the middle of the afternoon, much sooner than Emma expected him, and strode into the house, his face smoky with anger.

"Look at this! He exclaimed. "Just look at this. These bastards have stolen our work."

He slammed an unbound copy of a journal onto Emma's desk. It was the *Proceedings of the National Academy of Sciences*, a widely read, prestigious journal. Joe had bent it open so that the back of the binding was broken and it lay open to an article by Philip Schleicher and Martin Fox entitled, "Genetic Specification of Biochemical Reactions of Pigment Biosynthesis in *Neurospora crassa*."

"My God," Emma gasped. Her heart beating in her throat, she quickly scanned the paper while Joe paced wildly around the room.

"I can't believe this," Joe shouted. "They must have seen our paper when we sent it in."

"I need to read this more carefully after I calm down," Emma replied with a shaking voice, "but it's our pathway. They cite your JACS papers for that. The genetic mapping isn't nearly as thorough as mine and they use different names for the genes, but they get the same conclusions. And they make the claim that genes act through enzymes, one gene per enzyme, just like we did."

"Who are these guys anyway?"

"They're at Princeton. Schleicher is a well-known professor of genetics. I thought he worked on fruit flies. I don't recall seeing any genetics with fungi from his lab. I never heard of Fox. Maybe he's a grad student or a postdoc?"

"Well, they're crooks, that's what they are. They must have seen our manuscript, seen how good it was and recommended to the journal to reject it, so they could buy time to throw this, this *garbage* together."

"We don't know that. I suppose it's possible that they were working on this too, on the genetics, I mean, and when they saw your structures, they just put it all together—like we did."

"Well, God damn it! They'll get all the credit for our—for *your*—beautiful insight into how genes work. This was our best chance—maybe our only chance—of ever gaining recognition as world-class scientists. I hate it, I just hate it."

Enrico ran into the little bedroom that doubled as an office. "Daddy, what's wrong?"

Joe doubled his fists, scowled, and was unable to answer.

"We just got some bad news about our research, honey," Emma said softly. She bit her lip and fought tears. She didn't want to frighten Enrico, who surely could not understand why his parents were so distraught.

Joe whirled around. "Just promise me this. Promise you'll write to the editor of the *American Journal of Genetics*. Ask him if these, these guys—Schleicher, he's the big deal professor, right?—ask him if he reviewed our paper and came up with all that crap to get it rejected. Ask him that, OK?"

"All right, Joe. I'll do that. Just calm down. You're upsetting Enrico. I'm as disappointed as you are."

FOR THE NEXT several days Emma fought depression and anger. She taught her classes, but felt flat, as though she were automatically repeating phrases from previous years. The beauty of the spring was gone, as though a glowering black storm had blown away the blossoms and obscured the sun. Joe was so angry that they couldn't talk about the offending paper.

Emma forced herself to read Schleicher and Fox's paper carefully and took notes on the many similarities between it and their rejected Hansen and Bellafiori manuscript. Then she carefully composed a letter to Professor Cornelius Burke-Jones, a faculty member at Yale and the editor of the journal that had rejected their manuscript.

After detailing the many ways in which the two papers reported the same findings and conclusions, she wrote, "The many remarkable duplications between the two manuscripts are sufficient to raise the question of whether our manuscript had been read by Professor Schleicher prior to the publication of his PNAS paper with Dr. Fox. If so, that information may have been used to influence the content and conduct of the research that they published. Alternatively, if they were pursuing the same line of research independently, a motive would have been provided to reject our manuscript so as to gain time for them to claim priority by publishing their work before we did. If such occurred, it would be a highly improper abuse of the review process. Those suspicions would be removed, of course, if we have your assurance that neither Professor Schleicher nor Dr. Fox were asked to review our manuscript or had access to it."

Emma went on to grumble, "I note that our manuscript was held to a standard of proof that the Schleicher and Fox publication was not. That is, publication of our submission was denied until we could provide proof that the biochemical steps in pigment formation that we identified—and whose identification was used without independent verification by Schleicher and Fox—were catalyzed by enzymes. No such evidence is to be found in their paper. We, however, have now obtained such evidence for two of the three biochemical steps identified in our work."

She and Joe fussed about the wording of the letter, and finally agreed on the final draft. They signed it and put it in the mail. Emma felt fully justified in writing it, but wondered whether any good could come of it.

They waited for a reply. In the meantime, their mood was darkened further by the news from Europe. Already in April German forces had occupied Denmark and, after a short one-sided war, conquered Norway. Then in May a massive German invasion of Belgium, Holland, and France began. The speed and violence of the attacks were unstoppable. The term *Blitzkrieg* became part of everyday speech.

By mid-June, as Emma and Joe waited anxiously for a reply from the editor of the *American Journal of Genetics*, Nazi flags were flying over Paris and the conquest of the Continent by Germany was certain. England lay open to attack and seemed defenseless. Emma and Joe argued: she continued to defend her pacifism, although with wavering confidence, and Joe insisted that Hitler had to be defeated.

"I know it's an evil regime," Emma cried, "but I cannot, I cannot bear to see us go to war again. If I were to lose you . . ." And her voice broke and she buried her face in her hands.

FINALLY, IN LATE June the letter came. Emma recognized the return address and carried it unopened over to Joe's little office next to the organic chemistry lab. They closed the door, and Emma nervously tore it open and read aloud:

"Dear Professors Hansen and Bellafiori:

"I am responding to your letter of May 22nd in which you raise certain questions about the review of your manuscript entitled "Genetic Determination of Biochemical Steps in Carotenoid Pigment Formation in *Neurospora crassa*", which was rejected by this journal.

"First, I must state that it would be highly improper of me to reveal the identity of the referees of this, or any, paper. The integrity of the review process is absolutely dependent on the use of anonymous referees, who cannot be expected to give their most honest, candid views, if they knew that their identities would be revealed to disappointed authors. I therefore decline to identify the reviewers of your manuscript.

"I recognize an unusual number of similarities in the content of your manuscript and the paper by Schleicher and Fox in the *Proceedings* that you reference. This is unexpected, I will admit, but you must recognize that instances of independent and simultaneous research undertakings and discovery do occur. One calls to mind the work of Darwin and Wallace on natural selection in evolution as an example. The coincidence is not *per se* evidence of misconduct.

"As to the different standards of proof required for your manuscript versus that that published by Schleicher and Fox, I can only point out that various journals use differing review procedures so that discrepancies in the standards applied inevitably occur. You may be unaware that the *Proceedings* only requires that a paper be approved and submitted by a Member of the National Academy of Sciences, who assumes full responsibility for the quality of the science. The *American Journal of Genetics* always seeks the views of at least two anonymous expert referees.

"If you have indeed addressed the scientific criticisms of the previous manuscript as regards evidence of enzymatic catalysis of reactions of pigment biosynthesis, I would encourage you to submit a revised manuscript documenting this new evidence. This is significant work, and I can assure you of a fair and objective review for publication."

Emma and Joe sat in silence for a moment.

"I think he ducked your question," Joe said, with barely controlled anger. "If Schleicher had not been a reviewer, he could have told you that, couldn't he? That doesn't reveal who the reviewers were. The fact that he didn't do that means that Schleicher was a reviewer, don't you think?"

"Maybe." Emma sighed. "I guess we'll never know for sure. I've thought about this. Even if he was a reviewer, what could we do about it?"

"Tell the whole scientific world!"

"You think they would listen? The two of us from a little Midwestern college? And he's a big Princeton professor. I don't know. Maybe we should just lick our wounds and go on. The letter hints pretty strongly that they would publish our paper now. With the new evidence."

"Yeah, well, I think he's got a bad conscience, so now he's willing to take a paper that he should accepted before." Joe stalked around from behind the desk and grabbed Emma by the shoulders. "We—*you*—discovered something really big, damn it, and now we get to publish a me-too paper."

"Well, it's a good paper. Let's publish it. It's better than nothing."

"What about the Pigment C to A conversion? We never demonstrated it *in vitro*."

"No, but the evidence that enzymes catalyze the other two steps is solid. You'd have to be pretty perverse to argue that the first two steps are catalyzed by enzymes and the last one isn't. C'mon. I'm going to write the revision."

Joe had to leave for six weeks of summer military training the following week. This annual disruption in their lives had not been too difficult for Emma in the past because she generally had little or no teaching duties during the summer, but this year the shadow of the series of disastrous defeats of the Allies in Europe and the growing intensity of aerial attack on England filled Emma with anxiety. If America joined the war, she would surely call up the reserve officers, Joe among them.

She distracted herself by working on the revision of their manuscript. The fundamental content was the same as in the rejected manuscript except for a new section that contained the proof of enzymatic catalysis of two of the reactions. The *pigD* and *pigB* genes, Emma concluded, clearly specified enzymes. Although it was not directly demonstrated, she drew the inference that the *pigC1* and *pigC2* genes also did so.

In the Discussion Emma reiterated the major conclusion of the paper: that many, perhaps most genes specify enzymes or other proteins, one gene per enzyme. She could not ignore the already published work of Schleicher and Fox, of course, so she mentioned it tersely. She prefaced her words by emphasizing that her and Joe's work had been conducted "independently and without any knowledge of the simultaneous research of Schleicher and Fox." The complete agreement between the results of the two independent investigations, she stated "provides strong confidence in the validity of their conclusions, which we agree have far-reaching consequences."

The revised manuscript was ready for Joe's reading when he returned from military training. He read it hastily, as though he had somehow lost interest in it, and told Emma to submit it to the *American Journal of Genetics*. He was distracted and agitated.

"All the regular Army officers are convinced that we are going to get into it. We'll never let the Germans take England. And there's real problems with the Japs out in the Pacific."

"But Roosevelt has been saying all along that he won't send our boys into war, that we would just send weapons and aid."

"Yeah, we'll see what he says after the election."

THE 1940 FALL semester at Harrington College seemed superficially like the previous twelve beginnings to the school year of Emma's experience. Young men and women filed along campus sidewalks. Freshmen wore green beanie caps, as they had for years. Biology students crowded Emma's office seeking advice or permission to enroll in one of her courses. The many mature shade trees underwent their annual fall riot of yellow, brown, red, and orange, then dropped their leaves in crisp, oaky-smelling piles.

But there was nervousness in the air. Reports and photographs of the horrendous bombing of English cities filled the newspapers and radio waves.

Joe fumed at news of Italy's military misadventures in North Africa. "Not only are they trampling all over where they have no business, they're incompetent. It makes me ashamed to be Italian."

A draft for one year of military service began in October and sent a shiver of unease across the campus.

Joe and Emma taught their classes and tried to live a normal life with Enrico. Both had received raises—the first since they were hired—as the College's finances improved. Papers for Joe's promotion to Associate Professor were forwarded to the Dean. The opposition he had expected from Professor Köhler had not materialized. Perhaps he had forgotten his anger at Emma's attack on Hitler's racial policies; perhaps even he had turned in disgust away from the Nazi regime.

And they waited. Waited for news from the editor of the *American Journal of Genetics*. Finally, in November the decision letter arrived. Emma tore it open, not even waiting to take it to Joe's office. She feared an explosion if the revised manuscript was rejected.

The manuscript was accepted for publication. One reviewer expressed concerns about the evident duplication of previously published findings, the editor wrote, but another reviewer recommended acceptance of the paper "as a welcome confirmation and extension of the ground-breaking work of Schleicher and Fox. The more detailed genetic analysis and direct evidence for enzymatic catalysis of the steps in pigment formation are valuable contributions." Because the editor was "aware of the simultaneous and fully independent conduct of your research and the far-reaching consequences of your conclusions," he intended to disregard the first reviewer and accept the paper.

"Why doesn't it feel more satisfying?" Emma asked after Joe had read the letter. "This is beautiful, important research that was done under very difficult circumstances."

"It is, sweetheart," Joe replied. He was calm; all of his anger had drained away. "I'm proud of it, of us. But in science, priority is everything."

CHAPTER 21
1941 -1942

FOR A TIME it was possible to believe that, despite the horrors of war across the oceans, life for Emma and Joe would be happy and peaceful. The dreariness of winter gave way to the warmth, tender greens, and cheerful blossoms of spring on the campus and streets of Harrington. The pleasure of introducing her students to the wonders of biology, of watching their faces glow with new understanding, returned for Emma after the depressing events of the previous year. Enrico was now reading simple children's books, but still insisted on curling up with Joe or Emma for readings at bedtime. *Winnie the Pooh* was a favorite. Emma had little time for genetic experiments, but worked with Joe on attempts to isolate precursors to the colored pigments that they assumed were accumulated in her *albino* mutants.

Their *Am. J. Genet.* paper appeared in print in March, and they received a surprising number of requests for offprints. The Dean assured Joe that his promotion to Associate Professor with tenure needed only final approval from the Board of Trustees, and that the new paper made the case certain. He also told Emma that he intended to begin the review of her credentials for promotion to full Professor.

"It should have been done before now. You and Professor Bellafiori have set a new standard for our faculty," he remarked during a private meeting in his office. "Most have been content to simply teach their classes or perhaps write a textbook, but you have proven that Harrington faculty can also conduct serious scholarly work, and can do so without neglecting your teaching."

The news removed a little of the sting of having lost the claim of priority for their discoveries about the mechanism of gene action to the Princeton group.

EMMA HAD BEEN dreading this moment. She sat nervously in a large ornate meeting room in Chicago's Conrad Hilton Hotel awaiting the start of the conference on new concepts in genetics. She had traveled to Columbus to find an appropriate suit for the occasion and finally settled on a navy blue one with white piping on its wide lapels and a small white pillbox hat instead of the wide brimmed fedoras that were now in style. It had a knee-length skirt and was snugly tailored with wide shoulders and narrow waist, buttoned over a white blouse and a pale blue scarf at the neck: fashionable, but subdued—and too warm in this stuffy room. She needn't have bothered. She was the only woman in the room, and the many men there only glanced at her briefly, as though she were out of place and of no consequence.

Professor Philip Schleicher strode to the lectern with a confident, even aloof, manner. Until this moment she had no idea what he looked like. He had arrived in the hall just before the session began. He was a tall, slender man with silver hair, dressed in an elegant three-piece gray suit and black bow tie. He adjusted his glasses, softly cleared his throat, and began speaking in a clear, confident voice. "I wish to present to you today the results of our genetic experiments with the ascomycete *Neurospora crassa*, experiments which we propose establish a direct biochemical function for genes, namely the specification of enzymes: one gene per enzyme."

Emma's fists tightened. She knew what he was going to say. She knew the experiments he would present; she had studied his paper carefully. Oh, yes, she knew the story: it was *her* story, hers and Joe's. She knew it was correct. She and Joe had determined the structures, mapped the genes, and proposed the same bold conclusions many months ago. Yet she now had to sit and listen to this man claim it all for his own, and every scientist in the audience would accept his claim without question.

So why was she here, here in this large hotel ballroom at a national genetics conference? To confront Schleicher with her suspicions? To demand an equal share of credit for the important new ideas that he was now expounding? No, she had decided. Provoking a scandal would probably do more harm than good. She would simply tell this gathering of scientific peers what she and Joe had done and how they had done it. And point out that they had done it entirely independently and without knowledge of the work of others. That would have to be sufficient.

"You have to go," Joe had said when she showed him the invitation to give a research talk at the conference in Chicago in June of 1941. "Just go and present our work. Tell 'em we did it independently. Answer questions. Talk to people. By God, let everyone know that we are co-discoverers of this."

"Maybe you should give the talk. The invitation was addressed to both of us. If you did it, they'd take it more seriously."

"Why? Because I'm a man?"

"Yes. You know that's true."

"Well, damn it. That's all the more reason why *you* should go and give the talk. This is your work. Make them recognize that. Make them take *you* seriously. If I go, they'll be distracted. Besides, you were the intellectual driving force behind all this. I was just your chemist."

"Oh, Joe, you are so much more than my chemist."

Joe grinned. "I know that. But I'm serious. You should give the talk. You're the geneticist. This is a genetics meeting. You deserve this recognition. I can talk about the chemistry at the American Chemical Society."

"But what about Enrico? I'll have to be gone for three or four days."

"Go! I'll take care of Enrico. Besides, if I go to Chicago with you, we'll have to visit my family and take Enrico along. I'm not up for that whole circus."

"I've never presented a research paper at a national meeting before. It'll be really difficult. I've got to squeeze the whole story into twenty minutes."

"You can do it. You're a teacher, a great teacher. Now get to work on it."

The session on new concepts in genetics was organized with a featured speaker—Schleicher—who was given fifty minutes to make his presentation, followed by four lesser lights, Emma scheduled last among them, who had twenty minutes to give their talks. Each talk was to be followed by a ten-minute discussion session. The arrangement obviously favored the impression that Scheicher and Fox were the discoverers of the new one gene-one enzyme concept and that Hansen and Bellefiori had merely confirmed it, but the invitation to speak at the conference gave Emma and Joe a chance to gain exposure of their work to the best geneticists in the country. This alone was a unique distinction for Harrington College faculty. Joe was right: the opportunity was not to be declined.

So, here Emma sat sweating in her new suit, waiting for the chance to present her carefully rehearsed talk while Professor Philip Schleicher of Princeton University grandly and sonorously gave his lecture. He projected a transparency slide that showed the chemical structures of the intermediate pigments on the way to the final pigment neurosporoxanthin—Joe's beautiful structures of Pigments A, B, C and D, but, of course, Schleicher gave them different names—and pronounced, "This, we conclude, is the pathway for the biosynthesis of the fungal pigment, based on our genetic analysis and the structures of the molecules from the chemical literature."

Emma seethed. He had not even mentioned that Bellafiori and Hansen had first isolated the pigments and determined their structures. In fact, their names were not spoken at all until the very end of the lecture, when Schleicher said, "We were gratified to learn from a recent publication that Hansen and Bellafiori had replicated our experiments, confirmed our findings, and agreed with our conclusions."

That stung too. The use of the word "replicated" implied that they had simply repeated the work of the Princeton group after the fact and gotten the same results, when Emma believed that the reverse had actually occurred. Schleicher's presentation was followed by vigorous applause and an excited discussion. Emma listened carefully, but said nothing.

After the discussion of his paper, Prof. Schleicher gathered his papers, collected his transparency slides from the projectionist, and headed for the door at the rear of the auditorium. He clearly didn't intend to remain to hear Emma or the other speakers. Fueled by a sudden flash of anger, Emma followed him out into the corridor. She had promised herself not to do this. She knew that it couldn't possibly end well.

"Professor Schleicher," she called out. "I have just one question."

He turned, scowled. "Yes? Um . . . do I know you, Miss?"

"I'm Emma Hansen, professor at Harrington, you know, of Hansen and Bellafiori."

"Oh."

"Just tell me truthfully, did you review our paper for the *American Journal of Genetics* in 1938?"

A glassy, cold look veiled his dark eyes. "I have no idea of what you're talking about, Miss, and I seriously doubt that you do either." He turned his back and strode down the hall.

Shaking, Emma returned to the lecture room. She barely heard the next short research talk, but gradually forced herself to regain her composure. When her turn to speak finally came, Emma mounted the steps to the stage and stood briefly at the lectern quietly, seeking to calm her nerves. Her throat was constricted and her hands trembled. She had taught classes for years with confidence and ease, but addressing an audience of fellow scientists for the first time was unnerving. A portion of the audience had departed after Schleicher's presentation, but there were still perhaps a hundred faces looking up at her, not one of them a woman's face.

She had to tell her story quickly and efficiently. As she began speaking about her science, the tension flowed out of her body and her voice became clear and steady. She emphasized that she and Joe had worked alone and without any knowledge of what she called "parallel research going on in another laboratory." She explained how her mutants had allowed Joe to isolate the pigments using novel methods and to determine their chemical structures. She showed her genetic maps without taking the time to present the supporting data and presented their conclusions about the enzymatic steps of the pathway and the corresponding genes that determined them. Finally, she described their new evidence that two of their three postulated steps were definitely catalyzed by enzymes in cell-free extracts. At the end, she spoke the detested name. "On the basis of our findings we concur with the one gene: one enzyme hypothesis for gene action put forth by Professor Schleicher and would generalize it further to propose that genes also specify other proteins that are not enzymes."

Polite applause followed, but no questions.

Emma gathered her papers, her nerves still vibrating, and stepped down.

An older man approached her: Bernard Dodge, who had been so helpful back when she was a Ph.D. student. "Emma, that was absolutely beautiful work," he said as he grasped her hand. "Amazing that you and Bellafiori could accomplish so much working alone at a small college. Congratulations."

"Thank you. It's so good to see you again. I'll always be grateful for all the help you gave me when I first starting working with *Neurospora*."

"Oh, that was nothing. Pity, though, that you will have to share the credit with the Princeton group. Remarkable coincidence, that."

"Yes, wasn't it?"

JOE AND ENRICO came into the house, flushed and laughing from their romp in the fresh December snow.

Emma, her face wet with tears, looked up at them from the kitchen table.

"Sweetheart! What's wrong? Is it your father?"

"No, no. It's . . . it's . . . the Japanese have bombed Pearl Harbor. It just came over the radio."

"Pearl Harbor? Where's that?"

"It's a navy base in the Hawaiian Territory. They said a lot of ships have been sunk or are on fire. Listen, they're just repeating it over and over."

They stared at the arched-shaped wooden box with its dials and grill. Even through the static the excited urgency of the announcer's voice vibrated as he related the terrible news.

Joe paced back and forth. "The sneaky bastards. I thought it would be the Germans that dragged us into it, not the Japs."

"Oh, now we'll go to war for sure. And you'll have to go, won't you?"

"Mommy, please don't cry!" Enrico piped and ran to wrap his still cold arms around her

"I suppose so, yes. I am an officer in the reserve, and, damn it, our country's been attacked. But, but, we've talked about this. I'm in the army, not the navy. I'm thirty-five years old and a chemist. They won't send me into combat. I'll probably end up at some weapons depot or proving ground."

"Well, I know it's selfish and unpatriotic, but I don't want you to go at all. I couldn't bear to lose you. Not after what happened to Henrik."

But Joe did go to war and soon. He was called up for active duty in March of 1942 and after a short training period was assigned to the Aberdeen Proving Ground in Maryland, as he had predicted. He wrote cheerful letters to Emma and enclosed printed letters with simple text and hand-drawn pictures for Enrico.

"The Army sure knows how to waste people, time, and money," he grumbled to Emma. "They don't need a Ph.D. chemist for what I'm doing (which I am not allowed to tell you), but please be assured, sweetheart, that I am safe. The only explosions around here are in deep bunkers."

In June of 1942 Emma received a phone call from her brother Bjorn informing her that their father had died, so she and Enrico took the train to Stanton Falls. The cars were filled with young men—boys really—in military uniform, smoking cigarettes and joking as though they were going to a picnic instead of to slaughter. Some of them smiled at Enrico and patted him on the head, as Henrik and Joe must have done on their way to war when they saw children.

Their train arrived just in time for them to go directly to the undertaker's establishment in Stanton Mills for the customary viewing the evening before the funeral. A gathering of the Hansen's friends and neighbors stood in a large formally decorated room where they spoke quietly and soberly. Emma no longer recognized most of them nor they her.

At one end of the room under soft light lay her father's body in an open coffin, its interior lined with frilly cloth, the sort of material he would never have tolerated in life. Despite the undertaker's cosmetic art, the wastage of age and disease lay exposed on her father's face, his cheeks sunken, his nose carved to a thin beak, his eyes closed in unsuccessful imitation of sleep.

Emma stared at him, waited for emotions to come and was shamed when they did not. This flinty man's loins had given her life; his labor had fed, clothed, and sheltered her. When she was a schoolgirl, he had quietly protected her peculiar pursuits, even if he didn't understand them. Had he loved her? He never said. Had she loved him? She never said. It was too late for words now.

Enrico stood nervously beside her, tugged at her hand. He was the only young child in the room.

"Can you see Grandpa? Do you want me to lift you up?"

He shook his head no. "I saw," he whispered. "Grandpa isn't going to wake up, is he?"

"No, sweetheart. He has died. Remember, like the dead robin we found in the yard? Everything that lives, stops living sometime. It's how nature works."

"Me too?"

Emma's eyes stung and she knelt to embrace Enrico. "Don't worry. It won't happen for a long, long time."

Tears ran down Enrico's face. "Willie at school said the soldiers that went off to war are going to get killed. Is Daddy going to get killed?"

Now Emma, in spite of her best effort to protect Enrico, was crying too. "No, no, honey. Daddy is safe. Grandpa was just very old and sick."

Emma turned from the coffin and, holding Enrico firmly with her left hand, shook hands with Bjorn, Susan, and their nearly grown sons, who seemed embarrassed by her obvious grief, whose causes they mistook. Beside them stood her sister Kirsten, whom she had not seen in many years.

Oddly, Kirsten's husband Kurt and her daughters were not with her. She was now in her late forties, and the years had not been kind: her hair was graying, her face lined and hardened. Was she still angry with Emma for not having attended their mother's funeral fifteen years earlier?

Kirsten's eyes widened at Emma's tears. She offered a limp hand. "Well, better late than never."

"Please, Kirsten, can't we put that behind us?"

Kirsten shrugged, inclined her head to indicate a desire to speak privately. At the side of the room she whispered, "I suppose you know, he left the farm, everything, to Bjorn, nothing to us."

"No, I didn't know, but . . . well, I guess . . . since Bjorn has been running the farm all this time . . . Bjorn and Susan and the boys . . . I suppose it makes sense. The oldest son usually inherits the farm. It hurts not to get anything; I can see that, but I guess I didn't expect much. I've been gone so long. It's all right with me."

"Well, it's not all right with me. He should have left it in equal shares. Kurt was so mad, he wouldn't come to the viewing. Bjorn could have bought us out. Prices for milk, corn, and meat are way up now with the war and all. And it's going to be a long war, it looks like. He'll make a lot of money."

"Oh, God, how can you say that? My husband is in the Army now. If the war goes on long, it'll take Bjorn's and Susan's boys. Just because you have only girls. I don't give a damn what it does for farm prices!"

Kirsten turned without speaking and walked away. Does death always bring out the worst in families?

After the funeral the next day, Emma asked Bjorn to drop her and Enrico off in Stanton Falls two hours in advance of her train's departure for Chicago, so she could visit the Oosterfelds. Bjorn delegated the task to his older son Peter, who was happy for the chance to drive the family car. The youth's striking resemblance to Henrik unsettled Emma, and he in turn was shy because he hardly knew his aunt and little cousin.

Emma broke the silence with what she hoped was a gentle question. "How do you like high school, Peter? You're a junior now?"

He shrugged. "Yeah. It's OK. I wanted to get on the basketball team, but practice is after school, and Dad said I had to be home for chores. I'm sixteen now, so I can drop out."

"Oh, don't do that. You'll be so much better prepared for the future with more education. I guess you'd expect me to say that, but it's true."

"I don't see how school helps me much, 'cause I don't know what I want to do. I don't like farmin' much. Maybe if I could have my own place. Couple years, if the war's still goin' on, guess I'll join the army."

"Well, I hope it's over and you don't have to go. And we get Joe home again. Peter, war is terrible. It just about killed your Uncle Henrik. It did destroy him mentally."

"What ever happened to him? They never talk about it."

Emma bit her lip. "He just disappeared. We don't know what happened. I think he jumped a railroad car and became a hobo, but no one really knows. Did anyone tell you that you look just like him? I was so fond of him. It makes me want to hug you." She lost the battle against tears. Peter fell into an embarrassed silence.

EMMA MOUNTED THE familiar stairs at the side of the grocery store, slowly to accommodate Enrico's short legs. Piet greeted her and Enrico at the upstairs door. He was even more thin and aged than the last time she had seen him.

"Come in, come in. We're so glad you came to see us. Sorry about your father. We couldn't come to the viewing or the funeral, because Hannah has been poorly. Heart trouble. She can hardly get around anymore, but, here, come say hello. She's lying down."

Hannah was lying on a sofa under a blanket, clearly very feeble and breathing with difficulty. She waved a bony hand toward Emma. "Come here, dear girl. And little Enrico. Forgive me for not getting up."

Enrico hung back shyly.

"You remember Hannah, sweetheart?" Emma said.

He nodded.

Hannah patted his hand. "Such a beautiful child. Your mommy is like a daughter to us, Enrico."

Emma gently kissed her cheek, thin and dry as crepe paper. They made small talk, avoiding the painful questions that hung in the air: with no family in the community how were they coping? How would Piet manage after Hannah died? Emma longed to tell them how grateful she was for their support when she had struggled financially, but even more, for their affectionate kindness, for their having been, in a way, parents to her, but she knew they would be embarrassed by such overt emotion. She wanted to say goodbye to Hannah, who would surely die before Emma would return to Stanton Mills, but the best she could manage before they left was to kiss the old lady again and say, "I hope you will be much better soon. Thank you for all you and Piet have done for me."

Emma was unusually quiet on the train as they returned to Harrington.

Enrico leaned close to her, then looked up, brown eyes imploring. "Mama, you be happy, OK?"

CHAPTER 22
1942 -1943

BY THE FALL of 1942 the war—it was now being called World War Two—had reached its tentacles into Harrington, Ohio. The number of students on campus dropped sharply. Rumors circulated that Harrington College was threatened with closure because of low enrollments and that only generous gifts and loans from Miss Harrington kept the College open.

For the first time in the history of the college, the majority of the students were women. Many men had volunteered for military service after Pearl Harbor; others had been drafted. All men under forty-five were registered for the draft and nervously awaited their fate. Arguments and resentments over deferments were common. Emma had never seen such attention to radio broadcasts and newspapers before. Strange names entered everyday speech: El Alamein, Guadalcanal, Stalingrad. Rationing of gasoline and rubber tires, sugar and coffee began. The news of death and destruction was everywhere, yet the little campus town was quiet. An air of nervous unreality prevailed.

Emma taught much smaller classes and fewer of them—not many coeds enrolled in biology that fall. Without Joe to encourage her and help with their domestic chores, her genetic experiments faltered, then halted. Although Enrico, now in second grade, was in school all day, Emma needed to be with him as much as possible when he was at home. He missed his father grievously. He became more serious and fearful than he had been before. He held imaginary conversations with Joe and hoarded his father's letters in a cigar box. He occasionally wet the bed, which he had not done since he was three.

Only through separation had Emma learned how deeply she had fallen in love, how her life had been transformed. Once so self-sufficient, she felt herself moving through her days automatically, puppet-like, in black and white instead of the vivid colors that were now being used in movies.

Joe's ready affection, expressiveness, and energy had become a part of her life. His enthusiasm and encouragement drove her research when she became discouraged. And, oh, how she missed him physically, his frequent embraces and kisses, the intense pleasure of their lovemaking and blissful gratitude as they drifted into sleep afterward. He wrote faithfully every week, a letter for Emma and another letter for Enrico. He joked about the stupidity of military life and routines, and constantly reassured them of his safety. On infrequent weekend leaves he visited Washington, Baltimore, and Maryland's Eastern Shore and wrote vivid accounts of his experiences.

Emma did not hide her longing for him in her letters, but she felt it was her duty to seem as cheerful and independent as she could.

IN EARLY NOVEMBER Emma received a phone call from a weary and depressed Piet Oosterfeld informing her that Hannah had died. Although Piet protested that it was unnecessary, Emma made the train trip through the dreary late fall countryside to Stanton Falls for Hannah's funeral. She offered Enrico the choice to stay behind with Mrs. Schroeder, but he refused and hung closely to her side during the two-day trip. Of her family, only Bjorn and Susan attended the funeral. Although Emma and Enrico stayed with them on the farm for one night, their conversations seemed stiff and hollow. Had they noticed that Emma grieved Hannah's passing more than she had her mother's and father's deaths?

After the funeral guests had drifted away, Emma took her leave from Piet.

"I know you'll be lonely, Piet, I wish I were closer," she said as she held his spotted and bony hand.

"Ah, don't worry, Emma. I'll be joining her soon."

"Oh, Piet, don't say that." Emma choked.

"It's all right, dear girl. You know, she didn't say much, but Hannah loved you like a daughter. As do I." They embraced, a bit stiffly, but with feeling.

"I'm a biologist," she said softly, "but some parents are not related to their children by blood. Like you and Hannah." Then she turned away, because she knew that tears would embarrass Piet and upset Enrico.

Piet Oosterfeld died a month later. There were rumors around Stanton Mills that it was by his own hand, but the coroner and the undertaker refused to confirm them. Emma was named the sole heir to the modest Oosterfeld estate, which provoked yet more gossip.

JOE WAS GRANTED leave for Christmas. It took him four days to get to Harrington because he first went to Chicago to visit his family. He reported that the trains were jammed with soldiers and sailors. He breezed into the house on a gust of cold snowy air in a thick brown Army overcoat, smelling of stale cigarette smoke, his cheeks flushed, and enfolded Emma and Enrico in his arms.

They had decorated the house with a small Christmas tree, candles, and holly. Emma had laid in supplies for favorite dishes that she knew Joe and she would enjoy cooking together. Joe and Enrico had wild romps. Joe and Emma made love with an intensity that attempted, but could not quite achieve, the expression of all that bound them together and they feared losing.

They were so keen to make the holiday a joyful one that Emma sensed that they were trying too hard. There were hints of artificiality, of desperation to their merriment. Joe seemed distracted. This was not the easy, natural way of their intimate lives together. What was this long separation, this war doing to them? Finally after a week together, two days before Joe would have to return to his unit, Emma massaged Joe's neck as they lay in bed together.

"Joe, something's wrong. What is it? Has something happened? I can feel it. Have you . . . met someone?"

"Oh, God, no, Emma. There will never be anyone but you. Don't ever think that. But . . . yes, there is something I've been dreading telling you. Because I know how you will worry. I didn't want to spoil Christmas with it."

"What, Joe, what?"

"Sweetheart, please try not to worry about this, but I have been reassigned to go overseas."

"Overseas? Where? What for?"

"It's all hush-hush. I'm not supposed to tell anyone. Not even you. But the Army's getting set to invade Italy from north Africa as soon as Rommel's been run out."

"Italy? Oh, no. They're not sending you into combat?"

"No, no. Not that. They found out that I speak Italian and some German. They want me to interrogate captured Italian soldiers, you know, for intelligence. Get 'em to tell us where troops and defenses are, orders they got, that sort of thing."

"That sounds dangerous to me. Won't you have to be where the fighting is?"

"No. I'll be behind the lines. They will bring the prisoners back to HQ. Word is, the Italians are pretty demoralized. They expect that a lot of them will be pretty cooperative. They're sick of fighting the Germans' war."

"Well, I dread it. I wish you didn't have to go over there. It was a lot safer at Aberdeen. I don't care if you were bored and your talents wasted." Emma buried her face on Joe's chest, kissed the beloved smooth skin. "When do you have to go?"

"I don't know exactly. When I get back, they're sending me to some special training to learn Italian military terms and learn about the kinds of information I'm supposed to get, all that. Then, I'll have to take a troop ship across the Atlantic—that should be some ride in the early spring—and join up with a unit there. The timing and attack routes are all big secrets."

"I don't want you to go," Emma cried. "I was so single-minded throughout my life until I met you. All I wanted was to study science, to teach science, to do research. I shut everything else out. Even my family, except for Henrik. And the goddamn war took him from me. You changed all that. And now it's trying to get you. You—you and Enrico—are the most precious things in my life now. More precious than all the science. I don't want you to go! I don't."

"Oh, sweetheart, my love, I don't have a choice. When you're in the Army, you have to go where they send you. You know that. But, believe me, I'll be careful. I'll be the biggest coward in the Army. I'll stay way back and make chit-chat with the *paisanos*. No heroics, I promise. Please, don't worry."

ON A HOT AUGUST afternoon in 1943 the doorbell rang. A boy on a bicycle handed Emma a Western Union telegram. He avoided looking at her and sped away without waiting for a tip. Dear God, no. Heart pounding in her throat, she ripped a yellow sheet from the envelop and read:

THE SECRETARY OF WAR DESIRES ME TO EXPRESS HIS DEEP REGRET THAT YOUR HUSBAND FIRST LEUTENANT JOSEPH F BELLAFIORI WAS KILLED IN ACTION IN SICILY ON FIFTEEN AUGUST CONFIRMING LETTER FOLLOWS—

Is it worse knowing or not knowing? Joe's body lay hastily buried in the unforgiving soil of Sicily. Emma would never see it again. Did the bullet pass cleanly through his chest and did he fall to the ground, his chestnut eyes wide with disbelief? Or was there an explosion that ripped his beautiful body into a bloody tangle of flesh, bones, metal, and khaki shreds, the former human recognizable only from his dog tags? Were there flames, burning gasoline torturing his scorched, suffocating body? Did he die quickly, his last sound a surprised grunt? Oh, God grant him—and her—that. Or had he lain writhing on the ground, crying out for all that he was about to lose, crying out for Emma and Enrico, for the joy of living, for help, for the pain to end? It was too horrible to bear, yet the images stalked Emma, attacked her at night, threatened her sanity.

The letter from Col. Brinkmeyer, Joe's commanding officer, didn't answer those questions. It simply stated that he had been killed by "a surprise attack on his convoy by German aircraft." He said that Joe had been "an excellent intelligence officer, effective in his work and popular with his fellow soldiers" and concluded with "profoundest sympathy" and asked her to remember that Joe had "sacrificed his life for his country."

How she hated that cliché. How many times would it be repeated to widows and mothers and fatherless children before this war was over? His country had *wasted* Joe's life. She had lost the love of her life and Enrico had lost his adored father. The world had lost a brilliant scientist and teacher. The bullets or shrapnel or whatever the hell they were had torn bleeding holes in her life. How in God's name could she go on living?

CHAPTER 23
1950

EMMA CLOSED THE folder, leaned back in her office chair, pushed her glasses up to her forehead, and rubbed her eyes. She was still getting used to her bifocals, she supposed, or was it simply fatigue from reading four senior honors theses this afternoon?

So many students asked her to direct their honors research that she could only accept four each year. This year two had chosen topics in traditional biology: one had conducted a study of the parasitic wasps that paralyze cicadas with their stings, lay their eggs in the bodies and store them away in underground burrows, and the other had followed the succession of microbiological species that developed in a rural pond over the course of last summer and this spring. Two others worked in Emma's lab on isolation and characterization of mutant strains of Neurospora that required amino acids for growth.

Her office door opened quietly. 'Rico. Only he came into Emma's office without knocking. He plopped his books onto her desk and bent to kiss her cheek.

"Hi, Mama. Sorry I'm late. Baseball practice went on longer than usual."

"Oh, I was so busy with these theses that I didn't notice."

Emma rose from her chair and embraced him. How she loved him. His smiling entrance was like the warmth of summer sun. He looked so much like Joe that her heart ached. At fifteen he was already taller than Joe had been and more slender, almost willowy, but he had the same dark curly hair and amber-brown eyes, the same easy grin. His voice had changed last year—it still startled her to hear a deep man's voice in the house—and his face was losing its boyishness. Dark shadows covered his upper lip and jaws.

He needed Joe to teach him how to shave, but Joe was gone, wasn't he? Joe would have been so proud of him. What would he have thought, though, when Enrico announced when he started high school that from now on he wished to be known as Hank—short for Henry—not Enrico or 'Rico? Too foreign sounding, he said. His friends complied, but Emma persisted in calling him 'Rico in private.

In the bleak days after Joe's death Emma wrote a list of reasons to go on living. The first item was Enrico. Then followed: Science, Teaching, and "Because Joe would want me to: Honor Joe." Now, nearly seven years later that list, tattered and tear-stained, was still in the corner of the blotter on her desk. The list did its job; it reminded Emma again and again of what she had loved and why she loved it. Gradually she not only went on living, she found purpose and muted happiness in life again.

As is common for an only child raised by a widowed parent, Enrico/ Hank developed into a serious, responsible, adult-like child, not wounded, but very aware of the possibility of being wounded, protective of the mother who had protected him. He was saved from excessive seriousness by having inherited Joe's playful, emotionally expressive character. He was quick to cry, quick to anger, quick to forgive. He expressed affection without inhibition and had many friends. He wasn't a natural athlete, but pursued sports with determination. Emma saw that the coaches of his sports teams often became father figures for him. If Joe were still alive, he'd surely have lured Enrico into his lab to work on his projects by now.

Emma squeezed Enrico's shoulder. "'Rico, how would you like to work in the lab with me this summer?"

Why had she not invited him to do this before? Perhaps she was wary of overwhelming her son. He was so much like Joe as it was; she resisted the urge to mold him into a scientist-collaborator like his father had been. The boy needed freedom to develop on his own path. Yet, it would be a joy to share her love of research with him.

"Would I have to give up baseball?"

"No, of course not. Your schedule would be completely flexible— whenever you are free and I'm in the lab too."

A frown crossed Enrico's face. "What would I have to do?"

"Well, you know I do genetics . . ."

"The science of heredity, yeah, but I don't know much about it."

"Don't worry about that. I'll teach you as we go along. I've moved away from pure genetics to using it as a tool for figuring out how cells work, how they take the simple chemicals we can feed them and convert them into the complicated molecules that cells are made of. It's called biosynthesis."

"Oh. So how do you do that?"

"The metaphor I like to use is an assembly line, like in a factory where an automobile is put together out of thousands of small pieces. Each worker puts on one piece and passes it on to the next worker. So, in the cell the worker that puts on a piece is an enzyme, a clever protein molecule that knows how to make a very specific chemical reaction go really fast."

"I thought protein was something you were supposed to have in your diet."

"It is. Proteins are really important components of all cells. I'll have to teach you more about proteins later, but for now, just think of them as workers on a biosynthetic assembly line."

"OK. But I don't see what genetics has to do with it."

"That's what we do in the lab. You see, the information needed to make an enzyme is inherited. It's carried on an inherited element called a gene. Every cell learns how to make its enzymes from its parents. Here's the important thing: for each enzyme, there's a single corresponding gene. Your Daddy and I were the first to prove that."

Emma's pride in that statement was clouded with residual anger. Phillip Schleicher. The arrogant swindler. Ah, well, no point in burdening 'Rico with all that.

"Really? Is that a big deal?"

"Yes, it is. I'm really proud of what we did. Anyway, here's how we use that knowledge. Suppose something goes wrong with the gene. It's defective; it can't make an enzyme that works. What happens then?"

"The assembly line stops."

"Exactly. The cells with the defective genes are called mutants, and they all inherit the same defect, so you can collect them. And you know that they are mutants because they can't make whatever the assembly line was making, whereas the cells with normal genes can."

"How do you know which is which?"

"You know how I grow my fungus cells—*Neurospora crassa*, they're called—on these Petri dishes?" Emma waved her arm at a bench in her office, where round, flat glass dishes were stacked.

"Yeah, you mean those dishes with little white spots on them?"

"Each spot is a pile of cells that all grew from a single cell. So they're all genetically identical. We call them colonies. Here's the thing. People have figured out that the fungus can grow on really simple medium, just some sugar and salts. They've got assembly lines for all of the hundreds of complicated molecules that they need to make new cells. And genes for every worker—each enzyme—on every one of the many assembly lines. So if we can isolate mutations that knock out each of the workers on a given assembly line, we can learn a lot about the assembly line and how it works."

"I don't get it. How?"

"Well, we isolate a lot of mutants that can't grow unless we add the end product of the assembly line—biosynthetic pathway—that we want to study. Let's say it's one of the twenty or so amino acids that the cell needs to make proteins. The parents can grow without it, but the mutants won't grow unless it's added to the growth medium. Some of the mutants knock out the same worker; some knock out different workers. We can tell which is which by mapping them. Different genes map to different locations. I'll teach you how that works. From that we can get a good idea of how many workers—enzyme steps—there are on the pathway."

"Seems like a lot of work just to figure out how many steps there are."

"It is, and what you really want to know is what each worker *does*: what chemical reaction the enzyme catalyzes."

"Yeah. Can you do that?"

"Yes. Here's the trick. Go back to the assembly line. Suppose one worker's job is to add the front wheels to a car, and he's not working but all the other ones are. Pretty soon a lot of incomplete cars with only their rear wheels pile up on the line, but no finished cars get made. From looking at what piles up, you can deduce that the missing worker normally does."

"Sure, that makes sense."

"So it often happens that the mutant strains that we isolate in the lab pile up a substance that's on the pathway to the final product. If we can isolate it and determine its chemical structure, we get valuable clues about how the pathway works. We would probably have to do that for several different mutations."

Enrico passed his hands through his dark curls. "Wow. I've got a lot to learn. I don't know any chemistry yet. Or genetics."

"Oh, 'Rico. I so wish your Daddy was here. He'd have loved to teach you. He was a master at the chemistry. I'd isolate and map the genes, and he would isolate the things that piled up in my mutants and determine their chemical structures. We were a great team."

Enrico searched Emma's eyes. He reached across the desk and patted her hand.

"So, without my biochemist—your Daddy—I work with scientists at other universities who are good at that kind of work," she continued in a husky voice. "It's not as much fun as Daddy and I had doing it ourselves, but it's actually more productive."

In fact, Emma had used the methods she had just described to Enrico to establish a nationally respected research program. She benefited from the finding of others that irradiation of the cells with an ultraviolet lamp could be used to increase the frequency of mutations instead of using x-rays, which were dangerous and difficult to control. She isolated and characterized mutant strains that were incapable of growing without the addition of essential compounds, such as amino acids, purines, or pyrimidines that are the fundamental building blocks of the critical large molecules of life: proteins and the nucleic acids DNA and RNA.

Without Joe to work at her side, she set up a series of research collaborations with biochemists at several universities who had the expertise needed for such work. She provided mutant strains to her collaborators and consulted frequently on their progress on unraveling the chemistry of the pathways and the study of the enzymes catalyzing individual steps in them. Emma was now the co-author on a growing number of research publications in the genetic and biochemical literature. She had become the most nationally prominent researcher on the Harrington College faculty, but Enrico was unaware of this.

"So what do you want me to do this summer?"

"Well, one of the assembly lines we don't know much about yet makes molecules called pyrimidines." Emma pulled a sheet of paper from her desk and drew a chemical structure. "That's called uracil. See it's a ring with four carbons and two nitrogens in it. The cells need it to make DNA, the stuff their genes are made of. Let's you and I try to find mutants of my bug that can't grow unless uracil is added to the growth medium. That'll get us started on figuring out how it's made by the cell."

"OK. You'll have to show me everything. I guess I never understood what you were doing in the lab all the time. Kind of like solving puzzles. It doesn't have anything to do with all the animals and skeletons and stuff like we have in the museum, does it? You know, at school they used to call me the kid who lives in a museum." Big Joe-like grin.

Emma laughed. "Did you mind?"

"Naw, I thought it was cool."

"The museum is not for my research. I guess it's mostly just because I love collecting things. Always have. I used to collect wild birds' eggs when I was a girl. Your Uncle Henrik and I. Then the collection got so big that I found I could use it for teaching general biology and stimulating interest in biology in school kids."

Over the twenty-two years she had been on the faculty in biology at Harrington College, Emma had accumulated a large collection of biological specimens: taxidermically mounted animals and birds—some quite large—carefully labeled boxes of dissected invertebrate and vertebrate species, bottles of creatures preserved in formaldehyde, skeletons, microscope slides and on and on. She had purchased many of these for use in her classes. Others had been given to her by grateful former students who were now biology teachers, researchers, or physicians.

Emma urged the Dean to establish a natural history museum to display the collection, but the Dean insisted that neither space nor funds were available. So Emma decided to create her own museum—in her home. She was no longer happy living in the home she had shared with Joe, so in 1945 she combined the money she had received from the Oosterfeld estate with the ten thousand dollars in G. I. insurance paid to her after Joe's death to buy a large Queen Anne style house, the home of a former president of the college, that was located just two blocks from the campus. There was plenty of room for her and 'Rico on the spacious first floor, so she converted the second floor bedrooms into a series of rooms dedicated to the display and study of her natural history collection. Hours were scheduled for students in the college's biology classes to troop up the grand wooden staircase to the upper level of the house to study the specimens, and once a month, she opened the museum to the general public. Biology teachers in the Harrington public schools were invited to visit the museum with their classes.

"Oh, look how late it has gotten," Emma exclaimed. "That's what happens when you get me talking about science. Let's go home and make supper."

"Yeah, Mama, let's go to the museum and gnaw on some of your old bones. I'm starving."

ON AN UNUSUALLY warm evening in late May, Emma sat at her desk in the large living room at the front of her house and puzzled over final examination questions for her general biology course. After so many years of teaching, more and more thought was required to come up with novel and original exam questions that probed the students' understanding.

The front door was open to allow cool evening air to flow in from the wide front porch. Moths, attracted by the light, threw themselves against the screen door. 'Rico had gone to bed in his room at the rear of the house. The rhythmic beat of the grandfather clock in the hall was interrupted by nine soft chimes. Already? It had only just gotten dark. Emma was calm, content, enveloped in the comfort of the life she and 'Rico had rebuilt from the ashes of war and death.

A soft tapping on the front screen door. "Emma? Is that you?"

There was something familiar about the voice. Where had she heard it before? Emma went to the door. She was not afraid to live alone, but she always kept the screen door hooked from the inside as a simple precaution. The visitor's face was obscured by the haze of the screen and the passage of time, so it took a moment for her to recognize him.

"Victor! My God, Victor Midlothian. What are you doing here?"

"I came to see you. May I come in?"

"Yes, yes, of course." Emma unhooked the screen, and Victor stepped into the room.

They embraced, first tentatively, then warmly. He was heavier than she remembered, and his face had lost its boyishness and become leathery with crinkles at the corners of his eyes. His hair, now more gray than brown and clipped short in military fashion, no longer fell rakishly over his brow, but the amusement in his eyes and his mischievous grin were unchanged. He would be, what, fifty-one now? A year older than Emma. He was still a handsome man.

She quickly pulled off her glasses, smoothed her dress, and waved him into the living room. "This is a surprise, Vic. I never expected to see you again."

"I know. It's my fault. I was lazy about writing. Too caught up in what I was doing."

"How did you even know where I was?"

"I was in Stanton Mills to take care of my folks' estate. They're both gone now, and I had to clear out the house, put it on the market, talk to the lawyer, that sort of thing, you know."

"Oh, I'm sorry. Both dead? I didn't know."

"I'm afraid I neglected them as much as I did you. I'm a little ashamed about that now." Victor rubbed his face with his hand and stared at the floor.

"Please, sit down, Vic."

"Thanks. Well, anyway, I asked around about you. Went out to the farm and talked to Bjorn. He told me you were a professor here. Wow.

A dream come true for you, huh? And this is quite a grand house you live in."

Emma shrugged dismissively. "It's bigger than I need. For just the two of us. We live downstairs. The upstairs is an informal natural history museum for the college."

"Oh. Bjorn told me that you were married and that you lost your husband in the war. I'm sorry. That must have been hard for you."

"It was. Very hard. Joe Bellafiori was the great love of my life. And my partner in science as well." Emma shook off the little wave of sadness. "But, what about you? Were you in the war? Or were you exempt because you were in the last war?"

"I joined the Army Air Force and spent the whole war training pilots stateside. They never sent me overseas. They said it was because I was needed for training, but I think they thought I was too old. Good thing. I trained a lot of pilots who never came back."

"Are you still in the Air Force?"

"Naw. I'm a pilot for American now. It's good money."

"Um, did you . . . ever . . . marry?"

The familiar grin. He shook his head. "You know me."

"I guess I do. Or did. People change sometimes."

"But a minute ago . . . you said 'we' . . . ?"

"I'm not remarried. Joe and I had a son. Didn't Bjorn tell you? He's fifteen now. A wonderful boy. I don't know how I could have gotten through those first years after . . . without him."

"Did you ever consider . . . uh . . . remarrying?"

"No. Not really." Emma shrugged. "I don't know. Joe spoiled me for any other man. Most men seem . . . well . . . intimidated. It would be good for Enrico to have a father, but . . . well . . . that's not enough reason, is it? I guess I've learned to be self-sufficient."

They fell silent, a silence that grew uncomfortably long.

"Vic, why did you come here?" Emma asked.

He shrugged, then fixed her eyes with his. "I don't know . . . I just . . . I guess . . . Emma, I have never forgotten you. I really wanted to see you again. There was something special between us."

"Was there?" Emma was warmed with a flash of anger. "You had a funny way of showing it. What's it been? Twenty-five years, at least, and not a word, not a letter. You were too busy flying your aeroplanes. Other women were closer to hand, I daresay."

Victor hung his head, twisted his hands between his knees. "I know,

I know. I was very immature. Selfish. I had a lot of growing up to do. Please forgive me."

"Oh, I got over it. You were fun and we had a good time, but I don't think I was really in love with you. No, no, not now that I know what *real* love is. And it certainly didn't make sense to think of marrying you—if you had even wanted to . . . which, admit it, you didn't."

"Ah, that's the fiery, independent Emma that I remember. You know, you haven't changed much at all. Still a very pretty woman. Very attractive. Would you ever consider . . . renewing our . . . friendship?"

"What are you suggesting, Vic? Surely not marriage?"

"Well, uh, no, I guess that wouldn't be practical. Not while I'm working as a pilot. But, maybe we could . . . see one another . . . now and then. I fly in and out of Cleveland sometimes. I could visit you then."

Emma stood up and shook her head. "I don't know whether to be flattered or angry. Things have changed. I've got a fifteen-year-old son sleeping in the next room—if he's asleep—and you . . . you come back after a quarter century and want to start right up where we left off. After all that's happened? I can't believe it."

Victor jumped up from his chair and held his hands out to ward off Emma's words. "Oh, no, no. I wasn't suggesting . . . I'm sorry. That would be . . . presumptuous. I apologize. Please don't . . . don't let it spoil the good memories we have. I am serious, though, if you are interested in . . . a friendly relationship. It might lead to something . . . more permanent. I still have . . .feelings for you, Emma."

Emma's feelings were too muddled for her to reply..

"I'm staying at the Hamilton Hotel downtown tonight. I'll tell them to give you my address . . . if you . . . change your mind."

When he was gone, Emma sat back down at her desk, but was unable to concentrate on exam questions. Replace Joe? No. A love life of that kind—maybe of any kind—was over for her. Or was it?

CHAPTER 24
1955

EMMA KNEW WHY the Dean Roberts had summoned her to his office. The secretary to the Biology Department had brought her, without comment, a copy of the *Cincinnati Enquirer* this morning with the page folded back to a news story headline:

LADY PROFESSOR'S SEX COURSE AT HARRINGTON COLLEGE

Emma had initiated a course titled "Human Sexual Biology: Love, Marriage and Childbearing" this year. As long ago as 1935, when she taught general biology while pregnant with Enrico, she had been aware that many of her students were woefully ignorant of sexual matters and that they were hungry for accurate, detailed information. She always included a section on reproduction when she taught human physiology, but not many students took such a specialized course.

She had invited her students to submit written questions or to visit her in her office, but she was overwhelmed by their responses and had to discontinue the practice. When she learned that Professor Alfred Kinsey at Indiana University was offering a "marriage and family" class that dealt frankly with sexual topics, she contacted him for details, which he gladly supplied, and she decided to offer a similar course at Harrington. The syllabus was described in terms sufficiently innocuous to avoid raising eyebrows in the Dean's office:

Anatomy of the human reproductive system

Physical aspects of marital relations

Varieties of sexual expression

Pregnancy

Childbirth and infancy

Once the course was underway, word spread across the campus, and many students came to the class who were not enrolled in it. A large lecture hall had to be located to accommodate them. Emma knew that there was considerable gossip about the candor and explicit detail with which she taught the course, but she chose to ignore it.

There were protests too. The pastor of the First Methodist Church of Harrington had complained to Dean Roberts about the teaching of immorality, and the Dean grumbled to Emma about angry letters and phone calls.

"Couldn't you tone it down a little, Emma?" he had asked her. "I respect what you are trying to do, but it's being misunderstood. I don't want the college dragged into a controversy about sex."

With characteristic determination Emma had ignored him and taught the course as she wished.

But now the sensationalistic article in the *Enquirer* threatened to embroil the College in scandal. A reporter had gotten word of Emma's "marriage and family" course, probably from the unhappy clergyman, and slipped into the lecture hall to observe several classes throughout the semester.

"Professor Hansen has abandoned all standards of decency and discretion," the reporter quoted the Rev. Dr. Whisnant as saying. "Her so-called 'love, marriage, and childbearing' course is laced with pornography and perversion."

"Even though male and female students take the course in the same classroom, the students were shown transparency slides of photographs of female and male external genitals, the latter even in a state of arousal. The students viewed a lengthy film of a woman giving birth with no detail obscured from sight. The course is a virtual how-to manual for every imaginable sexual activity. Techniques for arousing sexual excitement and performing conjugal relations were described in detail, as were several contraceptive methods. Professor Hansen described such practices such as masturbation, homosexuality, and prostitution as 'within the normal range of human sexual expression.' She discussed venereal diseases in detail and advocated means of avoiding and treating them.

"Professor Hansen denied that her course promoted immoral behavior. 'I expect the students to be guided by their own moral beliefs,' she said. 'The biological facts do not by themselves form the basis for moral decisions, but they allow anyone who is engaged in sexual activity to do so in an informed and positive way.'"

Emma vaguely recalled a conversation with a man, whom she had not seen before and seemed older than most students, who had questioned her about "promoting immorality" and "lascivious images and descriptions," but he had not identified himself as a reporter. She had assumed that he was a student who was troubled by the teachings of his conservative religious background.

The news story quoted her accurately, but she had also said, "Look, most of the students in the course will eventually marry, and some will engage in sexual activity outside of marriage, whether we like it or not. Isn't it better that they should be informed about sex, that they should know how to avoid harmful outcomes, that they should learn how to make sex a positive, pleasurable, and bonding experience? This is an educational institution, devoted to developing and sharing knowledge, not to perpetuating ignorance." None of that was quoted in the *Enquirer* article.

DEAN ROBERTS HAD a copy of the newspaper on his desk when Emma was ushered into his office.

"Professor Hansen, whatever am I going to do with you?" he asked.

"Why do you have to do anything with me?" Emma shot back.

"Surely you've heard about this report in the *Enquirer*?"

"Yes. They've sensationalized the whole thing. I think they should be ignored. Or I'd be willing to give them a statement justifying the value of this course. I explained all that to their reporter—who, by the way, never identified himself, just lurked in the back of my classes—but he chose not to print it."

"Well, I worried about this when we approved your syllabus. There's been so much fuss over Kinsey's books. And I have had numerous complaints before, as you know. I should have anticipated this."

"Are you now saying the course shouldn't be taught? Or are you just upset over the publicity?"

"Let me remind you that Harrington College is a private college. Although the college is no longer affiliated with the Presbyterian Church, many of our graduates and supporters are religiously conservative. The college is very dependent on the good will and financial support of our friends and alumni, some of whom are offended by this."

"Many?"

"I have had quite a few telephone calls."

"Tell them to call me."

"Oh, I don't think that would be wise."

For the first time during this tense interview, Emma laughed. "You're probably right about that. I have no sympathy with ignorance. Or with people who are afraid of sex for that matter. Kinsey has been teaching a course like this for years."

Dean Roberts shrugged. "Privately I am inclined to agree with you. But . . . I do have to worry about the public perception of our college."

He cleared his throat, rose from his desk, and walked over to Emma and sat near her on a side chair. "Professor Hansen, Emma, you are one of our most distinguished faculty members. Students flock to your classes. You have even opened a natural history museum in your own home. Your record of original research publications is the most impressive in the college. And the recent award of a grant from the National Science Foundation was the first for Harrington . . . "

"But . . . ?"

"I'm afraid that, in the best interests of Harrington College, the Human Sexual Biology course will be discontinued at the end of the semester."

"Hmmm. Forgive me, sir, but I don't feel that serves the best interests of our students." Emma considered adding that she thought it was downright cowardly, but held her tongue.

"I was sure you would not agree with me, and I've thought about this a bit. If you were . . . ah . . . to wait a year, give the fuss some time to blow over, then offer a . . . non-credit course of similar content . . . uh . . . off campus . . ."

"The college wouldn't object to what I do privately . . ."

"Um, yes, exactly so. No connection to the college."

"You might consider approaching the Unitarian church near campus," Dean Roberts continued. "Their sanctuary would probably be large enough, and they, uh, have the reputation of being, uh, open-minded. Mind you, it would be wise to be somewhat . . . less . . . explicit."

Emma took a deep breath. "Dean Roberts, your responsibilities are different from mine, I understand that. My duty is to pursue the truth, to fight ignorance, to stimulate our students to think critically with the use of the best information they can get. I know you share those values—you'd never have approved the course if you didn't—and I know that you have to protect the college. I guess I can live with your proposal, although I don't like putting the course off for a year."

"To let controversy pass, don't you see? It's in your interest too. I have had many who are calling for your removal. Even though you are tenured, the statutes would allow for that."

Emma bristled. "You're not threatening me?"

"Oh, no, no. Just . . . work with me, all right?"

A FEW DAYS later Hank bounded up the porch steps and through the front door of Emma's house with a white bag stuffed with dirty laundry over his shoulder. He was near the end of his sophomore year at Harrington. He and Emma had agreed that he should live in a dorm at the college, despite the extra expense, because it was time for him to learn to live more independently and they wanted him to experience campus life. However, he came home most weekends, usually bearing laundry, to visit Emma. They often cooked an evening meal together, and they ate in the dining room.

"So, Mama, how's the famous sex professor?" He laughed as he threw down the laundry bag and embraced Emma.

"Oh, is it all over campus? The news story, I mean. Everybody already knew I taught that course."

"Yeah. Everybody thinks it's funny. There were a couple of reporters hanging around, looking for wild sex parties. Orgies at Harrington College. It's ridiculous."

"Are you embarrassed, 'Rico?"

"Oh, hell no. Lots of the kids don't know you're my mom because we have different last names, so I tell 'em, 'That's my mom.'"

"Then what do they say?"

"Mostly they think it's cool. They can't believe their parents would ever be so open about sex. Then, it's funny, the next thing they ask is how's come my last name is Bellafiori instead of Hansen. So I explain about my dad."

After supper Hank became quiet, which was rare for him. Emma knew her son so well. He had something on his mind, something they needed to discuss.

"So, what is it, son? I can see the wheels turning. Is it about my sex course and all that?"

Hank shrugged, but did not reply.

"Is it about you and Wendy?"

Hank and Wendy had been dating steadily for the past year. She had been a dinner guest with Hank a few times. She was an attractive, lively girl, but oh, so young, still unformed. As was Hank. Just kids. Neither was ready for a serious commitment. Emma knew she shouldn't meddle, but, well, she wanted to be sure that Hank didn't make a poor choice. He was so passionate, impulsive—like Joe.

"Well, sorta."

"Are the two of you sexually active? Is that it?"

"Mom!"

"Oh, I know it's none of my business, but, 'Rico, it is. There are so many ways to get it wrong. I just want what's . . . right . . . for you."

Hank reddened and stared at the floor.

"You can talk to me about this. I'm the sex professor, remember?"

"Well, it's embarrassing . . . well, yeah, OK. Maybe we do wanna . . . I mean, just necking gets awfully frustrating. It makes you want more."

"I'm sure it does. Do you feel as if you really care for each other? You don't want to hurt her—or get hurt yourself—if you break up later." Intimacy led to commitment, Emma mused, and 'Rico needed to be free to back out.

Hank shrugged. "How can you be sure about that?"

"You probably can't, but you should talk about it. Understand whether Wendy is assuming that it will lead to marriage. Most girls do. They feel as though they've been spoiled for another man after they've had sex with one. That's silly, but that's how it is. I like Wendy. She's a bright girl. Has a nice personality. But you're both very young. Only twenty and both of you have two more years of college to go. Marriage is for people who are emotionally mature and financially self-sufficient."

"Can't you just have sex for fun, even if you're not planning on getting married?"

Emma mulled over her reply. Should she tell her son about Victor and Herschel? She decided against it. "Well, yes, lots of people do, but the kind, responsible thing to do is to be sure that you both agree that that's what you're doing. You have to understand, sex is powerful stuff. You can't always predict how it's going to affect your feelings. In the best cases it creates love, it deepens love, it generates great intimacy and trust. That's what I had with your father. I admit that we were . . . intimate . . . before we got married. It makes you want to marry, even if you hadn't planned to. But sometimes one of you is more in love than the other.

"And, son, if you and Wendy decide that you're going to have sex, come here. You can have privacy here at our house. I'll stay at the office. I don't want you getting kicked out of college because you got caught sneaking into a dorm room or making love out on the grass somewhere. And, for heaven's sake, use contraceptives. Every time. Can you get them OK?"

Hank, now blushing again, nodded. "Yeah. Gas stations have machines, you know."

"Well, this has been quite a day. I guess you made me practice what I preach."

"Have I . . . upset you? I mean, being so . . . randy and all?"

"No, it's just biology after all. A force that perpetuates the species. You come by it naturally. It's just that, oh, 'Rico, I'm still getting used to the idea that you're a young man, not my little boy any more."

ON A TUESDAY morning in mid-October Emma turned to page three of her newspaper and spotted a headline that read

PRINCETON PROFESSOR WINS NOBEL

"The award of the 1955 Nobel Prize for Medicine and Physiology to Princeton biology professor Philip Schleicher was announced in Stockholm, Sweden this morning. Schleicher was honored for his groundbreaking studies of the biochemical mechanism of gene action, specifically for the demonstration that each gene encodes a specific protein inside the cell."

Emma didn't read the rest of the news story. She didn't need to; she knew the rest. Her throat tightened; she bit her lip and tossed the newspaper aside. It was an old wound that she thought had healed, now ripped open after so many years. Damn it! But for the delay of a few months, the unnecessary obstacles that had denied publication and a claim of priority, that Nobel Prize would have been her and Joe's Nobel Prize. They had done it alone and they had done it first. Yes, first! But not in the eyes of the world. That honor was now enshrined forever in the name of Philip Schleicher.

The research findings of Hansen and Bellafiori would be relegated to a footnote, if they were to be remembered at all. They had merely "replicated" or "confirmed" the original discoveries credited to Schleicher. It stung like hell. At least Joe had not lived to experience this final insult.

She and Joe had gotten it right too. The accumulated research of the seventeen years since they first submitted their work for publication proved that. Emma's collaborative research with other investigators had demonstrated the one to one correspondence between genes and enzymes many times, as had the work of many others working with a variety of different species. Already a decade ago Avery, MacLeod and McCarty had shown that the genetic material—in bacteria at least—was DNA. They had done it just as James Sumner had suggested to her back in 1925: by isolating pure genetic material. And now, just two years ago, the stunning insights that flowed directly from the elucidation of the structure of DNA by Watson and Crick that explained with remarkable clarity and simplicity both how DNA could be replicated into exact copies when cells divide and how DNA could encode the information to specify the structure of proteins within its own chemical structure. The question *how does it work* had now been answered at a fundamental level. Emma and Joe's work—and Schleicher's—had merely been steps along the path to the deeper understanding that now emerged.

Did it matter *who* did the research that led to this understanding? No, not to the collective enterprise of Science itself, not a whit. All that mattered was that the findings were robust, reproducible, and led to new predictions that could be tested experimentally, findings that provided a deeper and lasting view into the intricate workings of the natural world.

Science was a huge, complex fabric woven of many strands. It was like a massive stone edifice, of great strength and beauty, constructed of myriads of stones of many sizes. Did it matter who put the stones in place? No, it only mattered whether they sustained and perfected the structure.

Some stones were so critical to the stability of the walls that they would bear the masons' names forever: Newton, Kepler, Einstein, Darwin, Pasteur, who knows, perhaps even the newcomers Watson and Crick. But most of those who had placed stones were soon forgotten. It simply did not matter who they were. It was like life itself. As a biologist she should understand that all that mattered was that the species continued, that new cells, new individuals replaced the old ones. We live and grow, reproduce and die. Individual lives were generated and discarded with reckless abandon. Eat or be eaten. Survival of the species requires only that reproduction outrun death. The individual does not matter. There is no malice, no favoritism, only serene indifference.

But to the individual it matters. Oh, hell yes, it matters!

CHAPTER 25
1968

I SHOULD BE out there with them, Emma mused, as she watched from her office window the band of students marching with their picket signs and chanting anti-war slogans outside of the Administration Building. I have more reason to hate war than they do. War destroyed the spirit of my brother Henrik and drove him into mad exile, running from what he would never escape. He would be over seventy now, but surely he was long dead, buried in an unmarked pauper's grave. I will never know. War killed the great love of my life, my husband, the father of my son, my closest scientific collaborator, my playful, spirited lover. Dead twenty-five years. It would never cease hurting. Yes, I could give these children reasons to hate war.

They were sending them off to foreign lands to be slaughtered again. They were drafting young men from college campuses again. It never stops. But this time, the mood was different from the two world wars. The blind patriotism was absent; bitterness and dissention filled the air. The students of the past were too weighted down by the Great Depression, too caught up in the fervor of World War, to take to the streets like this.

Emma had been around college campuses for more than half a century now. These students were different. They were confident, angry, confrontational, idealistic, and more than a little self-righteous. President Johnson, scarred and vilified for expanding the war, had recently chosen not to run for re-election. There had been assassinations, riots, and burning in the cities. But the war went on. Yes, I should be out there, a gray-haired lady professor nearing retirement, a respected researcher, a popular biology teacher who once was notorious as the college's sex professor,—ha!, those lessons had been taken to heart. I should be out there carrying a sign with them, show them that at least some of their elders agree with them.

But Emma did not join the demonstrators. A feeling of weariness and resignation lay over her, a numbing cloud. She had been arguing against war since her high school days—to little effect. She had fought barriers and resistance every step of the way to acquire her education, to obtain an academic appointment, to establish her research, and to gain recognition for it. There had been bitter disappointments and losses along with her successes. She pushed her glasses up onto her short, gray hair and rubbed her tired eyes. Perhaps it was time to give up a lifetime of struggle. Time to rest. Did she even know how to do that?

At least she could take pleasure in the private world of her little family. Enrico (who even Emma now called Hank) and Wendy had invited her to dinner to celebrate her granddaughter Maria's tenth birthday. At the age of thirty-three and as the father of three children, Hank was safely beyond the reach of the draft. Emma was selfishly grateful for that. She could not bear another loss to yet another war.

Emma had hoped that Hank would follow her into biology or perhaps his father's path into chemistry, but he chose to major in mathematics and physics and discovered that he loved to teach. He took a Master's in education at Ohio State and returned to teach at Harrington Central High School, where he was now the Assistant Principal. He and Wendy married right after graduating from college and a year later Maria was born, followed by two boys, now four and six years old.

Emma wondered whether Hank and Wendy's decision to return to Harrington to make their lives was motivated by Hank's desire to remain close to her and to protect her as she grew older and continued to live alone in her big old house-museum next to the campus. If so, she was glad for it. They were often together for family dinners and holidays. She took great pleasure in her grandchildren, though she had to admit to herself that the eldest, Maria, had become her favorite.

The girl shared the intense curiosity and acute observation of the natural world that Emma recalled from her own childhood on the farm. From an early age she had coaxed Emma to take her on nature walks where she pointed out birds and their nests, trees, and plants, signs of the activity of small animals that many would overlook. She loved Emma's upstairs rooms full of specimens and taxidermy, and Emma patiently explained them to her, as she did to the biology students who still visited twice a week. For the past two years Maria had taken to coming to Emma's house alone after school, and Emma set up an informal tutorial for her. Her birthday gift was a student microscope. Perhaps now, she thought, I will get my biologist. It will be easier for her than it was for me.

"I HEAR IT'S getting kind of rough out on the campus, Mama," Hank said as he, Wendy, and Emma settled into the living room after dinner. "Blocking traffic in the streets. Broken windows. Apparently the local police have asked for help from the State Police."

"Well, that's too bad. Everyone gets distracted from the important message when there's violence. I was just thinking this afternoon that I should be out there with them. Maybe if some older people joined in, the hotheads could have been restrained."

"Would you really join the demonstrations, Emma?" Wendy asked.

"I don't know. No. I've never been a political activist—I had enough walls to bang my head against as it was. But I agree with them. We need to get out of Vietnam. All that senseless killing."

"Well, maybe after the election," Hank offered.

"Humpf. Don't bet on it."

"Are you looking forward to summer, Mama?" Hank asked. "Going to work in the lab again?"

"Yes, but I have to start thinking about winding things down. I will certainly have to retire in two more years. The Board of Trustees made an exception to the mandatory retirement at sixty-five rule for me, but they will surely not do it again."

"Are you going to miss teaching? Or does it become repetitive after a while?"

"It could, but I keep revising the content. For the first year biology course, the rewards always came from arousing the students' excitement about the intricate beauty and complexity of living systems. Of helping them see how clever Nature is. Genetics has changed so much over the years, it's a completely different course now. Molecular genetics they call it. You remember that I persuaded the biology department to hire Morris Friedkin three years ago. He and I teach genetics together. He's a bacterial geneticist, but he knows a lot of biochemistry too. My goodness, there was no such thing as bacterial genetics when I started. No one knew that bacteria had sexes. And he does a lot of work with bacteriophages. It's all I can do to keep up."

"So you're trying to nudge the biology department into modern biology?"

"Right. And I've been working on the chemists too. They finally hired a biochemist. An enzymologist. They were so conservative, so backward about it. For heaven's sakes, your father was really a biochemist. Way back then."

"So what about retirement, then? What are you going to do when you stop teaching? Will you still work in the lab?"

"I hope so. I may give up my dear old Neurospora, though. I like Friedkin. He's offered to teach me how to do genetics with his funny little bacteriophages. You know, you can't even see them under a microscope. You only see where they've been by the holes they make in bacterial cultures."

"What about the natural history museum in your house?"

"I'll keep it open for biology students, school children. The college has no place for it. That's another project. I'm going to work with the college to try to raise funds for a new science building. Biology and chemistry together, the way they should be. Modern teaching labs, space for senior honors and faculty research. A couple of rooms for the natural history museum."

THREE WEEKS LATER Emma collected her mail as usual from the rack of pigeonholes in the Department of Biology office. Among a few letters and a genetics journal was a letter marked CONFIDENTIAL. The typewritten return address on the envelope was unfamiliar and included no sender's name. What was this? Emma returned to her office, sat at her desk, carefully opened the envelope with a letter knife, and read:

Dear Professor Hansen,

Although a good many years have passed, I daresay you will remember that I was the editor of the American Journal of Genetics *who handled the review and publication after revision of your paper with the late Professor Joseph Bellafiori entitled "Genetic Determination of Biochemical Steps in Carotenoid Pigment Formation in Neurospora crassa." The passage of time has amply confirmed that this paper presented truly groundbreaking discoveries. The manner in which it was handled has weighed on my conscience for a long time, for I believe that I was unwittingly involved in a great injustice to you and Dr. Bellafiori. I pushed the matter to the back of my mind, as one is inclined to do with acts of which one is ashamed, but it was brought forcefully to my attention again when the Nobel Prize was awarded to Professor Philip Schleicher. The news of Prof. Schleicher's recent death sets me free to share with you my knowledge of certain improprieties in the review of your paper. It is pressing that I do so now, as my physicians tell me that I may not plan to live longer than another year. I write to you in the strictest confidence, which I trust you will honor.*

"As were you and Prof. Bellafiori, I was shocked when Prof. Schleicher's paper appeared in the Proceedings of the National Academy *some ten months after your paper was submitted to* Am. J. Genet. *and rejected. The similarities in the content and conclusions of the two papers were remarkable—too remarkable to be overlooked. I can now tell you that, as you suspected, Prof. Schleicher was in fact a referee for your paper and that he recommended rejection in the strongest terms. I did not retain his review, but I recall having to excise much of the language because it was so dismissive of 'the extravagant and inadequately documented claims of some lady professor at a midwestern cow college.' Schleicher was a highly respected geneticist at a distinguished university, so I felt compelled to accept his judgment, the more positive comments from the other referee not withstanding. When I later read the* Proceedings *paper and saw that Prof. Schleicher had reached the same conclusions as you and Bellafiori on the basis of similar evidence and that he had not met the exceptionally demanding standard of proof that he had insisted that you provide, I knew that a wrong had been committed in which I had unintentionally participated. But the damage was done and irreparable without a major scandal. Schleicher's paper gave him priority in claims to the new discoveries. The ethical rules of our journal did not permit to me reveal the identity of referees.*

One cannot know, of course, exactly what occurred. We cannot know the extent to which Prof. Schleicher may have used the information he gained from your unpublished manuscript to influence the content of his own paper. It is scandalous to think that he actually plagiarized its contents, and I have no proof of that. I have long believed, however, that at the very least, he recommended rejection of your paper so as to delay its publication and to gain time to publish his own research first. That ploy was successful, and he was rewarded with the highest recognition for those discoveries. I believe that you and Prof. Bellafiori should have received equal, if not exclusive, recognition for them.

Perhaps I should have spoken up at the time, but I did not. I confess that I was unwilling to become embroiled in an ugly public exchange of accusations and denials. For my cowardice I beg your pardon. I also request that you keep the contents of this letter in confidence. I see no good coming from airing these old wrongs after nearly thirty years. To do so would unnecessarily sully the reputation of the American Journal of Genetics. *Furthermore, it is quite clear that no scientific errors that require correction resulted from Schleicher's action. I simply want you to have the private pleasure of knowing what you hopefully already know, that you have been one of the great pioneers of modern biochemical genetics.*

Sincerely,

Cornelius J. Burke-Jones, Ph.D.

Professor Emeritus of Genetics, Yale University

CHAPTER 26
1995

IN THE END I compromised. It seemed to be the best I could achieve. It wasn't the full, ringing vindication that Grandma hoped for, but she might have settled for what I did. I don't know. She wasn't here to advise me. She had voluntarily ended her life a week after I last saw her ten years ago.

A year after I first communicated with them, the Board of Editors of the *American Journal of Genetics* agreed—after considerable negotiation—to publish the complete text of the Hansen-Bellafiori paper "Genetic Determination of Biochemical Steps in Carotenoid Pigment Formation in *Neurospora crassa*" exactly as it was submitted to them for publication in November of 1938. The paper was preceded by an editorial note, which read:

> We have recently become aware of certain irregularities that occurred during the review of the following manuscript, which was submitted to this journal by Professors Emma Hansen and Joseph Bellafiori in November of 1938, that lead us to the extraordinary decision to print the contents of that manuscript verbatim as it was submitted. We believe that, absent these irregularities, the manuscript would have been accepted and promptly published after the normal review process. The contents of the manuscript, here reprinted, justify the conclusion that Professors Hansen and Bellafiori had provided in 1938 strong evidence for what has come to be known as the one gene-one enzyme hypothesis, which was a crucial insight in the development of modern molecular genetics, and that therefore they deserve to be regarded as independent co-discoverers of this concept with a credible claim of priority to the discovery.

I had provided the journal with the exact copy of the manuscript from Grandma's files. They refused to print the letter from the former editor, Burke-Jones, or Grandma's letter demanding that his letter be published. The name of Philip Schleicher did not appear anywhere.

"We cannot countenance besmirching the reputation of a renown scientist when he is not in a position to defend himself," the journal's current editor argued, and I reluctantly agreed.

As part of the compromise, I had to promise not to send Burke-Jones' letter to the *New York Times*, but I saved all of Grandma's papers, including the incriminating letter. Just last week a diligent and persistent science historian telephoned me, asking questions, and I will show her everything. As Grandma predicted, the truth will be known.

The extraordinary act of publishing a manuscript nearly half a century after it was first submitted attracted quite a lot of attention, though, and I believe it has led to a reappraisal of this bit of scientific history. Here at UC San Francisco, where I do research in molecular oncology, I am occasionally asked if I am related to the Bellafiori of the Hansen-Bellafiori paper, and it is always a thrill to reply, "They were my grandparents, both of them."

I am confident that the growing recognition of the importance of their research led to the decision of Harrington College to name its new science building Hansen-Bellafiori Hall. Dad and Mom and my brothers and I were invited to attend the dedication this year, and, since I am the only biological scientist in the family, I agreed to give a short talk about the nature and importance of their work. At the end I remarked, "Emma Hansen was not only a pioneer in genetic research, she was a pioneer in advancing the role of women in science and in professional life in general. 'Why would we waste half of the brains, half of the imagination in the human race?' I can recall her asking. Why indeed? And Joseph Bellafiori was also a pioneer in his cheerful acceptance of a woman as his equal partner in science and in his life. Let us follow their examples."

The next day after the ceremonies were over, I wandered the campus alone. The new building had set aside three rooms for a natural history museum that included most of the familiar objects from Grandma's big old house.

The worried-looking baby boy still floated in his formaldehyde, as did an array of snakes, fishes, flatworms, and amphibians. A great horned owl presided over a menagerie of forty species of Midwestern birds nicely mounted in glass cases in a room where stuffed foxes, beavers, badgers, and squirrels roamed beside fossilized skeletons and boxes of crustaceans. Most of the collection has been carefully catalogued, preserved, and stored in banks of drawers, where students can withdraw them and examine them in an adjacent room that is equipped with tables and microscopes. I could feel Grandma's gentle hand on my shoulder as I wandered among the collection.

But she is dead now. Gone for ten years. I like to think of her in heaven: running through a fragrant field of clover with Henrik in search of a bird's nest to raid, looking up from her microscope and happily recording what she sees in her notebook, showing her genetic maps to a grinning Joe. Maybe she even teaches classes in angelic sexuality. (Do they have sex in heaven? It could hardly be heaven if they don't.) She and Joe are surely cataloguing the natural history of their celestial home. *What is it made of? How does it work?*

But that's sentimental nonsense. Grandma didn't believe that and neither do I. She is beyond knowing, beyond caring. Only the memory of her persists, the work she did. Her body is gone; only the atoms that made up her body are immortal. They have been disassembled and re-knit into a million new forms. She left instructions to be cremated, and her ashes were scattered on the Harrington College campus. Carbon dioxide from the combustion of her body was fixed via photosynthesis into the leaves of trees, grasses, perhaps even into the wisteria that still grows on the porch of the old house near the campus where I spent my afternoons after school.

The water vapor rose up into the atmosphere and later fell as rain on the cornfields and cow pastures of Illinois. The verdant lawns of the campus are nourished by the minerals from her ashes. Perhaps an atom or two made its way into a scarab beetle patiently rolling a ball of dung or into a gracefully swimming paramecium cell; maybe a single carbon atom found a home in a molecule of the brilliant red neurosporaxanthin pigment that decorates the bread mold *Neurospora crassa*. Not very likely, I know. Fanciful, to be sure, but it is the only kind of immortality that Emma Hansen expected.

But she lives on. Her genes live on. I carry them. They sometimes govern my actions in ways that I only dimly understand. I carry her genes, and I will pass them on. I plan to have a large family. These are good genes, these Hansen-Bellafiori genes.

Good genes. They live on.

Author's Notes

The Lady Professor is a work of fiction. All of the principle characters are fictional; no resemblance to actual persons, living or dead, is intended.

However, certain real scientists, none presently living, appear in the novel and play significant roles in Emma's early research career. Two of the most important of these appear in Chapter 8: Barbara McClintock and James Sumner. Both were present at Cornell University during the time period of the novel, and both were then performing the research they describe to Emma. They worked in relative obscurity for years, but both were eventually recognized by the award of Nobel Prizes. Their contrasting ideas about fruitful approaches to the investigation of biology were central throughout the twentieth century. Barbara McClintock faced all of the barriers to women in science that were placed in Emma's fictional path. Her remarkable story has been well told by E. F. Keller in *A Feeling for the Organism: The Life and Work of Barbara McClintock.* W. H. Freeman, New York and San Francisco (1983). Despite the handicap of having lost an arm as a youth, James Sumner eventually succeeded in isolating a pure crystalline enzyme, urease, and demonstrated that it was a protein.

Bernard O. Dodge was a USDA scientist who actually performed the early genetic characterization of the fungus *Neurospora crassa* described in the novel (although a few years later) and eventually passed this research topic on to others, most importantly to Carl and Margaret Lindgren and George Beadle. The work in Emma's fictional Ph.D. thesis on genetics of *N. crassa* was later performed by the Lindgrens, and Emma's preliminary cytogenetic characterization of this species was actually published in 1945 by Barbara McClintock. Genetic studies with *N. crassa* eventually yielded some of the cornerstones of modern molecular biology, as detailed by R. H. Davis in *Neurospora: Contributions of a Model Organism.* Oxford University Press, Oxford and New York (2000).

Many other real scientists are briefly named in this novel, always with the intent of accurately portraying the roles they played in the science of their times. These include, in order of appearance in the novel, Robert Koch, Gregor Mendel, C. B. Hutchison, T. H. Morgan, Paul Ehrlich, Justus von Liebig, Roger Adams, Mikhail Tswett, J. H.

Northrup, M. Kunitz, Otto Warburg, Alfred Kinsey, O. T. Avery, C. MacLeod, M. McCarty, James Watson and Francis Crick.

Stanton Mills, Illinois and all persons living in or around there are imaginary. Hancock College and Harrington College are fictional inventions, as are all persons described as members of their faculties or students. Cornell University is a real and very fine research university, of course, and was indeed an early leader in higher education for women. Professor Osborne, Leonard (Lenny) Hallowell, Rosa Levin, and Herschel Greenspan are fictional persons.

All of the scientific research described as having been done by Emma Hansen and Joseph Bellafiori is fictional, although care was taken to invent activities and findings that would have been feasible in the time period and places described. Much of the research ascribed to Emma and Joe during their years at Harrington College was actually performed by real scientists in various locations and times during the twentieth century. Emma and Joe's imaginary work on the genetics and biochemistry of carotenoid pigment biosynthesis was invented for this novel because it would have been (just barely) feasible for two very energetic and imaginative scientists to accomplish at the time with limited resources, and it would have had the far-reaching consequences ascribed to it. The pathway for pigment biosynthesis was, however, drastically altered and simplified from the actual pathway in *N. crassa* to make the fictional science easier for a lay reader (and Emma and Joe) to comprehend. Joe's adaptations of Mikhail Tswett's procedures for column chromatography and paper chromatography were developed by others, especially by A. J. P. Martin and R. L. M. Synge, some years after the time period of the novel.

There is no *American Journal of Genetics* and no editor, Burke-Jones or otherwise; these are fictions. Other scientific journals named in the novel exist, but, of course, did not publish the fictional scientific papers described in the novel.

Readers who are familiar with the history of molecular genetics will recognize at once that the "one gene-one enzyme" hypothesis, ascribed in the novel to Emma and Joe and their fictional rivals Philip Schleicher and his co-worker Martin Fox, was actually developed by George W. Beadle and Edward L. Tatum on the basis of studies with *N. crassa*, although not from the genetics of carotenoid pigment formation; Beadle and Tatum were honored with the Nobel Prize in 1958 for this work. It must be emphasized in the strongest possible terms that this novel's imputation of unethical conduct to a fictional character, Prof. Schleicher, during the review for publication of the novel's imaginary research on the "one gene-one enzyme" hypothesis, does *not* suggest any kind of impropriety on the part of Beadle and Tatum or any other real scientist. Such is certainly not the case. The work of Beadle and Tatum is beyond reproach scientifically and ethically. This novel must not be construed to suggest otherwise.

The pseudoscience of eugenics was considered scientifically respectable in the first half of the twentieth century and was widely taught in high schools, colleges and universities. The quote in Chapter 6 from Charles B. Davenport's 1911 book, *Heredity in Relation to Eugenics*, is verbatim. Davenport was a prominent scientist and leader of the American eugenics movement; he was the Director of the Cold Spring Harbor Laboratory and was elected to the U.S. National Academy of Sciences in 1912. Eugenics has been largely discredited today, but the question of the degree to which behavior and personality are genetically determined remains an area of vigorous scientific debate.

The Lady Professor is above all the story of the life and loves of a woman who is determined to build a career in science at a time when women were generally barred from such careers. The obstacles and prejudices she faces in the novel are not invented. Many—though not all—of these barriers to women in science have been removed today, and the world of science is much richer for it. *The Lady Professor* is also a novel about the human side of science. What does it feel like to do science? It is not science fiction (a genre with which I am rather impatient), but what Carl Djerassi has called "science in fiction." As Emma reflects at the end of Chapter 24, science is a great, impersonal, self-correcting international cultural monument that cares only about the truth. But science is performed by humans; it is a very human activity and subject to the foibles and imperfections of human behavior, as this novel makes clear. The attempt of very imperfect actors to build perfect structures lies at the core of what makes us human, whether we are scientists or writers.

Urbana, Illinois
June 2014

Robert L. Switzer is Professor Emeritus of Biochemistry at the University of Illinois at Urbana-Champaign. He earned a B.S. in Chemistry from the University of Illinois in 1961, a Ph.D. in Biochemistry from the University of California, Berkeley in 1966 and joined the University of Illinois faculty in 1968. He is the author or co-author of 138 original scientific research articles, reviews and book chapters and the co-author of the textbook *Experimental Biochemistry* (W. H. Freeman). He was a Guggenheim Fellow and is a Fellow of the American Academy of Microbiology.

In recent years Robert has turned to a career in creative writing. His non-fiction memoir *A Family Farm: Life on an Illinois Dairy Farm* was published in 2012 by the Center for American Places, Columbia College, Chicago. He is currently working on a new novel and a collection of short stories. *The Lady Professor* is his first published novel.

Robert and his wife Bonnie, an artist, live in Urbana, Illinois. They are the proud parents of a son and a daughter and four grandchildren.

CPSIA information can be obtained
at www.ICGtesting.com
Printed in the USA
FFOW04n0423020717
37288FF